Unfinished

Ian Nicholas Manners

Unfinished Business

Ian Manners.

Two Hunters Publishing

Published in Great Britain by
Two Hunters Publishing
Stokes Farm, Binfield Road, Wokingham,
Berks, RG40 5PR
www.2hunterspublishing.com

ISBN 978-0-9543263-1-9

Set in Baskerville by bookplugs.com

Printed in England
by Cox & Wyman Ltd, Reading

This book is dedicated to my two daughters, Hannah and Akinyi, and my son Geoffrey. I would like to thank everybody who has helped me with this book.

1

THE DRONE OF a single-engine plane broke the calm from behind him as it flew overhead, eventually disappearing out to sea over the horizon. Minutes later another appeared. This time from the left cutting across his view as it flew parallel to the shore and south towards Diani Beach.

Several crows cawed as they called each other from one side of the compound to the other. The engine of a lawnmower spluttered into life as the gardener in the house next door began cutting the grass. The sweet smell of fresh cut grass filled the air. Sean inhaled deeply and breathed out slowly.

The sun glistened on the water as he looked out over the ocean. The sky was very blue and with hardly a cloud in sight. The sea was almost flat and very calm but several white-capped crests of larger waves could be seen beyond the reef. Nearer the shoreline the water rolled in slow motion gently onto the beach. Sean savoured the moment as he breathed in again, smelling the salty air. It was a glorious sight at the start of another day in Mombasa, Kenya.

He felt incredibly lucky to have such a beautiful home and lifestyle after the recent three years of turmoil that had blighted him. He watched rather enviously as a young couple strolled along the shore hand-in-hand, momentarily turning and kissing each other's lips before continuing on their way. Although he was happier than he had been in a long time his heart ached to share his life with another woman. The pain of losing Akinyi was easing day by day, though he would never forget her. His sadness at the failure of his relationship with Njeri also hurt him, but he knew he had to move on.

Nearly two years had passed since Sean Aloysius Cameron returned to Kenya with Achieng Samantha, his second daughter. It was now May 1996. As he sat on the wooden veranda enjoying a leisurely breakfast he watched as his daughter, Achieng, her name meaning sunshine – so named in honour of her dead mother's Luo heritage – was playing happily in the small garden leading down to the beach. She was now five years old. Her golden skin shone in the early morning sunlight. Her hair, braided long, was in traditional African style. It was a mixture of her natural black hair and lighter-coloured extensions. She was singing as she played. Sean couldn't quite make out the words but it sounded faintly like a traditional Luo lullaby. He had deliberately employed a Luo maid doubling as a nanny in order to teach Achieng her mother tongue. He wanted her to grow up knowing about her late mother's culture and traditions. He knew little Luo himself and she often teased him about his lack of knowledge of her language. His own capability was limited to enough Swahili to carry on a general conversation. His big problem when it came to languages was that for some unfathomable reason he kept mixing the little he remembered of school French and Spanish with Swahili and Luo, creating a jumbled mess.

He finished his cup of coffee and called out: "Achieng, hurry up. It's time to take you to school."

As she looked up and smiled that great big smile of hers, his heart melted as it had done a thousand times before.

"Coming, Baba," she shouted as she skipped happily back across the garden.

Sean held out her small school bag. She took it and proceeded to pull it onto her back.

"Come on, slowcoach," she giggled as she took his hand and began pulling him towards the car parked in the compound to the side of the house. They climbed in and Sean removed her rucksack before he made sure Achieng was safely strapped in her child seat. He then pulled his own seatbelt across his shoulder and clicked it into position, and turning the ignition key the engine roared into life. His car was a four-wheel-drive Land Rover Discovery, favoured by many ex-pats in Mombasa, as it dealt with the appalling roads, which more often than not were full of potholes and breaking up.

As he reversed slowly he glanced across and admired his house. It was a four-bedroom bungalow with whitewashed walls and a red tiled roof, a common design in the select area of Nyali where they now lived. When he had bought the house a year previously it had been rundown and derelict. Sean had renovated it with the help of Opiyo, his gardener-cum-handyman, a Luo like Akoth the nanny. It had taken the best part of nine months to complete the renovations to Sean's satisfaction. It had been hard work trying to combine refurbishments with the task of starting his new marketing business in downtown Mombasa.

After a slow start, Sean had secured the Mombasa Tourist Board business as one of his main clients and also a couple of hotels, where he managed their marketing and public-relations budgets. Although not wealthy he was comfortably off. He still owned his house in Richmond, back in England, and it provided a good rental income, enough to cover the small mortgage, tax and insurances. Once they were paid there was a small profit left over. Additionally he owned a small matatu bus in Mombasa that made a very good profit. Matatus were one of the cheapest forms of travel for the locals.

Throughout the journey Achieng chatted freely to Sean about meeting her friends at the school she attended. She had learned the alphabet and was developing her handwriting skills. She was proudly telling Sean what she expected to do at school that morning. Normally Sean returned home for lunch after collecting Achieng, but that day he had a meeting so he had arranged for Opiyo and

Akoth to collect her in the family estate car. Sean trusted them both implicitly, and Opiyo was a very experienced, safe driver.

It didn't take long before they arrived at the school. Sean found a parking space in amongst the numerous cars belonging to other parents. The school had a large multi-cultural cross-section of children from diplomatic families or the families of local businessmen and professionals.

As Sean lifted Achieng from her car seat she clasped her hands tightly around his neck, almost choking him in the process. Although she enjoyed school this had become almost a daily event, as she hated to be apart from him. However as soon as she was with her young friends in the classroom Sean was soon forgotten.

Nikki, the senior teacher in Achieng's class greeted him: "Good morning, Mr Cameron, Achieng – how are you both today?"

"Very well, thank you," responded Sean politely as Achieng buried her face in his chest. "Sorry, she's doing her shy bit again, Nikki." He paused. "Come on, say good morning to Miss Greene."

Achieng giggled nervously as she pulled her face away from his chest.

"I'm not shy. Good morning, Miss Greene," she said in a soft voice, holding out her arms for Nikki to take her. Nikki duly did so. She was about average height, possibly five feet seven, with short blonde hair cut in a stylish bob. She was lightly tanned from the sun and was very pretty. Sean guessed she was in her mid-twenties. He had been told by another parent that she was on a two-year contract at the school and had been born and brought up in Sussex. She was a typical English southern-counties girl. Beyond that Sean knew little else about her.

"My daddy loves you!" Achieng suddenly piped up.

Nikki blushed.

"Come along, Achieng, time for class," she half-whispered, clearly embarrassed, not knowing what else to say. She laughed nervously. Sean, equally embarrassed, shuffled uncomfortably as he tried to ignore the comment.

"Bye, sweetheart," he called to Achieng, blowing her a kiss as he turned and walked from the classroom, wondering where on earth she had got that little idea. He chuckled nervously to himself.

"Bye, Miss Greene."

As he drove the remaining four miles into town he began thinking about Nikki Greene in a new light. She was certainly very attractive, thought Sean.

§

Shortly after nine o'clock Sean arrived at his office. It was situated on the second floor above a parade of shops on Moi Avenue. The cool of the air conditioning was a welcome relief from the scorching sun and humidity outside.

His personal assistant greeted him in Swahili as he walked in: "Habari, Sean."

"Good morning, Mary."

He walked to the water machine and poured himself a cup, and, draining it, quenched his thirst. He sighed as he refilled it before slumping in his chair, looking across at Mary.

"Is there anything of interest in the post?"

"No, only a couple of invoices. However there's a fax from a James Annan for you, marked urgent."

Sean raised his eyebrows. "Where is it?"

"On your desk."

Mary smiled sweetly, noticing an unusual impatience in Sean.

He picked up the fax and began to read it:

> Dear Sean,
> I have some urgent business in Kenya. I need to see you as soon as possible. I am arriving on BA 065 from Heathrow on 16th May via Nairobi. My connecting flight

to Mombasa is at 10.35 on the 17th so I'll be there at 11.25. Hope you can meet me. I need to talk to you. No need to reply.

Best wishes, James

Sean put the fax down. "Now I wonder what that can be all about," he said to himself, feeling rather annoyed at James's assumption that he was on call. He hadn't seen James since the leaving party at his parents' house the night before he had returned to Kenya with Achieng and Louise, his older daughter from his first marriage. Louise had stayed for a month's holiday before returning to her mother in England. Other than an exchange of Christmas cards there had been no contact between James and himself since. Both led busy lives but were lifetime friends.

"What time is my appointment with Dixon and where is it, Mary?" asked Sean, not noticing the impatience in his voice again.

Something is troubling Sean, thought Mary. "It's at 12.30 p.m. at the White Sands Hotel. The file on Brad's company is also in your in-tray."

Sean wondered why Mary sounded irritated. He observed her for a few moments. She was an elegant woman in her early forties. She was from the Giriama, one of the largest tribes of people from the coast. She was dressed formally in a black skirt and white blouse. Her shoes were classic in style and made from patent leather. There was obviously an Arabic influence somewhere in her background, he thought.

He picked up the Dixon file and began to study it. Unable to concentrate fully on the project, his thoughts drifted back to James and his own recent past. A day didn't pass without thinking of his beloved Akinyi, Achieng's mother. Life had moved on and his pain was easier to bear but he could never forget. Achieng was a constant reminder of her mother. He was determined not to miss out on her upbringing in the same way that he had missed out on his elder daughter

Louise's, who was now studying for her GCSEs in England. She had visited him and Achieng during her school holidays. It was true he probably spoilt Achieng a little too much but he was now playing the role of father and mother to her, or at least he was trying the best he could. His thoughts drifted to Nikki Greene. He had become very aware of how attractive she was. Perhaps he would ask her out to dinner in the not too distant future.

Mary watched Sean daydreaming. She hadn't seen him in such a reflective mood before. She wondered briefly why Sean seemed so disturbed. Eventually she interrupted.

"You'll be late for your meeting with Brad Dixon if you don't hurry up."

Sean looked up. He frowned as he looked at his watch. "Yeah," he said quietly before he stood up, stuffing his files into his briefcase. He smiled at Mary as he left.

"See you later. Wish me luck. The success of this meeting should help me to pay your wages at the end of the month," he joked, returning to a more relaxed demeanour.

Mary half-smiled, not quite sure whether he was being serious or not.

"Kwaheri [goodbye]," she said softly.

Sean's meeting went well with Brad Dixon, and after dropping him at Moi International Airport he called Mary on his cell phone to tell her he wouldn't be coming back to the office. It was by then 4.30 p.m. and he wanted to spend an hour or so playing with Achieng on the beach before it got dark.

When Sean arrived home Akoth was in the kitchen preparing dinner. She looked up as Sean entered.

"You're home early, Mr Sean."

She carried on with her work. She was a typical plump Luo woman in her early fifties. She had never married and longed to have children of her own. Achieng was a great substitute for the child she never had. She loved her dearly and cared for her every need. At the same time she disciplined her when necessary. The love was mutual. Akoth was always cheerful. She had a big smile that revealed an almost perfect set of white teeth, except for a slight gap between the top two front incisors. Her hair was curly but closely cropped.

"My appointment finished early, where's Achieng?" he called to Akoth as he walked through the back door.

"She's playing with Opiyo in the garden. He's showing her how to carve an elephant out of wood."

"Oh, by the way, we'll be having a guest on Thursday night. Can you prepare the guest room?"

"Yes, Mr Sean."

After Sean changed into his swimming shorts and a tee shirt he stood on the veranda briefly watching Opiyo and Achieng. Opiyo was a tall, muscular man. His hair was crew cut. He had very dark, almost black skin, as was typical of a Luo from near Kisumu on the edge of Lake Victoria. Before joining Sean he had spent ten years in the Kenyan Army as a physical-training instructor. He was thirty-two years old.

A crow cawed and broke Sean's concentration. Achieng looked up and smiled as she saw her father watching her from the veranda.

"Baba, Baba, Opiyo is showing me how to make an elephant out of wood," she said excitedly, as she pointed to Opiyo's hand. She waved for Sean to come, indicating a piece of wood that was already taking the shape of an elephant.

"That is very impressive, Opiyo," Sean praised him, as he strolled across the lawn. "Get yourself changed for a swim, my friend. You can finish that tomorrow."

Sean regarded Opiyo as a member of the family. Opiyo duly stopped carving. He carefully wrapped the wooden elephant in a bag and disappeared off to his room to get changed.

"I'll be back in a minute, Mr Sean."

"Come along, Achieng," Sean shouted, as he grabbed her hand and ran towards the gate leading to the beach. "It's time for a swim."

2

THE BIG SILVER plane banked steeply to the left of the airport before turning back towards the main runway, ready for the final approach. Sean was sitting in the viewing gallery, watching as the pilot of the 737 eased the plane into position, dropping the undercarriage ready to land. The roar of the engines reached fever pitch as the pilot threw the engines into reverse thrust, causing the plane to brake sharply. It slowed down and came to a halt at the end of the apron, before turning and taxiing to the stand adjacent to the airport buildings.

The front door of the plane opened as the ground staff pushed the steps alongside ready for the passengers to alight. Several minutes later a steady stream of people began climbing down the steps before walking across the tarmac to the terminal buildings.

Sean spotted James as he appeared at the top of the steps. His big muscular frame almost obscured the whole of the doorway. Even from a distance Sean could see that he was in great physical shape. He walked with a distinct military swagger as he strode across the tarmac.

Sean, who was by now standing up in the viewing gallery, turned and headed for the meeting area outside the arrivals gate. It would probably be about twenty minutes before James collected his baggage and cleared customs. Sean hoped that the customs officers wouldn't delay him too long. More often than not they caused hassle for the arriving passengers, particularly their fellow-countrymen returning from foreign lands. Sean was always amazed how so many customs officers would make up the rules as they went along. Either confiscating items or charging small fines that invariably ended up not in government coffers, but rather their own pockets instead. He watched the tired faces of the arriving tourists and the happy faces of Kenyans returning from Europe and meeting their families. The babble of voices and laughter drowned out the piped music that was playing in the background.

James eventually appeared carrying a large holdall. He was quick to spot Sean. He put his hand up in acknowledgement. Sean moved forward extending his arm and the two friends shook hands vigorously.

"By god, Sean, you're looking well. The climate is obviously doing you the world of good!"

Sean was only a couple of inches shorter than James. He had also managed to keep his body in good condition. He got plenty of exercise at the local squash club and gym and the almost daily swimming with Achieng kept him very fit. James noticed that Sean's blond hair had been cut shorter than usual, giving way to a little greying around the temples. His normal pale skin had darkened in the sun.

"You're looking good yourself," countered Sean. "So come on, tell me what brings you to these parts?" he asked suspiciously.

"Oh, I'll tell you all about that soon enough. First I need a shower and a change of clothes. It's been a long flight. I'm tired."

The two friends were soon in Sean's car heading back to the house, passing through the hustle and bustle of the local traffic.

It was James's first visit to Mombasa, though not to Kenya. Unbeknown to Sean he had been in the country on a couple of occasions previously. Both times with the SAS up near the Kenya-Somalia border. He had been a training liaison officer to the Kenyan Army. He taught anti-guerrilla techniques and trained in how to deal with the Somali bandits who made cross-border raids on the local villages. Both stints were at the end of the 'eighties and early 'nineties, shortly before the Somali war escalated into the disastrous Operation Restore Hope led by the Americans in 1992.

Within twenty minutes they were back at Sean's house. Sean blew the car horn at the gate to warn Opiyo and the askaris of his arrival. Shortly afterwards the metal gates clattered noisily as Opiyo pulled them open, allowing Sean to drive through into the compound. One of the askaris carefully closed the gates behind them, making sure he secured the big padlock.

Sean introduced James to Akoth and Opiyo, who almost bowed to him as they shook hands. They showed him a deference some black people normally reserve for white people in Africa. Sean chuckled to himself as he noticed Akoth seemed to be admiring James's physique.

"Welcome, Mr Annan!" they announced in unison.

Opiyo collected James's holdall from the back of the car and showed him to his room.

"I'm off to collect Achieng from school," Sean called out. "I'll be back for lunch in half an hour."

Sean arrived at the school and watched Achieng as she played with her classmates on the climbing frame in the playground. She hadn't noticed his arrival. He looked across the playground and he could see Nikki Greene standing beneath a lone palm tree observing the children. Sean ambled slowly up to her.

"Hello, Nikki," he began, trying to sound as casual as possible. "I've been thinking about what Achieng said the other morning."

Nikki flushed slightly and smiled nervously. "Oh, you know what children are like, Mr Cameron, they say the craziest things sometimes." She half-stuttered, feeling a nervous lump in her throat.

"Nikki, how would you like dinner with me at the Tamarind on Saturday night?"

Nikki had already made plans, but dinner with Sean at the world-famous Tamarind was a much better option. She had secretly fancied him for a long time. He had those rugged good looks that made him very attractive to the opposite sex. The small scar on his left cheek, a legacy of the battle in the Black Forest, only seemed to enhance them. She also admired the way in which he brought up Achieng.

"Yes, that would be lovely, Mr Cameron, or can I call you Sean? Mr Cameron sounds too formal if we're to go out to dinner together."

Sean smiled. "I'll pick you up at eight – but where do you live?"

Nikki gave her address – the Reef Road close to the Fisherman's Inn in Nyali.

"Bye, Nikki, I'll see you on Saturday."

A nervous excitement coursed through his body as he walked across to where Achieng was playing.

"One more go, please Baba," she pleaded as she watched her father approach.

"Okay, but make it quick, we've got to get back for lunch."

No sooner had they arrived home than Achieng rushed into the sitting room to be confronted by what was to her a huge body dozing in an armchair.

"Baba, Baba!" she cried as she ran back into the kitchen where her father was talking to Akoth. "Baba, there's a big black man asleep in the chair in the sitting room!" she shouted breathlessly.

"Don't worry, he's your Uncle James. Go and wake him and tell him lunch is ready."

"No, Baba. I'm too scared to go on my own."

She grabbed his hand and began to drag him towards the sitting room. As they entered, Sean could see James stretched out in an armchair. He gave him a gentle tap on his knee.

"Come on, James, time for lunch." He gave him another shake. This time James stirred and looked up.

"Sorry, but I've been catching up on some well-deserved shuteye." As he rubbed sleep from his eyes he noticed Achieng half-hiding behind her father. "And who is this little princess then?" He smiled at Achieng.

Achieng meanwhile stared with wide eyes as James rose and stretched to his full six-foot-two. She stepped back showing signs of fear.

"Hey, sweetheart, this is your Uncle James. Don't you remember him? You met him at Grandma and Grandpa's house before we came to Kenya."

Achieng said nothing. She looked completely dumbstruck. Sean knew this was typical of Achieng's behaviour when she met a stranger.

"Don't worry, James, she's lost her tongue," he teased. "You'll be glad she has because within half an hour she won't stop talking. Come on, let's go and have some lunch," said Sean as he led the way.

"Then I'll explain why I'm here, Sean. First let's catch up with *your* news."

§

No sooner had Akoth taken Achieng off for her afternoon nap than Sean and James moved to the veranda overlooking the Indian Ocean. The tide was out and several people had taken advantage of walking across the sand that now stretched almost half a mile or so out as far as the reef.

In another three hours the water would return to within fifty metres of Sean's garden wall, which ran alongside the full seventy-metre frontage of his land. Sean employed guards, or "askaris", in Swahili, to protect his property. One of them was currently sitting in the shade under a clump of trees to the right-hand-side of the garden. It gave him a good overall view of all the land to the front of the property.

"Hey, dude, it's a breathtaking view!" James exclaimed. "I understand why you wanted to come and live here now – but isn't your lifestyle a far cry from how most of the rest of the population lives here?"

Sean nodded his head in agreement. "Sure, I'm lucky, but I make my own luck. I work hard to pay for all of this. I can't change how other people live in Kenya. All I can do is bring up Achieng in the best way I can and make sure she has a good education. Maybe when she grows up her generation will change the politics and economics of their country for the better."

Although Sean was becoming more and more disillusioned with the current government in Kenya he was determined to continue to live there. Day by day he was increasingly frustrated with the muggings, car-jackings, and how politicians were making so much money with their crooked dealings. He was waiting for the day when a new government would be voted in, which would, hopefully, begin to change the infrastructure of the country for the better, clamping down on the corruption that had become a way of life. Only time would tell if there was to be a change for the better.

"Hmm," contemplated James "I guess we can go on talking about Africa's problems forever," he said, with tired resignation to his voice.

"Tell me, James, why are you in Kenya?"

James paused. He wanted to keep Sean in suspense for a while longer. He smiled and at last he began to talk. "It's a long story. I've been working on a project for a client. As you know I now have a security company. This includes guarding celebrities and properties, implementing security procedures for private companies, surveillance and even private detective work."

Several birds cawed in the background. There was a rustling noise as the breeze whistled through the leafy trees. James sipped his tea and explained that he'd been employed by a director of a Tanzania casino to investigate the huge losses he'd been making.

"But don't casinos sometimes make a loss? Surely they can't always win?" asked Sean somewhat naively.

"Well yes, occasionally they can lose, but only when a punter is on a lucky roll. Some of the wealthy gamblers might have a huge win but that is soon offset by their losses when they return and gamble away their previous good fortune."

"What about the professional gamblers though?"

"You mean the ones that earn a living out of it? Admittedly some professionals make enough to live off but they're the smart ones who only play percentages. Guys like that are few and far between. If they start making heavy losses one night they have the sense to pull out and come back another time."

"So where do I fit in with all of this?" Sean asked with a puzzled look on his face.

For a moment James studied Sean. "I don't know that you do yet, but let me tell you what's happened so far."

Three months previously a senior government official from the Tanzanian High Commission in London had contacted him. A Tanzanian-born director of the Golden City, a new casino complex near Dar Es Salaam, wished to meet him to discuss an undercover operation that he wanted James to run.

At their meeting he explained to James that he suspected some of their staff appeared to be running a scam and were stealing quite considerable sums of money. He had been unable to prove anything and he wasn't sure which members of staff were involved, but he had a list of prime suspects. What he wanted James to do was send in one of his staff to work as a croupier in the casino and try and find out which of the staff were actually involved.

"So who did you employ that knew how to work as a croupier?"

"By coincidence I employed a former colleague from the SAS, by the name of Martin Donaldson. He'd worked for me during my time in the Regiment." He paused as he took another sip of tea.

"Prior to joining the Army, he'd trained as a croupier and had worked briefly for a casino in London. He joined me when I first started the business. He had a penchant for gambling and experience of being a croupier, so he was the obvious choice."

"Gambling is one thing but actually dealing the tables must surely be completely different?"

"Yes, but at least he knew how to play some of the games. I sent him on a two-week refresher course to brush up on his skills as a croupier – that was at one of the industry training schools in Hertfordshire. I'll tell you more about Martin later."

"What then?"

"Once we'd provided him with false references he applied for a job at the Golden City."

"But couldn't he be given a job without going through those normal channels? What if he'd been turned down?"

"Bloody hell, Cameron, sometimes you're too naive for your own good," James laughed. "We had to get him to apply through the normal channels because we couldn't take the chance of raising any suspicions amongst the other staff. Everything had to appear perfectly normal."

"Was he accepted?"

James nodded his head. It was at this point that Achieng reappeared.

"Sorry, James, we'll have to continue this conversation later."

"No problem. Let's leave it till after dinner, when Achieng has gone to bed. In the meantime how about going for a walk along the beach with her? I could do with stretching my legs," he said as he rose from his chair.

"Good idea," responded Sean.

He picked Achieng up in his arms to give her a cuddle. She

was still sleepy from her nap and the walk would do her good also. As he did so a troop of Vervet monkeys ran across the compound in front of them. They were easily recognisable with their black faces fringed with white hair. Their long grey body hair was very distinctive. Sean pointed them out to Achieng who quickly stirred from her sleepiness. They watched in silence as two males loped along displaying their distinctive bright blue scrotum. It was an important signal of status within the troop. Achieng cooed softly as three or four babies tumbled across the lawn in a playful manner. Eventually they sprang back up and clung upside down to the stomachs of their mothers to continue their journey. Meanwhile several others in the troop foraged for leaves and seeds before they all disappeared over the wall into the adjoining property.

3

THREE MONTHS PREVIOUSLY James had made the short walk from the London Hilton, where he was staying in Park Lane, to the Tanzanian High Commission on Hertford Street. It was a clear but chilly February morning. As he walked the 100 metres or so he could hear the hum of the London traffic in the background. The road was full of cars either parked on the meters set out along the right-hand side of the street or in the spaces officially reserved for diplomatic vehicles.

After passing several other embassies he reached the Tanzanian High Commission. He walked up the three stone steps at the entrance and pushed open the big oak front door, turning almost immediately to the left. This time through an equally tall glass door with a highly polished brass handle. He entered a small waiting room that had a distinctly musty smell. Half a dozen chairs were lined up alongside the walls. A young man of about twenty was sitting in one of the chairs reading a magazine.

James muttered, "Good morning."

The young man responded with a smile.

A table had been put against the far wall piled high with tourist information brochures. To his right there was a glass screen, behind which a clerk was sitting, reading one of the daily newspapers. She quickly put it down when she saw James. She seemed wary of the tall black man who had now entered the room. She was a slight girl in her early twenties with a pale brown complexion. James could smell her cheap perfume as she leant over the counter towards him. She had a typical Arabic look of someone from the coastal region of East Africa. Her hair was rather untidily tied back with a clip. Her large dark brown eyes popped with expectation as she waited for James to speak. She smiled nervously and before he could open his mouth she greeted him.

"Good morning, sir. How can I help you?"

She spoke with a half-American and half-East African accent. The pitch of her voice was much deeper than James expected for someone of such a slight build. He was momentarily taken aback. He hoped she didn't notice his surprise.

"Good morning." James glanced at his watch. "I have an appointment with Mr Chidoli. My name is James Annan."

"Wait a moment, please," the clerk said picking up the telephone and saying something in a language that sounded different to the Swahili that James had learned from his time in Kenya. Probably a local dialect, he thought to himself. She replaced the receiver and beckoned James to sit down. He declined, instead picking up one of the tourist brochures that had been lying on the table. He skimmed through it, half out of interest and partly to kill time. A large grandfather clock ticked in the background.

His train of thought was interrupted a few minutes later when the clerk announced, "Mr Chidoli will see you now, sir."

She rose from her chair and moved to her left, unlocking a glass door adjacent to the window. She pointed to her right.

"If you go up those stairs and turn right at the top you can take the elevator to the third floor. Mr Chidoli will meet you there." She smiled. Not quite so nervously this time.

James smiled in response, catching another waft of her cheap perfume as he brushed past her.

He pushed the lift door open when he reached the third floor. Stepping out, he was confronted by a tall black man who greeted him in the crisp tones reminiscent of an English public school. He had the aura of a very confident, educated person. He offered his hand.

"Good morning. Mr Annan, I assume," he said with faint irony. "We have been expecting you. Welcome, please come this way."

The man didn't actually introduce himself but James assumed this was Edward Chidoli. He stood to one side as he ushered James towards the office.

James entered. It was a large office. Very typical of the many embassy offices he had been in during his time in the Regiment. There was a log fire burning in the huge fireplace. Standing in front of it was a short stocky black man with receding hair. The very high ceiling made him look much shorter than his actual height, which James estimated to be about five-feet-seven. He smiled when he saw James.

Mr Chidoli interrupted the silence. "Mr Annan, this is His Excellency, the High Commissioner to Tanzania here in London, Mr Henry Murundi."

They shook hands.

"Welcome, Mr Annan. It is a pleasure to meet you. Your reputation goes before you. You have been highly recommended."

James raised his eyebrows slightly.

"Mr Chidoli has told me all about you."

Murundi beckoned to James and Chidoli to sit down. He then took up his place behind a huge mahogany leather-clad desk. He sank back into a high-backed leather chair.

Chidoli, sitting to James's left, began talking:

"Mr Annan, you may wonder why we have invited you to see us."

"The thought had crossed my mind," James interrupted, displaying a hint of his dry sense of humour.

"Let me tell you then," continued Chidoli. He showed no sign of irritation with the interruption. "As you already know, my name is Edward Chidoli. I represent a new casino complex in Tanzania based about thirty kilometres up the coast from Dar Es Salaam. It was opened shortly after Nelson Mandela became President of the Republic of South Africa in 1994."

James listened intently, not wishing to interrupt. He was somewhat confused about the mention of Mandela's name and his connection, if there was any.

Chidoli explained the link with South Africa. In December 1979, Sun City, a massive Casino complex, was opened in Bophuthatswana to avoid the anti-gambling laws of apartheid South Africa. Bophuthatswana was one of the African homelands set up by the then apartheid government in Pretoria to give the Tswana people supposed independence. It became a playground for wealthy gamblers from all over the world and rich South Africans who were starved of glitz.

The homeland, seemingly ruled independently from Pretoria, had a figurehead president, Lucas Mangope. It purported to give self-rule to South African blacks but was Pretoria's way of trying to pacify anti-apartheid resistance from governments from around the world.

Two years after Sun City was opened a second rival complex, the Palace, was opened by Sonny Diamond, a former employee of Sun City. Sonny Diamond ran the Palace for many years before eventually fleeing South Africa to avoid facing charges of tax evasion and fraud.

Chidoli continued: "Diamond's finance director, Victor Marais, took over the running of the casino for a few months before he too had to flee the country shortly after Mandela came to power."

At this point James broke his silence. "What happened to Diamond and why did Marais have to flee?"

"Diamond fled to Mauritius where he owned a hotel complex. He didn't return to South Africa but when Mandela came to power a warrant was issued for his arrest and he was extradited back to South Africa to face charges for tax evasion and fraud."

"What happened to him?"

"He was found guilty on three counts of tax evasion but not guilty of fraud, due to insufficient evidence. He was fined 5,000,000 rand and ordered to pay costs. Furthermore he was ordered to pay the South African Revenue Service 10.5 million rand!"

"Wow, that's one hell of a lot of money!!" exclaimed James. "So he didn't go to prison then?"

"Oh yes he did! He was sentenced to seven years but it was reduced to five on appeal," replied Chidoli.

"And what of Marais, what about him?"

"Marais was a well-known money launderer, drug runner and racketeer. You name it, he was involved in it. He was a really nasty individual. He was also under investigation for tax evasion and fraud. When Mandela came to power Marais plotted his own escape route."

Murundi interrupted at this point: "This is where Tanzania comes into the equation. Marais sold out his shares in the Palace and invested heavily in the Golden City development along with a group of disillusioned Afrikaners who didn't want to stay in the new South Africa."

"So what was the attraction of Tanzania for the Afrikaners?" queried James.

"Tanzania had only recently started to make changes since the years of rule under Julius Nyrere's influence. Afrikaners saw the system in Tanzania as moderate with the potential to develop a stable economy. By bringing in a great deal of money and investment they realised they could continue to live the lifestyle they had in South Africa without being hounded by Mandela's new government there," said Murundi with a deadpan face. He continued: "The new Tanzanian government under the leadership of Ali Hassan Mwinyi, who had been handed power by Nyrere when he retired in 1985, turned a blind eye to much of what many of the Afrikaners were already doing, even before Mandela came to power, because we needed foreign investment. Many Afrikaners had left South Africa before Mandela's landslide victory there and applied for residency in Tanzania."

Chidoli glanced furtively at Murundi and took over: "Benjamin Mkapa, who was voted in as the new President of Tanzania in the first free elections in 1995 was very disturbed about Marais's residency in Tanzania. He was well known for his stance on corruption. The authorities in South Africa were applying for Marais's extradition and Mkapa couldn't afford any scandals so soon after the election."

At this point Chidoli sat almost bolt upright in his chair. "I am the only Tanzanian-born director of the Golden City Casino. Marais has to have a Tanzanian national on the board of directors. It is a common business requirement where foreign investment is coming into the country."

James noticed beads of sweat appearing on Chidoli's forehead. He seemed to be very agitated. James wondered whether he was telling the truth. Chidoli took a handkerchief from his jacket pocket and wiped his face. He continued. This time he raised his voice:

"It's nothing to do with greed and me wanting to take over from Marais. I simply don't want foreigners to take advantage of my country's economy and take money out of the country, I want them to re-invest here." He said this with a steely look in his eyes. He claimed to be genuinely concerned about his country but James couldn't help thinking there might be a hidden agenda.

At that point Murundi got up from his desk and threw a few more logs on the fire. The wood was very dry and within seconds flames crackled up. The smell of freshly burning wood filled the air. Murundi returned to his desk, straightening his tie as he did so. Chidoli began again:

"The casino has recently sustained heavy losses. I've suspected for a long time that something was not quite right but I didn't have enough evidence to catch the suspects red-handed. Secondly we suspect that Marais himself is behind a scam to get rid of more money without declaring it and paying tax. It also gives him a chance to get the money out of the country."

"So there's a political motive involved as well as an economic one," said James.

"Yes, but furthermore a large proportion of the staff were from England or are former employees of Marais from the Palace. They are likely to know all the casino scams that ever existed."

"Jesus!" whispered James under his breath. "How do you propose that I become involved?" He was playing for time so that he could weigh up the situation in his own mind.

Murundi lit up a cigar and coughed as he inhaled. "Does anyone mind?" he said, waving the cigar in the air as he spoke. James and Chidoli shook their heads. They were hardly in a position to object.

"We would like you to put one of your men into the Golden City posing as an employee," Chidoli responded.

"By coincidence, one of my staff has experience as a croupier. He's an expert in dealing blackjack. He learnt how to play when he worked in a London nightclub with a casino attached, but unfortunately his expertise does not run to other games."

"Don't worry," interrupted Chidoli. "There's an industry training school in Hertfordshire that can make him into a fully fledged croupier in a couple of weeks."

"I'm sure Martin Donaldson is the very man."

"What I need to know are your terms of business, Mr Annan."

"My normal charges for a job of this nature are $25,000 (US) per month per man. I will also require a down payment for a deposit for three months' work for two men as a guaranteed non-returnable minimum."

"That works out at least $150,000!" Chidoli quickly calculated.

"Plus of course reasonable out-of-pocket expenses. I will require a float of $10,000 for expenses. I will invoice you on a monthly basis in arrears and whatever I spend, plus or minus the $10,000, must be topped up at the end of each month. For each man I will invoice on an ongoing monthly basis until the work is completed."

Chidoli looked astonished. He obviously hadn't expected such a high figure. His breathing had become noticeably quicker. James waited in expectation, deliberately not saying anything. Eventually Chidoli spoke:

"You are a hard man, Mr Annan." He smiled as he removed his gold-rimmed spectacles. "It must be your African heritage. I don't think I've much of a choice." He rose from his chair and offered his hand to James. James stood up and they shook hands on the deal. James was surprised that Chidoli didn't even try and bargain. He found it rather unusual for an African not to try and negotiate.

"Gentlemen, I think this is where my involvement ends for the time being," Murundi interrupted.

"I will keep you informed of developments, sir," said Chidoli sternly.

Murundi stood up and shook hands with James. Chidoli remained behind as James left the room.

As James walked slowly back to the Hilton he wondered why Chidoli had not met him on his own. He was confused as to why Murundi had become involved and why they had met at the High Commission. He wondered whether the relationship between Murundi and Chidoli was deeper than it appeared.

4

THE RHYTHMS OF the night had already started. Sean and James were sitting on the veranda. In the background they could both hear the croaking of the bullfrogs mingled with the clicking sound of the crickets. The noises mixed with the sound of the wind as it whistled through the branches of the palm trees that stretched out before them. They watched in silence as the almost full moon lit up the sea with the waves gently breaking on the shore.

Achieng was tired after their swimming and Akoth had given her an early supper and put her to bed. This time Sean and James had dinner alone. Over dinner James had given Sean a briefing of his meeting with Chidoli and Murundi.

"Next time, Sean, I'll bring Yolanda and the kids and make a holiday of it. They would absolutely love it here," said James enthusiastically, turning away from the magnificent view.

"Yes, James. I would be delighted to see you all. It's a shame you haven't been before now."

"Ah, I've been so busy," sighed James, "setting up my business and so on, I guess it's been the same for you."

Sean nodded his agreement.

"So where do I fit with all this? I don't understand," puzzled Sean.

"I want you to fly down to Dar Es Salaam and visit the Golden City as a punter. When you're there I want you to find out as much general information as you can without raising any suspicions."

"Why are you asking me? What's happened to Martin

Donaldson? Surely he's better placed than me to get the information you require?"

"Hmm, there's more than a slight complication." James paused. "There's a lot more that's happened in the last few months. Things don't always go according to plan," he said ruefully, his voice trailing away as he said it.

"What do you mean?" Sean said cautiously, becoming more dubious about the whole situation.

James looked at Sean. He slowly stretched back in his chair. "It's a long story, but first I need a beer."

Sean got up from his chair and disappeared into the house, returning with two big bottles of Tusker beer, the local brew. James threw him a curious glance.

"There's no need for you to worry. I only have the occasional beer now. My drink problem's behind me," Sean said to reassure James.

"I hope you're right, my friend."

James began to tell Sean about Martin Donaldson. Like Sean and James he was the product of the English public-school system. A classics scholar whilst at school he failed his 'A' levels having had a bright future predicted for him by his masters. Top of his class up until the end of the first year of sixth form, he didn't do a stroke of work in his second year. An all-round athlete, he was particularly good at rugby, being awarded his school colours as the hooker in the first XV. His miserable failure at 'A' level caused him to leave school not knowing what he wanted to do with his life.

It was only under parental pressure that he decided to try his hand in the insurance world. It didn't take him long to realise that it was a job he hated with a passion. He resigned within three months. After a succession of temporary jobs to earn money to live he saw an advert for a trainee croupier with a London casino group. He applied and got it.

After attending training school he worked for a year at the Mayfair Grand in London. He soon became bored with it and took the surprising step of signing up in the Army as a private. It was a complete shock to his friends and family and completely out of character. Although he had been very rebellious at school he knuckled down and excelled in his initial army training. Before long he was offered the chance of going to the Officer Training School at Sandhurst. Six months later he passed out as a second lieutenant and joined the Light Infantry based at Winchester.

Slightly above average height with a wiry but well muscled body he showed great aptitude in the Army. His high IQ and his determination to prove to his parents that he was actually a high achiever allowed him to reach the rank of First Lieutenant quicker than most. Three years later he applied to join the Regiment and passed selection, his speciality being firearms and explosives.

Martin soon became well known as a ladies' man. His black hair and dark complexion made him look a Mediterranean version of the actor Pierce Brosnan. The resemblance was uncanny and it resulted in him having a string of affairs with London debutantes, aspiring actresses and models.

Martin eventually left the Army shortly before James in 1990, when he took a job as a greeter at a popular London nightclub. He missed the action in the Army and again he soon became bored. He continued working at the nightclub and it was only when James left the SAS in 1993 and approached Martin to join him in his security business that he left the nightclub.

5

MARTIN DONALDSON ATTENDED the croupier school in Hertfordshire for a revision course when the Golden City project came up. Whilst at the school he learned to deal blackjack and roulette very well. He also refreshed his memory on punto banco, baccarat and chemmy and how to operate a dice table. Edward Chidoli arranged the necessary references and produced a history of jobs through his contacts in the casino industry from a couple of small-town casinos in England. He had been careful not to get references from any of the big London clubs. It was more likely that staff that had been employed there moved more frequently around the world from one location to another. The casino industry was a very incestuous business. Chidoli had been very careful to check that none of the current employees at the Golden City had been employed at the casinos where Martin had obtained his false references.

"As I said, Martin's application was successful and at the end of the course he had flown to Dar Es Salaam."

"What happened then?"

"All went well for the first month. Martin hadn't noticed anything strange at the tables. There were no obvious overfriendly connections between staff and the punters."

"Have there been any discussions amongst the staff suggesting that there might be any fiddles going on?"

Martin had been trained in interrogation techniques during his time in the Regiment. He had been careful not to overplay his hand but generally he was able to ingratiate himself with his colleagues without being overfriendly with any of them. His methods of questioning had been very carefully planned. He had managed to slip leading questions into seemingly innocent conversations without making it sound like an interrogation.

"Would you like another beer? All this talking has made me very thirsty." James drained the last remnants in his glass.

Sean got up from his chair again and went to the kitchen where he pulled another couple of cold Tuskers from the fridge. Before he returned to the veranda he checked on Achieng. She was curled up on her bed sleeping peacefully under a huge mosquito net. He gazed at her still form for a few minutes before returning to the veranda. James by now had risen from his chair and he was leaning against the wooden railing looking out to sea, admiring the stars in the near cloudless sky above.

Sean poured James his beer.

"Cheers!" they said simultaneously and touched each other's glasses, raising the frothy-topped liquid to their lips, each taking a long swig.

"Amber nectar," said James as he put his glass down on the nearby table.

"What happened next? I still want to know what went wrong with your plans with Martin."

"Who mentioned anything had gone wrong with them?" replied James, sounding irritated for the first time.

"Sorry, I was only speculating."

James scowled. "According to Martin, at the end of the second month a group of croupiers began discussing the possibility of investing in a racehorse or two. Nairobi is only an hour-and-a-half flight away and there is a good racecourse there with regular racing."

"That seems a strange investment to make. I didn't realise there was a big racing industry here in Kenya!"

"It's not exactly a booming business but it's a standing joke that when there's a race meeting at the Nairobi course the jockeys change the horse colours and their own silks after each race, giving the horses and riders new names to make it look as though there are more competitors than there actually are!"

Sean chuckled. "Surely the horses must be knackered by the end of a meeting!"

"It's not quite that bad, but you can imagine that new racehorses on the scene are made very welcome and most important of all it's a good way of laundering money."

Astonishment again registered all over Sean's face. "You mean any money that had been ripped off from the casino was being used to buy racehorses. Surely they can't be that expensive? Are we not talking about millions of dollars being stolen? What the hell does a racehorse cost for Christ's sake?"

James placed a hand on Sean's shoulder. "It wasn't so much the cost of the horses, it was a way by which the gang of croupiers could launder the money suggesting huge winnings at the races! It stopped people from becoming suspicious about any change in their spending habits. If any questions were asked they could claim that they had won at the races."

"Jesus! So tell me how many croupiers were involved in the scam by that time?"

"Martin wasn't sure exactly but including himself he worked out there were nine!"

"Nine! So tell me how Martin got involved."

"He had been promoted one evening to Acting Inspector. So he was able to watch one of the other croupiers in action. In addition there was one gambler on the other side of the tables. He's British. His name is David Smith. According to Martin he had recently used the idea of the Bahamas cups in a casino in the Bahamas with minor success. He had learned about the cups from the coup that had previously been operated at the Palace Casino."

"How did he know about that?"

"He read about it in British and South African newspapers shortly after the original coup was discovered in 1985."

"Excuse me, but am I missing something here? What exactly are the Bahamas cups?"

"I suppose that would be helpful!" responded James. "Forgive me. Basically they are a hollowed out tin cup made to look like a pile of gambling chips. They are made fractionally larger than a real pile, maybe one or two millimetres in diameter larger. That way they are indistinguishable from the real ones and to make them even more authentic a real chip is stuck to the top of the tin cup. It is almost impossible to detect it with the naked eye."

"So how many chips are there in a pile?"

"There are five chips of any one amount. For example at the Palace Casino there were piles of chips of ten rand, twenty rand and fifty rand and so on."

"What was the point of a cup though?"

"What happens is the gambler will bet a pile of chips using the cup, or what appears to be a pile of chips and places his bet on the table. When he loses, the dealer will collect the cup and put it in the bank. When the gambler then wins, for example 50 rand in a pile of 10-rand chips, the dealer will very quickly lift the cup over a pile of 100-rand chips and make the payout back to the gambler. Fifty rand then very quickly becomes 400 rand and so on. It doesn't take long to shift an awful lot of money off a table. When the gambler leaves the table he goes and cashes up with the cashier. The cashier, the dealer and the inspector and possibly the pit boss need to be involved to make sure the whole operation runs smoothly."

"Tell me about the coup that was pulled off in the Golden City."

James looked at his watch. It was by then nearly midnight. "Listen, Sean, I'm really tired now. I could do with some shuteye. Let's continue this tomorrow."

Frustration showed all over Sean's face.

"You can't go to bed now without completing your story. At least answer me one more question and tell me more about the coup in the Golden City, and how Martin spotted the cups. What was the connection with the Palace Casino?"

James grinned, knowing full well he was prolonging Sean's agony. However, he went on to explain that during Martin's first shift as Acting Inspector, he spotted what he thought was one of the cups. The croupier "working the cup" was very clumsy with all the chips he was using that night. It was either through nerves or inexperience.

Martin, realising he had spotted something very unusual, decided not to take immediate action and report him to the management. It was only later in the staff bar after the end of the shift that he approached the dealer involved and asked him what had been going on.

"There's not much more to tell but there is a strong connection between the two casino coups from both sides of the table." James raised his eyebrows. "I'll tell you all about it tomorrow."

6

SEAN BRAKED HARD and swerved to his right spraying up a cloud of dust and debris narrowly missing the matatu that had pulled out in front of him, forcing him across the centre line in the road. The tyres on his car screeched on the tarmac. The smell of burning rubber filled the car. He sounded his horn in annoyance. The driver of the matatu returned the gesture. He honked his horn even louder and for longer as Sean changed down into a lower gear, accelerating past the bus, back on to the left side of the road. The driver's tout who was hanging out of the vehicle on the nearside shouted some abuse and waved his free arm at Sean in a provocative gesture. Sean checked in his rear-view mirror that Achieng was still tightly strapped and safe in her car seat. He accelerated faster so as not to get involved in any further altercation with the matatu. Several pedestrians looked on in amazement, shaking their heads in disbelief. It was another typical example of the poor driving standards along the New Malindi road leading back into Mombasa. It was 8.30 in the morning, a time when vehicles and people struggled to get to work on time. Two hundred metres further on Sean indicated to the left and slowed as he turned down the side road leading to Achieng's school.

Out in the garden several children were already playing as Nikki Greene and the other teachers greeted Sean and Achieng at the gate.

"I'm looking forward to seeing you tomorrow night," Sean said to Nikki quietly as he was leaving, careful not to advertise the fact to the other teachers.

"I am too!" Nikki replied enthusiastically, as her body tingled with excitement. She waved as Sean climbed into his car and drove off in the direction of his home. He was feeling very pleased with himself as he greeted James on his return.

"Fancy a run before it gets too hot? A couple of miles along the beach will do you the world of good."

Sean began a series of stretching exercises. He was already in shorts and trainers.

"Sounds good to me," James agreed. "I'll go and get changed."

Five minutes later they were jogging along the hard sand closest to the water's edge, and it took Sean back to the days when he last ran with James up on the Brecon Beacons, with full bergens on their backs. Mombasa was a far cry from that, he thought. He winced at the painful memories of his blistered feet and shoulders and the biting cold winter air on Brecon. They kept up a steady pace and after about three miles they slowed to a halt in front of some of the more popular beach hotels. There was a hive of activity as several tourists browsed at the little shops and curios set up along the beach.

"Time to stretch off," Sean ordered as they slowed to a stop to catch their breath. The humidity was already very high and he could see that James had struggled with the distinct lack of air as he ran. They began a series of stretching exercises, much to the amazement of the beach boys and tourists as they watched the muzungu and the big black man with interest.

Five minutes later they were on their way, back in the direction from which they had come. This time Sean deliberately quickened the pace, his arms and legs pumping vigorously. By now his tee shirt was dripping with sweat. In spite of the sea breeze on his face the humidity made him struggle to breathe with a controlled flow. As they neared home Sean broke into a sprint. James reacted quickly and the two ran side-by-side for the final 400 metres, at a furious pace, until they eventually came to a stop by the back gate.

"You bastard, Sean," James wheezed, as he gulped for air, his lungs exploding from the effort. "Getting revenge for the training in the Brecon Beacons, I suspect." He laughed deeply as the sweat streamed off both of them. Sean laughed too, trying his best not to show James he was suffering in much the same way. After warming down with a few more stretching exercises they sat down on the low wall overlooking the ocean.

Sean called to Opiyo, who was working in the garden: "Ask Akoth to bring some water and oranges, please." He turned to James, "At least tell me what happened next at the Palace Casino!"

Akoth appeared with a tray of water and some oranges that she had already peeled, and placed it on the wall beside them. They each took a glass of water and gulped it down to quench their thirst.

"First of all let me tell you about the Palace Casino connection in South Africa, and Alan Hudson, the gambler who was involved in the original coup."

James went on to explain that when the Palace Casino coup was discovered Hudson had disappeared. Apparently, he was held up at gunpoint in a Johannesburg hotel and robbed of a great deal of money, several of the Bahamas cups, and most important of all an address book containing a list of names, all with Palace Casino addresses.

The robbers, who it is alleged were Yugoslav gangsters, realised they had stumbled on something very interesting. They were opportunists, originally only after money. They had been following Hudson for several days. They knew he was a gambler who had been playing the tables in the Palace Casino. It is alleged the Yugoslav gangsters made off with about $40,000. Initially they didn't realise the importance of the address book but it didn't take them long to put two and two together and work out there was probably a scam happening at the Palace Casino.

Hudson realised the significance of losing the cups and telephoned Derek Julius, his gambling partner who was still at the Palace Casino, to warn him to leave. Hudson had the good sense to leave Johannesburg immediately and return to the States.

Sean drank a pint of water and picked up one of the oranges and began to eat it, sucking the juice from it before chewing the pith and skin. He looked at James.

"How was Julius involved?"

"Julius was a real slime ball. He was a lowlife from the East End of London. He had been stealing from casinos for years and had heard about Hudson and his Bahamas cups. Somehow he had made contact and approached him shortly after the Palace Casino had opened. Security was slack in the early days after opening."

"Okay, we now have a situation where Hudson and Julius are in the Palace Casino. Surely they needed someone on the inside to work the tables?"

"Of course they did. Julius already had a connection working at the Palace. A former lover of his, Angela Whittaker, had run several scams with him previously at some of the casinos she had worked at in London. She was one of the insiders he needed and she began recruiting a team who included her new husband, Barry. One of the others he recruited was in fact one of the senior managers, an Englishman by the name of Tony Stanley, with whom he had run a scam at a casino in the Bahamas."

"Are there that many dishonest people working in casinos? Are they prepared to steal and take the risk of getting caught?" Sean took another bite from his orange.

"You'd better believe it. The temptations put in front of them are huge. Imagine dealing with such vast amounts of money every day of your life. Once working in a casino normally honest people are confronted with a huge moral dilemma. On the other side even the most honest of gamblers who cross the threshold of a casino step into the twilight world of it, all dreaming of huge winnings. How many of them would steal even a few chips from a table if they were down on their luck and thought they could get away with it?"

"So did Julius warn the croupiers about Hudson's misfortune in Johannesburg?"

"No, he continued to work the tables. He regarded it as his chance to take even more money with Hudson out of the way."

"Surely someone must have queried Hudson's absence?"

"Barry Whittaker did but Julius explained that he had to return to the States to visit his sick mother."

Sean fetched some more water and James continued the story. Sean sat there absolutely fascinated by it. Julius operated the scam and chanced his luck for a further two weeks. Meanwhile the two Yugoslav gangsters took a trip to the Palace where they met with one of Marais's senior managers. Luckily for him he happened to be Tony Stanley. Unfortunately for them, Stanley himself was involved in the coup and was horrified to discover the Yugoslavs had a list of some of the names of the staff involved. Seizing his chance he persuaded them to part with the address book in return for a cash payment of 30,000 rand. It was quite a considerable amount of money in the early 'eighties as the rand then was worth about two to the pound sterling. He was also in the privileged position of having access to that amount of money immediately.

When the two Yugoslavs departed Stanley had to think quickly. He also had to find a way of replacing the 30,000 rand if he could at all. The following week there was a senior managers and directors' meeting to be held in Mauritius, where Marais owned a hotel complex. Stanley was due to attend it and he planned to take his wife, Lindsay, with him.

She was an inspector on the tables but was not involved in the coup. Stanley realised there was a real possibility of him being caught. Although he had paid off the Yugoslavs he didn't trust them and he didn't want them coming back to talk to Marais. It was imperative that he talked to Marais first. The meeting in Mauritius was a golden opportunity to inform Marais about the coup.

Sean interrupted. "James, come on, get to the point. How do you want me to be involved?"

"There is a casino in Mombasa. I want you to pay a visit there and learn how to play some of the games, particularly blackjack."

"Why?"

"It will take you a week to learn a few of the games and then as I said before, I want you to fly down to Dar and play the tables at the Golden City, posing as a rich but novice punter."

"Hang on a minute. Don't forget I have a business to run. Are you sure that's all you want me to do?" Sean remembered that particular week was Achieng's half-term week from school. "I can't let her down. We've planned to do so many things."

He remembered also Louise's disappointment when she was younger, when he kept changing their plans with his overseas trips. He swallowed hard, overcome with a similar feeling of guilt again.

"Sean, it will be so easy. You are the ideal man and don't forget you owe me a favour." He gave Sean a wry grin. He was embarrassed. He hated himself for calling in the favour at that moment.

Sean gave James a long hard look, remembering how much help James had given him to find Akinyi's killers. If it hadn't been for James he would never have found Achieng either. He owed him right enough. His look of anger turned to one of resignation, which slowly turned to a sheepish smile.

"Okay, James, I'll do it."

"Good on you, Sean, I knew I could rely on you." He slapped Sean on the back in celebration.

"One thing though. I'm going out to dinner on Saturday night. It's a long-standing arrangement and I can't get out of it," he lied, not wishing to miss out on dinner with Nikki Greene.

They raised their water bottles in acknowledgement and took another swig, draining them both as they did so.

"Who is the lucky lady? I guess I'll have to make my own arrangements for Saturday night. We can start your training at the casino on Sunday. I can't let you miss out on the chance of a love affair."

"No one you know," replied Sean rather curtly.

James flicked a fly from his leg and then broke the momentary silence. "What happened to Njeri? Do you still see her?" He knew full well that Njeri had returned to Kenya to start her own business on the north coast near Mombasa.

Sean winced noticeably. "She opened a very successful hair, beauty and massage salon."

"Have you two rekindled your romance?"

Sean responded abruptly. "No. Of course we haven't. You know as well as I do that any involvement on an intimate level ended once I discovered she went 'on the game' in Richmond."

"You must have seen her though," James pried, trying again, realising he had hit a raw nerve.

"Yes, we meet for a drink from time to time. In spite of all she did I have to admit I remain very fond of her. I'm simply very disappointed that when I gave her a good opportunity in Richmond she didn't take it."

James pulled at his wet tee shirt. "It seems she has now though with the success of her beauty salon. I wouldn't mind meeting her again. Can you call her and arrange to meet for a drink?"

"Yes, of course, why not?" replied Sean, quickly changing the subject as he looked at his watch. "Come on. I need to collect Achieng from school in forty-five minutes. Let's get changed. You can come with me."

They got up from the low wall and ambled back to the house. On their way back Sean turned to James. "One last thing. Are you sure that's all I've got to do at the moment?"

"It depends what else comes up," grinned James.

7

NIKKI LOOKED STUNNING as she answered the door to her apartment. Sean's face must have been a picture as he tried not to make it too obvious he had noticed her hourglass figure. Her usual garb at nursery of shapeless Polo shirt and black skirt was in sharp contrast to the low-fronted, short leopard-skin print dress she was wearing. Her matching high-heeled shoes showed off her shapely legs. He half-gasped as he greeted her.

"Good evening. Is Cinderella ready for the ball?" he joked. He deliberately tried to appear as casual as possible when all the time the adrenaline was rushing through him like an express train. "You look good," he said, as if he had to convince himself that he wasn't dreaming.

"You don't look so bad yourself, Prince Charming," she giggled as she set the tone for the evening. At the same time she admired Sean in his finely pressed, mandarin-collared white shirt that was tucked into his tailored dark blue trousers. The day in the sun had topped up his already golden tan. He was certainly a handsome devil, Nikki thought to herself.

"Your carriage awaits, Cinders," he said as he offered Nikki his arm.

Sting's "Every Breath You Take" was playing on the CD in Sean's car as he drove steadily to the Tamarind. The Mombasa traffic was as busy as ever. The journey passed quickly as the two engaged in small-talk. Nikki even teased Sean about his poor effort at singing along with Sting. Singing was certainly not his forte but he felt he didn't have a care in the world as he warmed to Nikki's effervescent personality. As he breathed in slowly he savoured the perfume she was wearing.

On arrival at the Tamarind Sean was greeted by the maître d', who showed them to their table. All eyes were on them as the other diners cast admiring glances at the attractive couple. As they sat down Sean couldn't help noticing Nikki's large firm breasts beneath her dress. Her nipples looked hard and erect beneath the thin material. He tried to divert his eyes away from them. Nikki giggled again, as she watched Sean, knowing full well what he was looking at. He coughed nervously as he realised she was studying him.

"So what would Cinders like to drink, an aperitif perhaps, or would you prefer it if I ordered a bottle of wine?"

"Ooh, I would love some champagne," she purred excitedly. She smiled, fluttering her eyelashes at Sean.

"No problem."

He perused the list and turned to the wine waiter, who had been hovering at the table in expectation.

"A bottle of number fifteen, please. On ice, and I will have a mineral water."

The pair sat in silence as they studied their menus carefully. A live African jazz band played softly in the background. By the time the waiter returned with the drinks they were ready to order. The evening passed with much laughter and jokes. Sean felt very at ease with Nikki, as she did with him.

Nikki explained she had done her degree in sports science at Loughborough University. She played tennis to county standard and was good at a variety of other sports. After completing her degree she had decided to take two years out before trying for a job at a sports and leisure complex in England. Her uncle was an import/export agent in Kenya and it was he who told her about the job at Achieng's nursery. She saw it as a good opportunity to travel and see another continent before settling down to a serious career.

"And what brings you to this part of the world, Sean?" For some reason she was not expecting him to give a full answer. She suspected there were many things in his past that she would have to wait to find out about.

"Oh, that's a long story." He replied carefully, not wishing to commit himself.

She saw the pain in his eyes and wished she hadn't asked that question so soon, but the champagne had made her braver than she ought to have been.

"I'm sorry, I didn't mean to pry."

He noticed her sudden awkwardness and wanted to make her feel at ease.

"Oh please don't worry about that, I feel sure I'll be able to tell you the full story one day, but it really is a long and complicated one."

Nikki waited before continuing. "Tell me about your childhood and your family in England. What you do for a living and so on. You look like you could have been a top sportsman."

Sean was in peak condition physically for his age even though he had struggled with alcoholism, a couple of years previously.

"You are very observant." He smiled, not wishing to appear too bigheaded. "Yes, I played international rugby for Scotland and the British Lions and retired after Scotland won the Grand Slam in 1985."

"Wow! My younger brother would be really impressed with that. He plays rugby for the Harlequins," she said rather proudly.

"What position?"

"You've got me there. I'm not entirely sure but he's very fast and apparently scores lots of tries."

"How old is he?"

"He's six years younger than me. So that makes him nineteen. He's only recently left school and wants to turn professional, much to the opposition of my father," declared Nikki. "He wants him to follow a proper career path."

"He should turn professional. I wish I could have done so in my day," he said ruefully, realising how much money some of the top players were now commanding for pursuing a sport they loved.

The conversation turned away from sport and Sean explained about his business and some of his plans for the future. They continued their meal discussing all sorts of things.

Over coffee Nikki suddenly asked, "What about Achieng's mother?" She wanted to check that there was no opposition to her still around. Sean swallowed hard and again Nikki could see the pain in his eyes.

"She's dead!" he said bluntly. "She was murdered by neo-Nazis in Germany." He almost whispered the last sentence and turned his attention to the bougainvillea flowers that were on the table. He plucked one from the vase and leant across and placed it in Nikki's hair. He looked up and could see the shock on her face. He smiled as if to reassure her that he didn't mind her questions.

"Come on. I'll get the bill and if you like we can go dancing," he said, trying to introduce a relaxed atmosphere again.

"Yes, I would like that very much."

Sean hoped there would be some slow music played so he got a chance of putting his arms around her and holding his body close to hers. He was enjoying his evening and wanted the feeling of excitement to last forever.

§

It was 2.45 a.m. when Sean and Nikki finally returned to her apartment. Both were tired after the night of dancing at the Mamba Village Discotheque, a popular nightspot situated on the outskirts of Mombasa. Being a Saturday night it had been particularly busy and very hot. It was a long time since Sean had enjoyed himself so much. As he drove back to Nikki's apartment he felt his shirt sticking to his body from the sweat caused by the dancing. The air conditioning in his car was a sharp contrast to the heat of the disco and he shivered slightly as the coldness from his wet shirt touched his skin.

He sounded his horn as he reached the gates of the apartment complex. An askari opened the gates once he realised it was Nikki and directed Sean to a parking space. He pulled up slowly and stopped, leaving the ignition running, expecting to drop Nikki off so he could hurry home for a shower to warm his chilled body.

"Please come in for coffee, Sean." Nikki smiled seductively at him and touched his left knee as she began to open the car door. Sean looked at his watch and was about to protest.

"Come on, Sean," she insisted, assuming a position of control as she sensed his nervousness.

He switched off the ignition and climbed out of the car, following Nikki across the car park, through the small reception and up a small flight of stairs to her apartment on the first floor.

As she unlocked the front door Sean couldn't help admiring her body again as he stood behind her. Her dress was clinging tightly to her body and it further enhanced her curvaceous figure. He took a deep breath. Once inside, Nikki directed Sean to her sitting room. Crossing the room she switched on her CD player.

"Any preferences?" she asked as she searched through a pile of CDs.

"No, no, you choose." He wondered what music she would select to set the mood for the rest of the night.

"I'll be back shortly," she said as Sade's "Smooth Operator" began playing in the background. "Make yourself comfortable."

Sean sat down on the two-seater settee. As he looked around he noticed the room was filled with African memorabilia and a variety of ornaments. On one of the walls was a family photograph. A large Turkish carpet was spread on the tiled floor. On the far wall a colourful African batik depicting a variety of animals contrasted well with the whitewashed walls. It was definitely a woman's home. A variety of flowers in several vases added the final touches around the room.

By the time Nikki returned some ten minutes later Sean had warmed up and his shirt was almost completely dry. He felt relaxed and had removed his shoes. As Nikki entered the room he felt another rush of adrenaline. She had changed into a mid-thigh-length silk dressing gown. Although tied tightly at the waist it was falling open at the front revealing her firm breasts.

"Would sir like a coffee?" She placed a tray with a tall pot and two cups on the low table and sat down next to him. As she leaned across to pour the coffee she placed her forearm and right hand on his knee to keep her balance. Sean smelled her perfume as she brushed against him. Once she had finished pouring the coffee she turned towards him and threw her arms around his shoulders. She kissed him full on the lips. He was momentarily taken aback but quickly responded with a passion that Nikki had never experienced with another man. Her hands moved slowly from his shoulders and she began caressing the back of his neck. At the same time her darting tongue explored his. She withdrew briefly and gave a soft gasp as she drew breath. She stood up taking his right hand with her left and pulled him gently upwards beckoning him to her bedroom. Sean almost protested worrying about getting back home so late. It concerned him that Achieng might wake in the night and find that he was not at home. He dismissed the thought knowing she was in safe hands with Akoth and Opiyo, and after all James was also there.

His thoughts quickly returned to Nikki as he followed her to the bedroom. As they reached the bed she still had her back to him but deliberately let her dressing gown slip from her shoulders, revealing her perfectly formed and tanned body.

Sean leant forward and kissed her neck, running his fingers through her blonde hair. She let out a gentle squeal of delight and turned towards him unbuttoning his shirt. As he stooped and kissed her he drew her body to his and felt her firm rounded breasts below his chest. She tugged at his leather belt, releasing it and began to undo his fly, causing his trousers to drop to the floor.

He stepped out of his trousers and pushed her gently back on the bed. Within seconds their bodies were intertwined as one. They explored each other's bodies as they kissed passionately. He felt her rounded breasts with both hands. Nikki responded and exhaled. Very soon his tongue was gliding over her breasts and down across her stomach. She moaned in expectation as his tongue searched her bellybutton and tasted the small beads of perspiration that were appearing on her body. Sean inhaled and smelt her sweet perfume as his tongue moved down and explored her inner thighs. She clutched at his hair and her body arched up.

"Make love to me, Sean. Make love to me," she repeated as he slowly entered her.

8

TEN YEARS EARLIER Tony Stanley and his wife Lindsay flew from Johannesburg to Mauritius for the management meeting with Victor Marais. Tony had planned how he would approach Marais about the coup that had taken place in November 1985. He realised he would have to do his best to hide his nervousness from Marais. Any slight slip and he knew Marais would accuse him and Lindsay of an involvement. He hadn't told Lindsay but he had some information about Marais that would be their lifesaver.

On arrival at the airport in Mauritius they were met by a Marais company vehicle and were driven to their hotel complex at Le Toussroc. After checking in at the hotel, Tony telephoned Marais.

"Hello. This is Tony Stanley. I arrived an hour ago and would like to see you. I have something very important to discuss with you."

"Can't it wait until tonight's management meeting? I have several important appointments that I cannot cancel," replied Marais very curtly.

Marais was not an easy man to deal with and Tony did not like him at the best of times. He had seen his vicious temper on several occasions previously and he certainly didn't want to be on the receiving end of one of his outbursts.

"I have something very, very important to discuss with you alone and it cannot wait until this evening." Tony replied firmly enough to make Marais pay attention to the seriousness of it. He surprised himself with the steeliness and resolve with which he said it.

"If it was that important why didn't you phone me from the Palace?" Marais was even more aggressive than before.

Tony hesitated, collecting his thoughts. "It is not the sort of thing I could risk discussing over the phone." He tapped his fingers on the bedside table.

"Oh, very well!" snapped Marais, growing even more frustrated. "Be at my office in one hour. Don't be late."

The line went dead. Tony hung up and looked across at Lindsay who was sitting in an armchair on the other side of the room. She stared at him anxiously.

"What are you going to do, Tony? Do you want me to come with you?"

"No, no, it's okay, love. It's nothing I can't deal with on my own." He was doing his best to appear confident. "I want to make sure you're kept well out of it anyway." He glanced nervously at his watch. It was 1.30 p.m.

"Come on, let's go and have some lunch. I'll deal with things better on a full stomach."

A short time later Tony and Lindsay were down at the poolside, eating a light lunch. It was a beautiful hot sunny day and they sat in silence as they admired the calm of the Indian Ocean, gently lapping against the shoreline. The stillness of the flat blue sea helped Tony to ease his nerves in preparation for his meeting with Marais.

Other than one stiff brandy he drank only water. He knew he would need his wits about him. Although generally a cool character on the surface, he had never experienced such depths of fear at being caught out. Several times in the past, when he'd been stealing from casinos, he'd come close to being caught, but he had never worked for a boss like Marais before. He winced as he remembered some of the severe beatings his fellow-employees had taken from Marais and his security men for being caught stealing. They at least hadn't been caught for stealing the large amounts of money that Tony and his fellow coup members had been. He was greatly concerned and there was always the risk he'd be sacked. He finished his plate of food and wiped his mouth with his napkin, putting it down on the table next to his setting.

"Time to go," he said, rising from his chair. As he did so he leant across and kissed Lindsay full on the lips. It was an unusually tender display of affection on Tony's part.

"Good luck," she whispered in his ear.

"I think I'm going to need it."

Lindsay watched him as he strolled across the sun terrace and disappeared through the swing doors to the right of the cocktail bar. He was only a slight man and below average height. Lindsay suspected he was not the sort of man who would be able to deal with Marais's security men. She feared for her husband but not as much as for herself at the thought of being implicated in something she knew absolutely nothing about, until Tony had told her the day before. Tears welled in her eyes. The shame on her family would be too great for her to bear if there was any suggestion she'd been involved in the coup. She came from a very wealthy English family. Her father was a highly respected Labour MP and a multi-millionaire industrialist, and any scandal might be enough to cause him to have to resign from Parliament. Her mother and father had never liked Tony, who they regarded as a bad influence on their daughter. He was not the calibre of man they wanted her to marry. Tony had been brought up in an orphanage and had been in and out of trouble in his youth. After a series of odd jobs after he left school he eventually answered an advert in the local paper to train as a croupier. Although poorly educated he had a streetwise air about him that stood him in good stead when he entered the world of casinos. It wasn't long before he rose through the casino hierarchy from dealer to inspector to pit boss and eventually manager of a small concern in Stoke-on-Trent, before taking up his current position at the Palace, when it first opened. Despite his success Lindsay's parents still did not like or trust him, and when they married three years earlier they had refused to attend the wedding. Although she still remained in touch with them, she was very saddened by their refusal to accept Tony. She sat in quiet contemplation. She wondered whether they had been right about Tony after all.

§

Tony knocked on the door to Marais's office and entered without bothering to wait for a reply. Marais was sitting behind a large desk studying some papers. He looked up briefly as Tony walked in and pointed to a chair in front of his desk.

"Sit down!" he barked and returned to reading his paperwork.

Tony sat down. Looking around the office he admired the beautiful ornaments and sculptures that adorned the room. He thought to himself how he wished he had Marais's wealth. "Bastard," he muttered under his breath, thinking of how poorly he was paid for the amount of unsocial hours he spent working in the casino for Marais, and helping him to make a pile of money. Marais was well known for his meanness and rarely paid bonuses. Now was payback time, or so Tony planned. His intention was to ask Marais for a big payoff in return for information regarding the coup. Five minutes later Marais looked up from his paperwork.

"So what is it that you want to speak to me about so urgently?"

Tony gulped. He raised his eyes to the minder who was leaning with his back to the wall behind Marais's desk.

"I need to speak to you alone," Tony said, surprising himself with his steeliness. "Please!" he repeated. This time he lowered his voice.

"Okay." Marais clicked his fingers for his minder to leave. "Wait outside, Jappie. I'll call you when I need you."

Jappie responded slowly. He sneered at Tony as he left. His blond hair had been cropped very short. The scars on his cheeks and his hulking eighteen stones made him an imposing figure. A trickle of sweat slid down Tony's back. Tony turned and faced Marais. Their eyes met.

"I'm listening. What is it you want to tell me?"

"I think I have uncovered a coup at the Palace. It is currently in operation and I have a list of names of the croupiers involved..."

Marais interrupted before Tony could continue. "What!" he exploded. "Why the hell didn't you tell me about this before!?" His face changed to a red colour.

"Of course, had I known about it before I'd have told you," said Tony, feigning annoyance, but at the same time trying to control his equilibrium. He went on to explain to Marais about the two Yugoslav gangsters who had turned up at the casino with the address book.

"So how the hell did you persuade them to hand it over?" Marais was becoming even angrier, but at the same time was impressed that Tony had got hold of the book.

"Calm down."

Tony surprised himself at his own calmness and control and sudden lack of fear of Marais. He now saw his opportunity.

"Before I continue, I need your absolute assurance of my safe passage from the casino with my wife Lindsay."

Marais looked perplexed. "There's only one reason why you'd want to get out of the casino in a hurry – you're probably involved yourself. Am I right?" Marais deliberately lowered his voice to barely a whisper as he spoke the last three words. Tony looked at him in surprise. Marais was an exceptionally tall man and stood at about six-feet-five Tony couldn't help laughing out loud as he thought how comical Marais looked as he sat hunched in his great big leather chair wearing a ludicrous-looking khaki safari suit that didn't fit him properly. His white shirt was stained with sweat at the front. He had thick blond hair that looked almost out of control on the top of his head. For all the money he had he was not well groomed. He had an ugly face. His thin pointed nose seemed out of proportion to his face. As a result it did not enhance his looks. Marais fidgeted uneasily in his chair.

"What are you laughing at?" shouted Marais, almost apoplectic with rage. He wasn't used to people laughing at him or certainly not to his face. His blue eyes bulged.

"Nothing," said Tony abruptly. It must be nerves."

"What do you want?" Marais screamed again.

"I want £250,000 and a safe passage back to England for my wife and me."

"Go to hell, I'll have you arrested and you'll spend years rotting in one of our gaols!" said Marais raising his voice almost to fever pitch.

"No you won't," responded Tony very calmly. "First of all you don't know who is involved in the coup and before you are able to catch anyone and close it down a great deal more money will be gone from the tables." He calmly leant across Marais's desk and helped himself to a glass of water. Ignorant bastard for not offering me any, he thought to himself, feeling more confident than ever. Outside the sound of a speedboat engine could be heard starting up. It broke the unhealthy silence.

"What makes you so confident, Tony?" Marais used Tony's Christian name for the first time, presenting a softer approach.

At this point Tony played his trump card. He took great delight in watching Marais's face as he said, "I have something on you that I uncovered when you were working for Diamond. He wouldn't take kindly to finding out you were ripping him off for years and running two sets of accounts."

The colour drained from Marais's face.

"I don't know where you got that idea from. I ran a perfectly legitimate business for Diamond while he was still at the Palace."

He knew full well that he had been running the two sets of accounts. Not only would Diamond have him killed if he found out but he would also have to answer to Lucas Mangope, the President. If he found out also he would want a lot of answers to a lot of questions. Marais shivered as he began to sweat.

"I will tell you why. Because I have a copy of those two sets of accounts in a safe deposit box in England."

Marais was taken aback.

"Where the hell did you get those from? They're not much good to you there."

"That's where you're wrong," snarled Tony. "My lawyer is instructed to open that safe deposit box if anything untoward happens to me!" He knew he had the upper hand for the first time. He continued. "I am not a greedy man but £250,000 should do nicely," he sneered and sat back in his chair.

Marais looked defeated. He leant forward and pressed the intercom on his desk. A woman's voice replied: "Yes sir, can I help you?"

"Get hold of Williams and Joubert immediately. I want them here in my office now!"

Before his secretary could respond he cut the intercom.

"Wait outside. I want to speak to Williams and Joubert alone when they arrive," ordered Marais, bursting with anger. "I'll call you when I need you."

Tony looked at Marais and decided not to argue. He helped himself to another glass of water. As he left the room, Jappie pushed past him. He gave Tony a menacing look and closed the door behind him.

9

TONY WAS LOUNGING in a low-level sofa in the corridor outside Marais's office when he saw David Williams, the security manager, deep in conversation with his assistant, André Joubert, coming towards him. Joubert was a former South African secret policeman. They were both frowning as they hurried along the corridor obviously aware that something serious had happened for Marais's secretary to contact them on their pagers. They had both expected to spend a leisurely afternoon relaxing by the pool before their first meeting with Marais and the other managers that evening.

"Hi Tony, how's it going?" Williams asked as they both acknowledged him.

"Hi guys," Tony responded nervously.

Williams knocked on the office door and entered. Joubert followed close behind.

Ten minutes later Joubert came out with a very serious expression on his face. Tony noticed the butt of his pistol poking out from the shoulder holster he was wearing beneath his jacket. He momentarily felt fearful before he collected his composure and stood up. His legs had gone almost jelly-like but he managed to follow Joubert into the office. He began to wonder what would happen to Lindsay if Marais decided to have him killed. He felt a pang of guilt for the first time in his life. He truly loved Lindsay even though he had treated her badly at times. He imagined the even greater hatred Lindsay's parents would have for him if any harm came to her as a result of his actions.

As Tony entered the room he watched Williams and Marais, who were deep in conversation. A piece of classical music was playing in the background. It was loud enough for it to be heard above their voices. Jappie had already taken up his usual position behind Marais's desk. He had a deadpan expression on his face. Marais looked up.

"Ah, Tony, please take a seat. I think today must be your lucky day!" he announced with a smile on his face.

"What do you mean?" Tony was taken aback by his remark and complete change of manner.

"Luckily David here has persuaded me not to kill you and rush in and have all the people on the list arrested and thrown in gaol..."

Tony interrupted. "That would be difficult," he said with a sneer, "because I've yet to give you the book with the list of names."

"I can easily remedy that," Marais said aggressively. "Jappie, turn out his pockets!"

Jappie moved forward. At that point Joubert pulled his gun from his holster and pointed it at Tony. The colour drained from Tony's face.

"There's no need for that," he said nervously putting his right hand up in protest. "I'll give it to you willingly. Call off the Neanderthal, and as for you, André, put the gun away, there's no need for that either."

Tony swallowed hard. He could feel the trickles of sweat run down his back. Moisture filled the palms of his hands. Marais banged his fist down on the desk.

"Jappie, no!" At the same time he raised his eyes in Joubert's direction. Joubert looked disappointed but obediently put his gun back in his holster.

"Can't you turn off that wretched music?" asked Tony. "It's driving me nuts."

"No!" responded Marais. "Walls have ears. We don't need anyone to hear what's been said in this room."

Tony shook his head and with that he produced the address book from his trouser pocket and lobbed it on his desk.

"You've got a nerve. I've already paid 30,000 rand for that book and now you're blackmailing me to pay you more."

Tony grinned. "I guess I was lucky to be in the right place at the right time."

David Williams leaned forward and picked up the book. He opened it slowly. A look of surprise appeared on his face as he read out the names on the list. He knew all the staff at the casino relatively well. He obviously hadn't expected some of their names to be there. He regarded himself as normally a good judge of character and his estimation of people's honesty was usually correct, but on this occasion one or two of the names surprised him greatly.

Marais eventually broke the silence and began to explain to Tony what he planned next. David Williams and Joubert had persuaded him to have the tables watched for a few days. It would be long enough to gather enough evidence to arrest those involved. After that the plan was to explain to the staff that a training exercise would take place. Dealers would temporarily be promoted to Acting Inspector, Inspectors to Acting Pit Boss and so on. The Pit Bosses and Inspectors in turn would then spend a couple of days dealing the tables. Those not involved in the coup would then be cleared easily. If the gambler Derek Julius continued to work the cups he had in his possession it would mean others not on the list would be implicated.

"What about Lindsay and me?" asked Tony cautiously.

"I will announce your resignations."

"But how do we explain our sudden departure?"

Williams interrupted: "That's easy, it's common knowledge that you and Lindsay have been trying for a child with little success. Everyone knows she's had problems trying to conceive and has been on a London specialist waiting list for a long time."

Tony looked embarrassed.

"I agree, that's a good way of explaining instant resignations. But most important of all what about the £250,000?" queried Tony, becoming increasingly worried about his money.

"Another easy explanation," replied Marais. "I will today arrange for the transfer of £125,000 directly into a bank account of your choice anywhere in the world and two first-class tickets back to London from Johannesburg for you and your wife."

"Hang on a minute, what about the other £125,000? I thought we had a deal?"

"Tony, you have to show Mr Marais that you can be trusted," replied Williams. "On your return to London we want you to arrange for your lawyer to return the two sets of accounts to Mr Marais's lawyer. Then and only then will the remainder of the money be transferred to you."

He passed Tony a business card with the name and address of Marais's lawyer. Tony took the card. He studied it briefly and transferred it to his shirt pocket.

"I'd better not get this washed in the laundry!" he joked before changing his demeanour. "How do I know *you* can be trusted to give me the money?" he said angrily. He was greatly concerned that Marais would not pay him the balance.

"Have no fear. On receipt of the original set of books my lawyer will hand over a banker's draft made out to you. That is as good as cash!" Marais reacted venomously. He was becoming increasingly annoyed with Tony's attitude. Tony half-smiled. He was dreaming about how he was going to spend his new-found wealth.

"One more thing, Tony," Marais said, as he stood up and leaned across his desk. "Make absolutely certain that any photocopies you have of the accounts are destroyed!"

"And what if they're not?"

Marais stood up straight. He towered over Tony and

pointed his finger directly at him. His blue eyes flashed with anger. "You are a dead man!" he whispered hoarsely.

Tony shuddered.

That same night Lindsay and Tony took the flight back to Johannesburg accompanied by Williams and Joubert. On arrival Lindsay was taken away in a company limousine with André Joubert and checked in at the Holiday Inn. Meanwhile, Williams, Jappie and Tony took the short flight in one of Marais's Cessna aircraft back to the Palace to collect Tony and Lindsay's personal effects.

Williams had deliberately timed their arrival to coincide with darkness falling. This reduced the chances of Tony being seen by any other members of the coup as the management block was situated away from the general staff compounds. In less than an hour Tony had packed up everything he needed and was driven back to the small airstrip with Williams and Jappie still in tow. After a bumpy plane ride back to Johannesburg, Tony was driven at high speed to the Holiday Inn where he was taken to Lindsay's room on the fourth floor.

10

SEAN'S NIGHT OF passion with Nikki ended prematurely. Nikki woke at 6.30 a.m. to the sound of the alarm. She turned over and smiled at Sean as he woke. Bright sunlight was streaming through the windows and cast a shadow on their bodies as they lay on the bed.

"You are one sexy man, Mr Cameron. I hope you don't think I do this sort of thing with all the fathers at my school!"

"I hope not! You'd be worn out!" he laughed. "I certainly don't do this sort of thing with any of the other teachers!"

She giggled. "I can't imagine you in bed with Miss Crompton," she laughed again, referring to Achieng's rather frumpy, middle-aged spinster headmistress.

"Time to go," Sean said looking at his watch. "A quick shower is on the agenda and then I'm out of here."

"Time enough for a tea or coffee or would sir prefer some more energetic exercise before he goes!"

Sean blushed. "Much as I'd love to continue where we left off, I really must go."

Before he climbed from the bed he leant across and kissed Nikki tenderly on the lips, at the same time caressing her cheek with the back of his hand. As he pulled away and stood up she admired his physique.

"You really are a very unusual and interesting man." She was studying Sean very carefully. "There's a lot more to you than meets the eye, I think!"

Sean raised his eyebrows, said nothing and headed for the shower.

Ten minutes later he appeared in the sitting room looking

refreshed and well groomed. Nikki pointed to the tea on the table. “Help yourself.”

“Thanks. By the way, I’m having a barbecue today. There’s someone I’d like you to meet. If you’re free it starts at one o’clock. It’s very informal.”

“Oh, that would be lovely!” Nikki purred. “A chance to see my knight in shining armour once again. One o’clock it is.”

Sean drained the last of his tea. “Time to go,” he said as he put the mug back on the table.

At the door Nikki threw her arms around his neck and gave him a long lingering kiss.

“See you later,” Sean said with a big grin as he withdrew from her embrace. He pulled his car keys from his pocket.

Several minutes later Sean was at home. Achieng was already up and chatting to Akoth as she prepared breakfast.

“Baba, Baba,” Achieng called out excitedly as she saw her father. “Where have you been? I didn’t find you in your room when I got up.”

Akoth gave Sean a knowing look. She rather disapproved of him staying out all night.

“I got up early and had to go to the office,” he lied unashamedly.

“What was that for?” Achieng questioned him again.

“It’s none of your business.” Sean was amused by her persistence.

“I’m starving, when’s breakfast ready, Akoth?” He grabbed a warm croissant Akoth had taken from the oven. He broke it in two and stuffed one half in his mouth. Akoth playfully slapped his wrist.

“Mr Sean, I’ve told you before not to do that,” she scolded him. “It teaches Achieng bad habits.”

Sean looked suitably sheepish.

“Breakfast will be ready in ten minutes,” Akoth continued.

“Is Mr James up yet?”

“Yes. He’s on the veranda.”

Sean took Achieng's hand and led her outside to see James, who was sitting in the swing hammock reading a book.

"Hi James, how are you?"

"Morning," James replied putting his book down. "It doesn't look like you had any sleep at all."

Sean smiled, feeling very pleased with himself.

"Breakfast will be ready in a minute. By the way Njeri and her children are coming for a barbecue today. I'm sure she'll be very pleased to see you."

"Good. It will be interesting to talk to her. Is there anyone else coming?"

Sean beamed, slightly embarrassed. He cleared his throat. "There is actually. I invited Nikki."

"Who's Nikki, Baba?" Achieng piped up.

"You know who Nikki is. She's your teacher, Miss Greene!"

"Miss Greene? Why is she coming to lunch?" Achieng asked. "I told her you loved her, Baba!"

"Children are so typical!"

James laughed loudly, amused as he watched his friend become even more embarrassed.

§

Three and a half hours later Njeri arrived with her two children. As he opened the front door to her Sean kissed her gently on each cheek. She gave him a quick hug.

"Hi Sean," she smiled. "You know Grace and Thomas."

Her two children walked either side of her as she marched confidently into the house.

"Hello, Sean," they said one after the other.

"Hi guys. Achieng is in the garden. Why don't you go and find her?" He beckoned them to go through. As he did so he touched Njeri's forearm with his hand.

"Go on, children," Njeri encouraged them, realising Sean wanted to talk privately to her.

"I need to speak to you about something first," he said as he turned back to Njeri.

"Oh," she said suspiciously.

"Please. Spare me five minutes."

Sean pointed to his study and followed her in, closing the door behind them. Njeri sat down in the wicker rocking chair. Sean walked around behind his desk and sat in his swivel chair.

"It won't take long but I need a favour." He eyed Njeri carefully.

"Go on," she frowned.

"James is here for a few days."

"Mmm," she said pensively, "sounds like trouble if you ask me..."

"No, no, nothing sinister, I assure you. He wants me to help him on a project of his."

"Go on!" She was becoming more suspicious by the minute.

"The problem is, he wants me to fly to Dar Es Salaam a week tomorrow."

"That's rather sudden."

"Yes, it is, but he only contacted me the other day."

"And you want me to come with you?"

"No, no," he protested, not appreciating her sense of humour. "As you know it's half term the week I plan to be away, and I promised Achieng I'd take the week off and do so many things with her."

"Get to the point, Sean." Njeri was becoming frustrated with him.

"Well, now I have to go to Dar I'd like you to look after her here. Akoth and Opiyo are very trustworthy but if you stayed here with her and Thomas and Grace, they could all play together. I know there's an age gap but they love her dearly and treat her as a young sibling. I'll pay you for it..."

"No you won't!" Njeri interrupted him angrily. "I don't want your money!" Her eyes flashed. "Of course I'll do it!!"

"Oh, Njeri, you're a star! I knew I could rely on you. Come on, let's head for the garden, James is so looking forward to seeing you again." He jumped up from his chair.

Njeri rose slowly and followed him out. James had introduced himself to Thomas and Grace and they were all playing with Achieng. As James saw Njeri he got up and ambled over to greet her.

"You look better than when I last saw you."

Njeri gave a shy smile. She would always be grateful to James for rescuing her from the "red house" in Hamburg. She offered her hand and as she did so James bent forward and kissed her on each cheek. At that moment Achieng ran up to Njeri and threw her arms around her waist.

"Auntie Njeri, Auntie Njeri," she cried excitedly. "Come and play with me and Thomas and Grace." She giggled as she took Njeri's hand and dragged her to where Thomas and Grace were playing.

James and Sean looked at each other. James's eyes followed Njeri as she sauntered across to her children. Her hips swayed sexily from side to side. He turned back to Sean.

"Mmm," he said, "you couldn't go too far wrong if you hitched up with Njeri again. She's looking very, very well...and she certainly has some figure," he added quietly.

Sean shuffled uncomfortably, thinking of the previous night with Nikki. "I don't think so," he protested half-heartedly, not entirely discounting the thought.

At this point Akoth appeared with Nikki Greene walking behind her.

"Miss Greene is here, Mr Sean."

James had his back to them and half-turned to look at Nikki. "Phew!" he mumbled to Sean. "I can see why you only arrived home this morning." He turned round and extended his hand to Nikki.

"Hi, I've heard a lot about you."

Nikki's eyes darted to Sean. She wondered briefly whether he had discussed their night of passion in the inimitable male way. She dismissed the thought, thinking Sean was too mature for that. She flushed slightly. Her moment of anger subsided.

"I hope it's all good!"

Sean stepped forward offering his hand. Nikki took it and made an attempt to kiss him on the lips. Sean turned his head slightly so she ended up kissing him on his left cheek. Out of the corner of his eye he was aware of Njeri watching them closely. He began to feel awkward.

"Hi, Nikki, let me introduce you to a friend of mine, Njeri Mwangi and her two children, Thomas and Grace."

"Hello," said Njeri rather curtly, as a feeling of jealousy overwhelmed her. She suspected from the body language that this was Sean's new love interest.

Nikki smiled sweetly, deliberately taking Sean's hand in her own and squeezing it before letting go. She was claiming Sean as hers. She sensed that Njeri could be a love rival.

Shortly after lunch Njeri cornered Sean when he was on his own.

"And what is your relationship with Miss Greene?"

"I do detect you're jealous."

"Why didn't you ask Miss Greene to look after Achieng when you're in Dar?" she said emphasising the "Miss Greene" again.

"Because I know how much Achieng likes you, Njeri. I know she'll be in very safe hands and if a problem arises you'll be able to deal with it."

"Don't try and flatter me, Sean. Are you sure this project with James is not going to be dangerous?"

"Of course it isn't! I'll be in and out of Dar in less than a week. I've only got to spend some time gambling at one of the casinos."

"I hope you're right, Sean. I would hate it if anything happened to you," she said softly as she leant forward and squeezed his hand. "I must go now. I have some business I need to deal with. I'll leave Thomas and Grace here. I'll be back later."

Shortly after Njeri left, Nikki came to say her goodbyes.

"James tells me you're off to Dar Es Salaam tomorrow week," Nikki said, feeling very disappointed that she wouldn't be able to spend more time with Sean during half term.

"I was going to mention that but I'll be back by the following weekend. How about going out for dinner again on the Saturday night?"

"Sounds good but this time I'll cook at my apartment."

The thought of being back in Nikki's apartment caused a stirring in Sean's loins. She was a very passionate woman. He began to feel rather annoyed that he had to travel to Dar but he knew he owed James and knew there was no way he could get out of it. He looked forward to making love to her again.

"Well, you know what they say," said Sean. "The way to a man's heart is through his stomach."

"And other places as well," Nikki added, flirting outrageously.

§

It was very busy outside the casino in Mombasa when James and Sean arrived at 7.30 p.m. There had been a huge downpour shortly before and parts of the road were flooded, causing many of the vehicles outside to be parked haphazardly. A mixture of top-of-the-range BMWs and four-wheel-drives contrasted with a variety of battered taxis. A few hookers stood on the pavement leading up to the steps of the casino, in expectation of the arrival of businessmen to take them to play the tables, or of successful punters leaving with their winnings, to celebrate at the nightclub next door.

As they climbed the steps one of the askaris recognised Sean.

"Hello, Mr Sean, how are you?"

Sean looked up and acknowledged him. It was one of the men who had helped him and Opiyo to renovate his house.

"Hi, Charlie, how are you doing? When did you start working here?"

"Two months ago. I take any work I can get and this was the only job available. Welcome, it is good to see you. How is little Achieng?"

"Achieng is very well. She is growing up so fast. See you later."

At the top of the steps another askari moved aside and held the door open for them. Inside some piped music was playing in the background. It was almost drowned out by the noise of the fruit machines as several punters poured in coin after coin, hoping to win the jackpot.

"We've got time for a drink before we start," said James.

"No problem. The bar is up the stairs and we can overlook the tables from the gallery. I've been here a couple of times before with clients but I've only ever watched as they've played."

When they reached the bar, James ordered two Tuskers and they went and sat on two barstools in the gallery.

While they watched the activity below James went on to tell Sean about Tony Stanley's involvement at the Palace Casino and how Hudson had been held up at gunpoint at his hotel room in Johannesburg. Within a short time Sean had a comprehensive idea of what had been going on at the Palace ten years previously.

James had arranged to meet Chidoli at the casino but he had phoned earlier to cancel the appointment. He had remained in Dar due to pressing business commitments.

"James, tell me what you know about Chidoli."

"Not much but I checked with some of my contacts at the High Commission in Dar and they tell me he's the only Tanzanian director of the Golden City consortium."

"Can he be trusted?"

"That I don't know. What I do know is he paid me a deposit upfront and he has continued to pay me as agreed."

Sean nodded. "What about Murundi? Can you explain his connection with Chidoli?"

"I can't. I can only assume he's become involved because the Tanzanian government is very concerned about Victor Marais's alleged underworld connections."

"But what is your gut feeling?"

James grimaced. "I can't say I trust either of them 100 per cent but that is typical in my type of business."

The casino by now was filling up even more. Sean observed the tables below. They were mostly full of Indians and some wealthy Kenyan businessmen. Many of them were with female hangers-on who were clearly not their wives. He smiled to himself. The waitress arrived with the drinks.

"Cheers."

James raised his glass in a toast. Sean pulled his stool closer to the table.

"Here's to the success of our operation."

"Now is the time to tell me everything that has happened so far, James. If I'm to go to the Golden City I need to know what I'm up against. I suspect there are a few pieces missing from the jigsaw puzzle that you haven't told me about."

"Okay. I'll tell you everything, but first let's go and play some of the tables. We'll have dinner – then I'll tell you more about what happened at the Palace and the recent turn of events at the Golden City."

He picked up his glass as he stood up. Sean followed. A crescendo of sound emanated from one of the fruit machines as a cascade of coins fell into the tray. It was followed with the satisfied yells from the lucky gambler as he punched the air with excitement.

Sean took up a stool at one of the blackjack tables. Next to him a white American spoke noisily as he made his calls. The Kenyan blackjack dealer stood with a blank expression on her face. She was pretty but seemed to have trouble smiling. Her hands moved quickly as she drew the cards from the shoe. An inspector almost stood in her shadow. She called out the cards as she dealt them in front of each of the four other gamblers. One of them was an immaculately dressed and suave-looking African. Sean noticed his exceptionally long fingers as he picked up the cards.

An elderly Indian was standing on his left with a gorgeous-looking black woman. She stood behind him stroking the back of his neck. Large looped earrings dangled from her ears. Her long black dress fitted tightly to her body showing off her abundant curves. Next to the Indian was another white man, younger than the first and with darting eyes. He looked very anxious as he called his bets. Sean thought he seemed under pressure to get back on a winning streak. His pile of chips was dwindling fast. A look of disgust registered on his face as he twisted once too often and threw in his hand.

To Sean's right an elegant middle-aged black woman smiled as she drew her two cards. First she drew an ace and then a Jack, beating the dealer who drew a ten and a nine. She whooped with delight as the dealer paid out double, increasing the steadily growing pile of chips that lay in front of her.

The dealer cleared the table and Sean handed over 5,000 Kenyan shillings in exchange for some chips. The dealer took the money and placed it in the hole next to her. She deliberately made a big show of spreading the chips in front of the inspector who agreed with her count. At the same time the inspector noted how much Sean had bought, on the clipboard she held in her left hand. The dealer passed the chips to Sean and play began.

One hour later and 25,000 Kenyan shillings better off, Sean and James sat down to dinner in the casino restaurant next door.

"Beginner's luck!" James taunted Sean.

"Yes, thanks – but I do have some questions."

"Fire away, Sean."

"How on earth did they operate the Bahamas cups in the

Palace Casino if the dealer spreads the chips before handing across any winnings?"

"Full marks for being so observant. After the Palace Casino coup, that system was initiated to try and prevent a repeat of the cups being used."

"So, is there any connection between the Palace Casino coup and the Golden City?"

"Back in 1985 at the Palace, when the coup was discovered, twelve members of staff were arrested. Seven of them were men and five women. The five women were later released without charge. Although it was alleged they were as guilty as the seven men, the President, Lucas Mangope, didn't want to have the problem of European women languishing in one of his prisons in Mafeking. It would have caused too much uproar abroad."

"What about the men?" Sean interrupted.

"Six of the seven were persuaded to plead guilty in exchange for lighter sentences."

"What about the seventh?"

"The seventh was a man called Chris Powell. He categorically denied any involvement and pleaded not guilty."

"What happened when they were sentenced?"

"Mangope, the President, was so angry about the coup that he ordered the judge to pass down harsh sentences even on the six who pleaded guilty!"

"How many years did they get?"

"Three of the croupiers and one inspector got four and a half years each and the pit boss and cashier got six and a half years! Powell got six and a half years as well!"

"Wow!" breathed Sean loudly.

"Not only that, they all got fined 20,000 rand each, or another eighteen months in prison."

Sean grimaced and stretched back in his chair. He looked around the room below. The tables were filling up with even more gamblers and the level of noise had increased. Overhead ceiling fans whirred above them providing some respite from the humidity of the night.

11

ONE WEEK LATER Opiyo drove James and Sean to Moi International Airport, Mombasa. They were booked on a charter flight to Dar via Zanzibar. The added advantage of going via Zanzibar rather than the scheduled flight via Nairobi was that it gave James the chance to look at the coastline south of Mombasa and down across the Tanzanian border.

It was a clear day except for a few scattered clouds as the Gulfstream 41 flew low over them and then turned out to sea. The plane rocked slightly as it broke through the clouds. There were only eleven other people on the plane and it didn't take long before the air stewardess served a round of mid-morning drinks. As the plane climbed to approximately 17,000 feet and levelled off, James turned to Sean.

"Now I can tell you the full story of the Golden City."

"Go on." Sean felt rather frustrated that James had obviously held some more information back.

"Two weeks ago Martin Donaldson was arrested along with seven other staff from the Golden City. David Smith, the gambler, was also arrested."

"So where are they now?"

"They are on remand in a prison about fifty kilometres north of Dar Es Salaam."

"And what have they been charged with?"

"They haven't been charged yet!"

"How can they be held for so long without charge?"

"You of all people should know things happen differently in Africa," responded James as he peered through the window at the mass of sea below them.

"What about lawyers or the British High Commission? Have they not become involved?"

"Yes. The High Commission managed to get local lawyers to act for six of the staff and David Smith the gambler. Chidoli organised a lawyer friend of his to represent Martin Donaldson."

The seventh staff member was an American and the United States Embassy had organised a lawyer for him.

"So what is your role in all of this, James?"

"I'll be posing as a British legal investigator and will visit Martin and the other staff in prison along with Jacob Mwingara, the lawyer employed by Chidoli."

"And what do you know about Tanzanian law?" queried Sean with a hint of sarcasm in his voice.

"Absolutely nothing but Mwingara will soon fill me in on the basics."

Sean turned away and looked out of the window again. They had been in the air nearly half an hour and would shortly be landing in Zanzibar. As he peered out of the window he was amazed at how turquoise the sea looked far down below. The plane dropped altitude as the pilot prepared to land. He banked to the left and turned towards the small airport situated three or four kilometres south of Stone Town, the capital. Two minutes later they were on the ground. It was only a short stopover. Two passengers alighted, while a further half-dozen people boarded for the flight on to Dar Es Salaam.

Half an hour later they were back in the air. Sean took the chance to doze off before the final descent into Dar. After clearing immigration and customs, James was met by Chidoli's driver and taken in a large black Mercedes to his office on Sokoine Drive in the city centre.

Several minutes later Sean was picked up by a tour representative in a courtesy bus from the Hotel Bilicanas, one of the four on the Golden City complex. The tour rep also met two other passengers from the flight. Sean was the last to climb onboard the twelve-seater minibus. He introduced himself to the other passengers.

"Good morning. My name is Sean Cameron." He offered his hand to the first passenger, a tall dark-haired man with a bushy moustache who revealed a protruding set of teeth when he smiled.

"Thadeus J Delport," he declared in a strong American accent. He took Sean's hand, pumping it vigorously. Sean released his grip offering his hand again to the small Indian man who was sitting by the window. He leant forward to shake hands. A strong waft of garlic filled the air as he opened his mouth.

"Juresh Shah."

Sean flinched slightly as it hit him. He turned and sat down on the row of seats behind the driver. The tour rep slid the door shut to the side of the minibus and climbed into the front passenger seat. He turned to face his passengers.

"Good morning, gentlemen. My name is Mohammed and this is your driver, Saddiq, who will be taking us to the Golden City."

Saddiq turned and raised his right hand in acknowledgement. Mohammed continued: "I hope you enjoy your stay with us at the Hotel Bilicanas. If any of you require any help or information please do not hesitate to contact me through reception. It will now take about forty-five minutes before we get to the hotel." He turned and faced the front.

Sean was surprised how small Dar Airport was and the lack of traffic on the roads, though there were many people walking along the roadside and others were pulling wooden carts. A few people rode antiquated bicycles laden with personal belongings. He wondered how the people managed to pull the carts in such stifling heat. It was even hotter than Mombasa. The open windows on the bus provided a refreshing breeze, albeit warm. His shirt was soaked through due to the high humidity. It was already 36 degrees centigrade. Sean leant his head against the window and shut his eyes. He didn't sleep but began thinking about Achieng. He wondered how much she would miss him. It was the first time he had been away from her for more than a night. He reckoned that with Njeri looking after her, and Thomas and Grace there to play with her, she would hardly notice he was gone. He smiled at the thought of it. He wondered how Louise, his elder daughter in England, was. She was coming to spend her summer holidays with him and Achieng and he was looking forward to that.

The bus slowed down as it hit a bump in the road. By now the traffic had become much heavier as they reached the city. The noise of the traffic was a direct contrast to the quietness of it near the airport. A cacophony of horns sounded as drivers showed their irritation at the various examples of bad driving.

They were soon through Dar and on the coast road, though it was far enough away that Sean couldn't see the ocean. The landscape was very flat with mixed vegetation of scrubland intermingled with coconut palm trees and tall breathtakingly beautiful casuarina trees. Several people were out working the fields that had been cultivated. The road surface soon changed from tarmac to dirt. It was in fairly good condition but threw up terracotta-coloured dust as several vehicles overtook them at high speed. Every so often the drivers slowed down and took avoiding action to miss the various potholes that had been created by the recent heavy rain. Twenty minutes further on and the road surface turned back to tarmac. Sean thought this rather strange but soon realised why when he spotted a vast conglomerate of buildings over to his right. The Indian Ocean was also in sight for the first time so he knew he was nearing his destination of the Golden City.

§

James arrived at Chidoli's office on Sokoine Drive in the centre of Dar Es Salaam, which in the Swahili language means "the haven of peace". His office was very sparse. It was not at all what James expected of an apparently rich businessman. A ceiling fan whirred overhead to try and combat the high humidity. Chidoli's personal assistant, Anne Mtoni, greeted James. She was in her early thirties and was dressed in an immaculately pressed black suit and white blouse. She wore round black-framed spectacles that made her look more serious than she probably was. Her black hair was tied neatly back. She smiled sweetly as she introduced herself.

"Mr Chidoli will be with you shortly," she announced. "Would you like a drink?"

"Water will be fine, thanks."

Anne left the room and returned a short time later with a huge jug of water and two glasses. She placed them on the table in front of Chidoli's desk. James helped himself and sat down in one of the armchairs.

Five minutes later Edward Chidoli arrived. He looked flustered. He wiped his face with a white handkerchief. James stood up and they shook hands.

"Good morning, James. Apologies for being late but I have been at a meeting with Victor Marais. The man is a nightmare. He's almost impossible to deal with!"

"Oh," said James. He could see that Chidoli was struggling to contain his anger.

"As you know the eight Golden City staff and David Smith, the gambler, were arrested two weeks ago. They are now being held at the New Bagamoyo Prison."

"So what is Marais up to?"

"He is fuming. He wants to have the nine of them put up against a wall and shot immediately!"

"He can't do that!"

"Of course he can't but these Afrikaners think they can do anything they like. They come here and still think they can carry on living like they did in the old South Africa. Why I got involved with him in the first place I'll never know!"

Chidoli removed his jacket before sitting down behind his desk. He went on to tell James that the eight staff and David Smith were busily preparing their defence against the charge of stealing from the Golden City. They had all pleaded not guilty at the preliminary hearing. Marais's accountants had suggested that as much as US$3,000,000 had been stolen. As soon as that sort of figure had been mentioned, investigators from the Golden City's insurance company descended on the place with great rapidity. They were not prepared to be out of pocket with a huge claim being made against them.

Since the Golden City had opened in 1995 turnover and profit had been consistently good. However, the suggestion of $3,000,000 didn't equate. It had been estimated that the scam had been running for only the last six months. Marais was either skimming money himself off the top or trying to put in an exaggerated claim from the insurance company.

"So when can I see Martin Donaldson and the others?" asked James.

"I have arranged an appointment at the prison at 1600 hours today."

James looked at his watch. There were three hours to kill. "Have I time to check in at the hotel and get back to the prison by four?"

"You will have to be quick. I'll get my driver to take you."

He got up from his chair and walked to the door. He opened it and shouted for his driver. There was a scraping of chairs on the concrete floor in the room next door.

"I'm coming, bwana, coming."

"George, I would like you to take Mr Annan to the Serengeti Hotel on the Golden City complex. Then you need to take him to the New Bagamoyo Prison by 1600 hours."

"Yes sir, yes sir," George replied rather nervously, fiddling with his cap in his hands.

"Call me after the interview and we'll meet to discuss what you've found out."

James nodded. George took James's briefcase and headed for the Mercedes.

On the journey to the hotel James reflected on what he knew about Chidoli, whose coldness unnerved him. His manner had been almost robotic in their meeting.

§

The manager of the Hotel Bilicanas was waiting in reception to meet his new guests. The head doorman held the automatic sliding doors open in readiness for the new arrivals. He was dressed in white Arabian-style clothing with a red waistcoat gaily decorated with gold braid. A red kufi was perched firmly on his head. His four assistants were similarly attired, but with plain yellow waistcoats and yellow kufis. Their style of dress was in keeping with the building's magnificent Moorish façade. From the moment they had entered the hotel grounds Sean couldn't help but be impressed by the magnificently manicured lawns either side of the long driveway.

The driveway from the gateway right up to the long sweeping drive-by at reception was edged with brilliant white kerbstones and overhung with a series of manmade elephant tusks, every thirty metres or so. It reminded Sean of the artificial elephant tusks on Moi Avenue in Mombasa. Except that these ones were smaller and looked more realistic. The water flowing from a series of fountains alongside the drive had been synchronized to create a dancing effect. As it cascaded down and rose up again it glinted in the sunlight like sparklers from a firework.

As Sean and his fellow-passengers got off the bus the head doorman instructed his porters to take their luggage to their rooms. He offered his hand to Sean and the others.

"Welcome, gentlemen." His voice boomed with the confidence of a man who was very happy with himself and his life.

Sean looked around as he entered the reception area. It was adorned with beautiful Arabic-style artefacts. Luxurious low-level settees with soft furnishings were scattered around the area. A couple of guest-relations desks were set to the right-hand side. Seated behind each one were two very attractive black women dealing with some customers. A long reception counter was installed on the left. Several members of staff were busily dealing with customers checking in or out. Sean looked up into the atrium set in the middle of reception. A huge tropical palm tree rose through the centre of it, surrounded at the trunk by an assortment of brightly coloured tropical plants and smaller green vegetation. The floor was covered in expensive-looking white marble tiles. Sean shook his head in amazement as he had another look around. Moments later a swarthy-looking man headed towards him and his two fellow-guests, Garlic Breath and Buck Teeth. The man was very short. He walked on the balls of his feet, typically in the way that some small men do, to try and appear bigger than they really are.

"Good morning, gentlemen." He had a strong South African accent. "My name is Pieter Coetzee. I am the general manager here. It is my duty to ensure your stay with us is perfect."

His manner was very arrogant. He shook hands with Garlic Breath first, then Buck Teeth and then turned to Sean. His handshake was firm as iron in its grip. Sean felt he was deliberately trying to impress his strength on him as if he had something to prove. It was as if he was intimidated by Sean's size. His black hair was immaculately groomed and cut short. Sean took an instant dislike to him. His face was heavily pockmarked and burnished brown from the sun. He was dressed in khaki slacks and a navy blue blazer with a white button-down shirt. His red tie was tied tightly at the collar. Coetzee directed them to the reception desk so they could check in.

By the time Sean reached his room on the third floor, his luggage had already arrived. A porter was waiting patiently for him. He unlocked the door. The room was huge and also decorated in Arabian style. Apart from a kingsize double bed there was a low-level settee and two armchairs adjacent to the sliding patio doors that led to the balcony. The porter set Sean's luggage down. Sean tipped him two dollars and after explaining how the air conditioning worked he departed.

Sean walked onto the balcony and looked out at the huge expanse of Indian Ocean set before him. A swing hammock with sunshade was on the opposite side of the balcony. Four wrought-iron-style bistro chairs with soft cushions to the seats and backs surrounded a glass-topped table.

"Not bad," said Sean, "maybe James's project isn't going to be too bad after all."

He smiled to himself before returning to the room to take a shower. A short time later he was down at the poolside in readiness for an afternoon in the sun before hitting the casino that night.

12

CONDITIONS IN THE New Bagamoyo Prison were only slightly better than Martin Donaldson had imagined. He and the others had now been there for almost three weeks since their arrest. Martin's share in the scam since his involvement two months earlier had been US$5,000. He had worked out that if the others had been earning at that rate they would only have netted about $15,000 each. Assuming all the other seven and David Smith had been involved right from the start the total netted to date would have been only $150,000. Even if the original coup members had been earning double Martin's cut it would still be about ten per cent of the figure of $3,000,000 they had been charged with. All seven had decided to plead not guilty, even though they were all guilty as charged. They were arrogant enough to think that even if they were found guilty the Judge would only hand them down suspended sentences. Their lawyers had advised them that if they were given suspended sentences they would be immediately deported from Tanzania and returned to the UK and the USA respectively. Even The British High Commission's legal advisors had played down the seriousness of the sentences awaiting them if found guilty. However, Martin's lawyer, Jacob Mwingara, was a little more circumspect and had warned him that they could all be given long sentences. Martin had also entered a plea of not guilty, against Mwingara's advice.

Benjamin Mkapa, the new President, had recently been swept to power in Tanzania with sixty-two per cent of the vote in the general election. His party had promised a clampdown on corruption. It was unlikely the Judge would be lenient with the sentencing. According to Mwingara, the Judge had already held a meeting with the Attorney General. Direct orders from the President's office had indicated no leniency.

Martin hoped that James would sort out the mess he was in and somehow get him released soon. The last three weeks had been the most boring he had spent in the whole of his life. It had been even more boring than some of the undercover surveillance operations he had undertaken during his time in the SAS. He had read a couple of books but they were very difficult to get hold of in prison. Other than reading, there was very little to do except try and keep up with an exercise routine. There was no space in his cell to do that. It was only a small room, originally designed to sleep twenty prisoners. He was actually sharing it with thirty-nine others. There was barely enough room for everyone to lie down and sleep at night. Some even had to sleep sitting upright against the walls. He had been issued with two threadbare blankets. One was used to lie on the stone floor and the other to keep warm. The blankets were dirty and lice-ridden. Although the cell was swept out on a daily basis it was infested with cockroaches and other bugs. There was no protection from the incessant mosquitoes at night but Martin had fared better than some of the others who had been badly bitten.

His only chance of exercise was in the small yard outside where the prisoners on remand sat during the day. He was still in the clothes he'd been arrested in, a pair of black trousers and white shirt as prisoners on remand could normally keep their own clothes. Once they were convicted, they were issued with a uniform. It consisted of a coarse grey-and-white-striped two-piece suit with trousers and shirt. They weren't allowed belts or ordinary shoes, which might potentially be used as a weapon. Instead they were issued with very flimsy canvas shoes or they went barefoot. As a special concession Martin and the other croupiers had been allowed to keep their shoes.

David Smith joined Martin during his exercise routine. The others were not interested in exercising. He suspected their attitude would change if they were convicted, if only to break the monotony and relieve the boredom. Their workout consisted of sit-ups, press-ups and a series of stretching exercises to keep all their muscles toned. Martin was surprised at how fit David was.

When they had first been arrested Peter Archer, the self-appointed spokesman for the croupiers, had caused a great fuss and contacted the British press through the High Commission. He had drawn attention to the very low standards and conditions in the prison but all he succeeded in doing was making them into political pawns. This had infuriated the Tanzanian government.

Martin and David had taken the opposite view to the others and argued that they should keep a low profile and not draw attention to themselves. David seemed to Martin to be an unlikely instigator of a gambling fraud. He knew he had to gain David's confidence and somehow get him to open up about himself. Out of all the others he appeared to be most friendly with Peter Archer. Archer was from Stanmore in Middlesex and had been working at the Golden City as a pit boss since it had opened. He had previously worked for Marais at the Palace.

Since their arrests, most of the other croupiers had been visited by friends who worked at the casino. Many of them had brought food parcels and basic medicines. Martin however had not struck up any particular friendship during his time there and had no visitors. Peter Archer had at least organised for Martin's personal belongings to be packed up and stored away in anticipation of their release. Marais had already sacked all of them from their jobs, guilty or not.

§

New Bagamoyo Prison was not exactly new. It was opened originally in the early 1800s as a stop-off point for slaves who were brought by the slave traders from the centre of what was then Tanganyika to Bagamoyo Town. From there they were shipped to Unguja, which was the original name for Zanzibar Island. The word "Zanzibar" comes from the Arabic "Zinj el Barr" or "Land of the Blacks". From Zanzibar they were shipped onwards to other parts of the world into a life of slavery. Between 1887 and 1891 Bagamoyo was the capital of German East Africa. After a major uprising against the then colonial government in 1888, the capital was transferred to Dar Es Salaam in 1891. The name Bagamoyo derives from the Swahili word "bagamoyo or "throw down your heart". It was usually interpreted as a sad reminder that the town was once the terminus of the slave-trade route and the point of no return for slaves. Over the years the prison had been redeveloped and only a few of the original features remained.

Shortly before 4.00 p.m. James arrived at the main gate of the prison. Several guards armed with AK47 rifles confronted him. The most senior guard asked him for identification. He handed him his passport.

"Mr Annan, we have been expecting you. Mr Mwingara is here already. He is waiting for you in the guardroom."

James was given a brief body search and his briefcase was inspected. The guard handed him back his passport. James was then escorted to the guardroom behind the main gate.

"You must be James Annan," said the tall man standing beneath the ceiling fan. "I am Jacob Mwingara."

Mwingara was immaculately dressed in a grey suit. It was tailored to perfection and looked expensive. His hair was receding slightly. He had pale brown skin and a long pointed nose. His hands were long and slender. His nails neatly manicured. This guy certainly hasn't done any labouring, thought James.

"Mr Chidoli has explained your role here."

James raised his eyebrows.

"Where is Jonathan Greening from the British High Commission?" James asked. "I understood he would be in attendance."

Mwingara smiled. "Oh, Greening. He's always late. When you meet him you will understand why," he said with a hint of sarcasm. It was five past four. "We might as well get started. I have some important things to discuss with you before Greening arrives," Mwingara continued. He waved the guards away. "Wait outside. I will call you when we're ready to interview the prisoners. Send in Mr Greening when he arrives."

The guards looked at each other and hesitated before deciding to leave the room. James and Mwingara sat down beneath the fan. A gecko scuttled away up the wall behind them as James dragged in a chair in readiness for Greening's arrival. Mwingara went on to explain that a trial date had been set for 10th June. Currently the lawyers representing the others were preparing their defences. Although all of them had pleaded not guilty, Mwingara suspected that nearer the time they would change their pleas to guilty, after advice from their lawyers, in the hope of a more lenient sentence.

"Why were the croupiers arrested?" asked James.

"Edward Chidoli has suspected huge losses at the casino for a long time. He has spoken to Marais about them but at first he dismissed Chidoli's fears as rubbish."

"Why did he disbelieve Chidoli?"

"Marais felt his security measures were too good for any scams being run by the staff and for them to be stealing from the tables."

"How could he be so arrogant?"

Mwingara explained that after Marais's experience at the Palace in South Africa he never expected another scam to be operated. He didn't think any of his employees would risk his wrath. He had a fearsome reputation for violence when confronted with stealing by his staff. Although he seemed unperturbed by Chidoli's fears he decided to put all the tables under closer surveillance. He installed several extra security cameras without the staff's knowledge.

David Williams and André Joubert were the only two people other than Marais and Chidoli who knew about the extra cameras. While he was watching the tables Williams observed David Smith very closely. He felt there was something familiar about him and was convinced he knew him from the Palace. As a result of his suspicions he arranged for Joubert to get a set of fingerprints from one of the glasses Smith had been drinking from. Joubert contacted one of his former colleagues in the South African Police and sent the glass to him to run a test from previous records. It turned out they were a perfect match to a set of prints belonging to Chris Powell, a British citizen. Powell was the same Chris Powell who had been employed at the Palace as an inspector and was arrested in connection with the scam back in 1985. He was formally charged and found guilty and served time at Mafeking Prison. Although he had always vehemently protested his innocence he was portrayed as one of the ringleaders and served four years of a six-and-a-half-year sentence. He was released on parole for good behaviour and deported back to the UK in 1989. Nothing further was heard about him.

"You mean Chris Powell and David Smith are one and the same!"

"Absolutely right!"

"Does Martin Donaldson know about this?"

"No one knows except for Marais, Williams, Joubert, Chidoli and me. We haven't told anyone else and we haven't even told David Smith we know his true identity."

"Why ever not?" said James, looking very perplexed.

"Marais and the Chief Prosecutor want to use it at the trial if he pleads not guilty. It is their trump card to ensure he gets a very long sentence."

James thought for a minute. "I think I need to tell Martin about it when I see him. He may be able to get more information from David Smith if he knows about his past."

"It's probably not a bad idea but make sure Martin doesn't let anyone else know about it."

At this point a very flustered-looking white man walked into the room flanked by two guards. He was wearing an expensively tailored but crumpled cream-coloured safari suit. He looked about fifty-five, with dark hair and a ruddy complexion. His nose was red and the skin on his cheeks was broken and blotchy. "I apologise for being late," he said loudly in the plummy tones of an English public school. He straightened his tie and shook hands with Mwingara and then James. His hand was clammy with moisture.

"Had to attend a wretched lunch at the Commonwealth Club," he guffawed.

James caught a strong smell of gin and thought it must have been a good lunch. Greening sat down.

"I will be very brief, gentlemen. I must tell you the British government's stance."

The Foreign Office had been in negotiation with the Tanzanian High Commission in London and they were severely embarrassed that eight British citizens had been arrested in connection with the fraud. The British government proposed that the croupiers could serve any sentence in the UK. The Tanzanian government had found this to be totally unacceptable. They wanted to set an example and insisted that the sentences be served in full in Tanzania. Furthermore they wanted in particular to show that white criminals were not exempt from conviction. The Foreign Office realised that the Tanzanians would not negotiate. As an act of diplomacy they offered to pay all court costs and any costs incurred in imprisoning the British croupiers for the duration of their sentences in Tanzania.

As it turned out the British government were mightily relieved. It was a much cheaper option for them to cover the Tanzanian costs than bring them back to the UK to serve their sentences.

"What about the American involved?" James asked.

"I'm not one hundred per cent certain but I think a similar arrangement has been made with the US government."

"By the sound of it the nine have already been found guilty," James responded.

Mwingara stood up. "It is looking more and more likely. Come on, we must get on and interview the prisoners."

"One last thing," interrupted James. "You didn't fully explain how the nine were caught."

"After the extra cameras were installed, the American, John Daly, was spotted by David Williams using the Bahamas cups with David Smith on one of the tables. I think Edward Chidoli has explained to you how the cups work."

"Yes, but what happened then?"

"After his shift Daly was pulled in for questioning by Marais, Williams and Joubert. Marais threatened that if he didn't divulge the names of the others involved he would kill him!"

Greening interrupted: "He gave in rather too easily," he said somewhat scornfully, as if he would have resisted Marais's threats had he been in the same position.

Mwingara laughed. "If your life was being threatened by Marais and his cronies I think you would confess even if you hadn't done anything."

Greening reddened with embarrassment. "On second thoughts I guess I probably would." He also knew about Marais's fearsome reputation.

§

It was raining heavily outside. The three of them struggled to cover themselves with the rather dilapidated umbrella that the prison guards had lent them to protect themselves from the sudden downpour. At the prison officers' canteen James shook the umbrella before setting it down fully opened on the floor. A large pool soon appeared as the remaining water dripped off the surface. They were being allowed to use the canteen as a meeting place as it was the only room large enough to accommodate the three of them and the nine prisoners. They had an hour and a half before they had to vacate it to make way for the prison officers coming for a meal in the middle of their evening shift.

The walls of the canteen were painted in a two-tone green. The lower half was dark green and the upper lime green. The paint on the lower half was scuffed and peeling badly. Several fluorescent lighting tubes suspended on rusty chains partially covered in cobwebs lit the room. The ceiling was badly stained by water leaks that had left yellowy patches. There was a strong smell of stale tobacco mixed with the stench of cabbage that had boiled for too long. The room was full of flies that flitted to and fro. In the centre an ancient-looking fan whirred noisily from the ceiling. It looked at any moment that it would break away from the fixings and crash to the ground.

The croupiers were already there. Two guards with rifles slung across their chests watched over them. James saw Martin on the far side of the room leaning against the wall. He looked very glum but winked when he saw James. A half-smile appeared on his face. James displayed no sign of recognition. The other eight were lounging in metal-framed chairs behind a row of trestle tables. A prison orderly arrived with a jug of water and three glasses for James, Mwingara and Greening. James looked around at the prisoners. All but two of them were wearing the work clothes they had been arrested in, black trousers and a white dress shirt. Most of them were unshaven and their hair looked dirty and unkempt. Martin in contrast was clean-shaven, as was one other who, for some reason, James assumed was David Smith. They both looked fit and in good condition in spite of having spent almost three weeks in prison. Smith had a calm demeanour about him. His hair was peroxide blond, though black roots were beginning to show. Flecks of grey were appearing at his temples. The skin on his face was very dry. He was heavily tanned. Although he was sitting down, James estimated that he weighed about ninety kilos and was about five-feet-eleven. James looked around at the rest of the croupiers. Some chewed gum and some smoked. Most of them were trying to appear unfazed by their situation but their eyes didn't hide their fear. Mwingara and Greening sat down. James remained standing.

Greening was the first to speak. "Good afternoon, gentlemen. You are all aware of who I am and you have all met Mr Mwingara, who is representing Martin Donaldson."

"What about our lawyers? Where are they?" interrupted one of the croupiers. He was clearly angered that they weren't being represented at the meeting. He pulled at his cigarette, inhaling the smoke deeply into his lungs. He fidgeted awkwardly in his chair as he tapped his fingers nervously on the table.

"Mr Mallet, there is not enough space for all your lawyers to be here. I have been elected by them to act as their spokesman for you."

"Nice of them to let us know," an American voice drawled.

James assumed this was John Daly. He was the only person other than David Smith not wearing black trousers and a white shirt. He wore blue jeans and a loose-fitting Hawaiian shirt with a pair of Nike trainers on his feet, which were resting on a second chair in front of him. After his initial interview with Marais, Williams and Joubert, he had been allowed to return to his room and change. He thought he was free to go but was shocked when Marais had him arrested a few hours later.

Greening appeared to be unaffected by their defiance. "Gentlemen, I have with me James Annan, a legal executive for the British High Commission. He is here to help you and interview you."

"We are all innocent, so the sooner we are out of this hellhole, the better," shouted a voice from the back of the room.

A murmur of voices chorused their agreement. James stood perfectly still. He lowered his voice deliberately, trying to hold their attention.

"Gentlemen, I would be grateful if you would introduce yourselves and state the position you held at the Golden City, starting with you, sir." He pointed to the man at the back. James pressed the record button on the small tape recorder he held in his left hand. The man glanced nervously at his fellow-prisoners. He scratched the heavy growth of beard on his chin before he began speaking. "Peter Archer, Pit Boss."

One by one the prisoners introduced themselves.

"Matt Bradley, Inspector," the next one said with a lilting Welsh accent.

"Tom Mallet, cashier," said the man who had earlier asked about the other lawyers.

"John Daly, croupier," the American drawled. He was a thin wiry man with lank blond hair and a face like a weasel.

"Martin Donaldson..." he hesitated, and added "...croupier," as if he had forgotten he had been temporarily working as a croupier.

"Peter Porter, croupier."

"Steve Vickers, croupier."

"Jeremy Lascelles, croupier," he said with a surprisingly English upper-class accent that James didn't expect. He had long floppy brown hair with a middle parting that he kept pushing back with his fingers.

Finally the man who James assumed was David Smith

spoke: "David Smith, professional gambler." There was a hint of irony in his voice. He was wearing light grey chinos covered in stains. His pale blue short-sleeved shirt had a couple of small tears in the front.

"Thank you, gentlemen," said James. He turned off the tape recorder and picked up his briefcase. "I would be grateful if you would take it in turns to have a private interview with me. It doesn't matter who comes first."

He glanced at Martin. A babble of voices filled the room. The metal chairs scratched noisily on the stone floor as some of the croupiers stood up. Mwingara called for a guard to direct James to the small interview room along the corridor from the canteen. James followed the guard followed closely by Peter Archer.

13

A FEW HOURS later James was back at the Serengeti Hotel. It was another of the hotels adjacent to the Bilicanas on the Golden City complex. Chidoli was waiting for him on the drinks terrace overlooking the man-made marina. Several very large and expensive yachts were moored below. A large dhow that had been converted into a restaurant had a full complement of customers on board awaiting a meal and evening cruise southwards along the coast to Dar and back. An African band had begun playing and they were already creating a lively atmosphere. The occasional shriek of laughter mingled with the music, as the dhow slipped its mooring and moved slowly away. There were lights on in several of the other yachts. An elegant-looking Sunseeker was moored over on the left. It dwarfed many of the other boats alongside, including a Princess.

"The Sunseeker belongs to Marais," said Chidoli.

The melodic voice of a female singer grew softer as the dhow disappeared into the distance.

Around the terrace, low-level lights interspersed the palm trees and floral decorations. Underwater lights illuminated the kidney-shaped swimming pool that spanned the area between the terrace and the harbour-side restaurant, which was full with diners eating heartily before their move to the gaming tables at the casino next door.

James reported his meeting with the prisoners to Chidoli, explaining that most of them had expressed anger and indignation at being charged with stealing $3,000,000. They admitted to James that they had stolen approximately $30,000 each and they were therefore pleading not guilty on the grounds that the charges were inappropriate. Most of them felt they had not even committed any crime. They seemed to have a warped moral code that meant it was okay to steal from the casino. Their feeling was that the casino ripped off the punters anyway and they were somehow helping themselves to ill-gotten gains. Their view was that most of the gamblers were crooks themselves who had made their money illegally through drug trafficking, prostitution and other crimes.

Peter Archer, who had been the first to be interviewed, had been very helpful. He openly admitted that he had set up the scam with Tom Mallet and David Smith. Marais had employed both Archer and Mallet previously at the Palace. Archer, Mallet and Smith were the key players, the others were simply recruited to assist once they knew that the cups could be used with little chance of detection on the tables at the Golden City. According to Archer all the members of the gang were on equal shares.

"Do you believe him?" asked Chidoli.

"Frankly I don't. Smith, Archer and Mallet were taking the biggest risks as gambler, Pit Boss and cashier respectively so it is likely that they had a bigger cut."

"What of Daly, the American?"

"Daly! A real snake if ever I met one!"

"What makes you say that?"

"As you know he was the first to get caught and pulled in for questioning. It didn't take him long to admit his guilt and try and cut a deal with Marais. He claims Marais agreed not to have him arrested and charged but reneged on his promise."

"I can imagine he is raging about that," stated Chidoli.

"Come on, Edward, how are we going to get Martin out of this fix? He's staring at a long sentence if found guilty!"

Chidoli frowned. "I am sorry for that but there was always that risk."

James swallowed hard. Chidoli was his client and he knew he was being paid well but for the first time he felt he couldn't trust him. There was something about his change of demeanour. He appeared to be completely unperturbed about the predicament Martin was now in. It was as though he had the attitude that Martin was paid to take risks and his luck had simply run out. James was already planning an escape route for Martin in the event of him being found guilty. However, he had more important things to do at that moment. He had to find out what other things Marais was up to so he might be able to get Martin released by blackmailing Marais. He looked at his watch. He wondered whether Sean was already finding out information at the casino.

"James, we now have less than two weeks to the trial..." He paused.

James interrupted. "I know. I will find out about Marais's intentions and any other criminal activities he has been involved in. You can rest assured of that."

"You need to and fast! I'm getting pressure from above. The Tanzanian government suspect Marais is evading tax and now he has put in such a large insurance claim they wanted answers," sighed Chidoli.

James nodded. He knew it was his most challenging project since he started his business and potentially the most dangerous. Marais was an angry man and if he was forced into a corner with a chance of being deported from Tanzania he would become even more unpredictable.

"I'm sorry, James, I must get back for dinner with my family," Chidoli said as he stood up. "Call me when you have some new information."

James rose from his chair and they shook hands.

"Don't worry, I'm on the case. I'll get you enough to have Marais put away for a long, long time."

"I hope so. My government want to convict Marais as much as I do. They fear he will attract more Afrikaners of his kind to the country and they don't want that," he said icily.

Chidoli turned on his heels and headed up the steps to the exit. James breathed in. The pressure was on.

§

The next morning Martin was confronted by the other croupiers in the exercise yard. David Smith lingered in the background. Martin looked around and up at the watchtower behind him hoping that one of the guards was aware that a problem was about to arise.

Tom Mallett poked Martin in the chest with his right hand. At six-feet-two he was taller than Martin. Martin stepped back, not wanting to become involved in a fight.

"What's your problem, Tom?"

"Don't you mean, what's *your* problem?" Mallett said aggressively, poking Martin even harder in the chest. "Why is it you were the only one yesterday to have a lawyer representing you?" he said angrily.

"Yeah," drawled Daly. He moved behind Martin's right shoulder but far enough away from Martin to be out of reach from a flying fist. "Yeah," he repeated. "Maybe you're the guy who grassed us up to Marais." He sneered, trying to incite a reaction from Martin. Mallett nodded in agreement.

"What have you got to say about that? It's very strange that no sooner had you joined us that the coup was uncovered." He warmed to Daly's suggestion that Martin was responsible for them being imprisoned.

"Come on, guys," protested Martin. "I had nothing to do with that. It certainly wasn't me. It could be any one of you guys." He looked Daly squarely in the face. "What about you, Daly? I heard you were the first to be interviewed by Marais." He took a step towards Daly who immediately retreated, bowing his head to avoid Martin's stare.

"Explain that," Martin repeated.

Daly suddenly reacted. He looked up and moved towards Martin. He raised his fists in preparation to attack him.

"You bastard!" hissed Daly, swinging a right fist at Martin.

Martin reacted quickly, sidestepping to his left. He grabbed Daly's wrist with his right hand and jerked his arm downwards, taking him completely by surprise. Daly sank to his knees. A searing pain shot up his arm.

Suddenly a warning siren filled the air. The guard in the watchtower behind Martin had been observing the fracas down below. He expected a full-scale fight to break out at any moment. He released the handle on the siren and grabbed his rifle and fired a volley of warning shots skywards. Several crows squawked in fear as the noise of the shots echoed around them and flew off in the direction of some trees outside the compound.

Moments later, eight or nine guards appeared waving big wooden clubs in one hand and carrying riot shields in the other. They surrounded Martin and the rest of the croupiers pushing through the steadily growing crowd of Tanzanian prisoners who had gathered around them, seemingly very bemused at the muzungus (white men) fighting amongst each other. Behind them a sergeant officer appeared. He removed the swagger baton from under his arm and pointed it at the croupiers.

"What's going on here?" he shouted loudly above the din. The Sergeant raised his arm at the guard in the tower. The guard immediately reacted and pointed his weapon at the prisoners in readiness for any further disruption.

Peter Archer stepped forward and smiled at the Sergeant.

"It's nothing, sir, we had a minor disagreement."

The Sergeant looked suspiciously at Daly who was clutching his right forearm.

"What have you got to say about that?"

"It was nothing, I tripped and fell and damaged my arm," lied Daly. He winced with pain. He had been surprised at the speed and power of Martin's reaction.

"Then go about your business! Any more disturbances and you'll all end up in solitary confinement."

"It won't happen again," Peter Archer responded, easing the tension.

The Sergeant waved the guards away and shouted at the Tanzanian prisoners in Swahili to disperse. Martin moved away and sat down cross-legged against one of the wooden pillars supporting one of the two corrugated roof structures in the yard. They at least provided some shade from the scorching sun. He flicked away some ants that had begun to crawl up his leg. Archer and Mallett followed him and squatted down beside him.

"Martin, Daly could be right. Can you explain why your lawyer Mwingara was the only one here yesterday? It doesn't add up," said Archer.

"There's nothing much to say, Mwingara already gave you a perfectly reasonable explanation," replied Martin nonchalantly, flicking some more ants off his legs. By now the other prisoners had dispersed around the yard. Martin eyed Daly suspiciously across the yard as he saw him talking animatedly with the other croupiers.

"That was some move you pulled on Daly," Mallett interrupted.

"Oh, that. It was only a little trick I learned a long time ago," replied Martin dismissively. He was still watching Daly who by now was pointing over in Martin's direction.

"That looked more than a little trick. Where did you say you worked before the Golden City?" queried Archer.

"Yeah, I've only ever seen something like that in a Bruce Lee movie," said Mallett excitedly before Martin could reply to Archer's question. Martin looked at Archer.

"I didn't say."

A prison guard appeared, calling the prisoners to fall in line for the return to their cells. Martin stood up. He half-smiled at Archer and Mallett and joined the line of prisoners who were waiting to go back to their cells. As he did so Daly brushed past him, deliberately hitting him with his shoulder.

"I'll have you, Donaldson," he hissed.

Martin stared hard at him. A smile appeared on his face. "Any time, Daly," he said casually. He took a step forward to avoid any further confrontation.

14

"HEY SEAN, HOW are you doing?" called Buck Teeth loudly as Sean sipped a beer overseeing the blackjack tables in the casino later that night. Sean had deliberately tried to avoid his stare as Buck Teeth sauntered towards him.

"Oh, I'm sorry, I didn't see you there," he lied. "I was engrossed in that game of blackjack," he lied again. "Apologies, I can't remember your name. I'm terrible at that."

"Thadeus J Delport III!" Buck Teeth boomed. "You can call me T J, all my friends do." He slapped Sean on the back, almost spilling his beer in the process.

"Can I get you a drink?" Sean asked hoping Buck Teeth would find another friend for the evening.

"Bourbon and Coke on the rocks," was the booming answer. "Hey, are you a gambler too?"

"I enjoy an occasional flutter. I'm here for a few days' holiday."

"Jesus, have you heard about the scam that's been going on here for the last six months?" T J suddenly announced loudly.

Sean was taken aback. "No. Tell me about it."

Several other customers at the bar raised their eyebrows and looked at each other in astonishment at T J's revelations. The barman served him his drink.

"Come on, Sean. Let's take that table over there by the window."

Sean followed. Several sets of eyes followed them as they walked to their table. As they sat down T J took a slurp from his drink, wiping his bushy black moustache with the back of his left hand. He then leant forward towards Sean and began talking in hushed tones. It was a complete change from the noisy American that Sean had experienced so far. Sean frowned. He was intrigued by T J's change in style and demeanour. He wondered why he seemed to be so unnaturally loud.

"Who was the black guy I saw you with on the plane? Do you know him well?"

For a moment Sean wasn't sure how to respond. He hesitated for a minute to collect his thoughts.

"Oh him, he was only a guy I met on the plane. He's here on business I think."

"He didn't look like a guy you'd only just met," T J said in a much softer American accent.

By now all thoughts of a night's gambling on the tables had completely gone from Sean's mind. Thadeus J Delport III was certainly not the man he had portrayed himself as originally.

"I've travelled the world, Sean, and my guess is that friend of yours is or was in Special Forces." His brown eyes searched Sean's face for any sign of confirmation. "What's his name?"

"I told you, he's not my friend." Sean was becoming exasperated with T J's attitude. "I do seem to remember it was James something. Ah yes, James Annan I think." He was unable to hide a slight smile as his efforts at denial sounded so hollow.

T J leant forward. "Sean, I'll get straight to the point. I think you're a man to be trusted. I think also that you and James are well acquainted despite your denials. I think we're all in a position to help each other. I think we may all be here for slightly different reasons but may all have a mutual interest."

He sat back in his chair and clasped his hands behind his head. He stretched back and returned his hands to rest on the table in front of him. Sean returned his gaze. He wondered what James would do if he was confronted with a similar situation. He sipped his beer. He looked at T J over the top of his glass. A line of the frothy liquid settled above his upper lip. He put his glass down and wiped away the froth from his lips with the tip of his tongue.

"I guess I have nothing to lose if you tell me why you're here," said Sean in expectation. "Anything you say will not go beyond me..."

"Or your friend! I suspect our mutual interest is Victor Marais!" T J said unexpectedly.

Sean smiled.

T J began speaking again in hushed tones. "I am a drugs enforcement agent." He produced an ID card to confirm it. "I was previously a US Navy Seal. On my retirement from the service I joined US Customs and Excise and I worked for them for ten years. I was then offered a job sponsored by the US government to act as a freelance consultant to a number of African governments in East and Southern Africa."

Sean was surprised that T J was revealing all this information to him. He sipped his beer and said nothing.

T J admitted to being an expert in combating drug running, having worked on attachment during his time in the Seals for the Colombian and other South American governments. Along with other Navy Seals he had trained the Colombian Army and Police in methods to combat the drug cartels that were shipping cocaine to the US and Europe. The drug enforcement agencies were working closely with their respective Navy coastguards. It was his third visit to Tanzania.

"The information I have gathered has linked all the drug barons in the various African countries I have worked in, to Victor Marais. By all accounts Marais is the key to the whole operation. Additionally I have come across information that Marais has been smuggling gold from South Africa into Kenya and Tanzania via Zanzibar.

Sean looked wide-eyed in amazement. He was beginning to have a sneaking admiration for T J.

"There is much more to tell you," said T J, draining his glass, "but I need to speak with your friend James and you together. I suggest tomorrow at midday down at the marina. There is also something else I need to show both of you."

"I'm sure James will be interested in what you have told me."

He knew James would be pleased that he had made contact with T J but they had already been talking for too long. He had to start playing the tables to try and glean further information from the croupiers about the coup.

"By the way, you never told me what you know about the casino scam," Sean said, remembering one of T J's opening remarks.

"I'll tell you all about that tomorrow." He laughed loudly and reverted to his pretence as the noisy American tourist. "Lady Luck is with me tonight." He laughed again and rubbed his hands together in anticipation of a big win. "Roulette's the game for me. What about you, Sean?"

"Blackjack's my game."

Sean was deep in thought as they headed to their respective tables. He was not sure whether T J could be trusted. He also had to remember to stop referring to T J as Buck Teeth.

§

T J was already waiting for Sean and James as they arrived at the marina shortly before midday. He was dressed in white trousers, white shirt and blue boat shoes. A white sailor's cap with a green peak shielded his eyes from the sun. He looked the epitome of the all-American tourist ready to go on a boat trip. He greeted Sean and James in the guise of his original noisy persona. Sean chuckled as T J slapped James on the back. He shook his hand as he did so. It reminded Sean of the occasion when they first met at the airport.

James in his inimitable relaxed way went along with the noisy charade. Sean had already briefed him about T J's behaviour. He also told James that he could not understand why T J was acting as a noisy American and seemed like he was deliberately attracting unnecessary attention. James also found it strange as Special Forces personnel tended to be very inconspicuous on operations.

Sean and James had dressed very sensibly in shorts, loose-fitting shirts and trainers. They were not sure what to expect and they had no idea where they were going or where they might end up. James carried a small rucksack over his shoulder that he had filled with water bottles.

"Hi guys. I've taken the liberty of hiring a small boat." T J's voice boomed as he pointed to the speedboat moored up next to them.

"Nothing like doing the tourist thing," James responded dryly.

One of the workers from the boat-hire company held it steady as the three of them climbed aboard one after the other. T J took up the seat behind the wheel. James sat down next to him and Sean moved into one of the two leather bucket seats behind them. The worker released the rope from the mooring and tossed it gently into the back of the boat behind Sean's seat. T J pressed the starter button and the engine roared into life. He pushed the throttle lever slowly into reverse and eased the boat gently backwards as he turned the wheel to the right away from the marina wall. Then he pushed the throttle slowly forward and guided the boat between the marker buoys out towards the entrance to the marina. Sean looked back and watched as a number of different crews were busily working onboard or alongside the large yachts moored up. Many of them were clearing up the debris left from the various parties that had taken place the previous night. Here they were in a playground for the rich and famous. Several armed guards patrolled the perimeter walls of the marina.

A canvas canopy provided some protection from the

scorching midday sun. Sean put on his sunglasses to protect his eyes from the glare reflecting off the turquoise blue water. As they cleared the entrance to the harbour the sea became noticeably rougher. T J gave a burst of throttle as he turned the boat south towards Dar. He held the wheel with one hand and clutched his cap with the other as the boat bucked and lurched over the waves causing the engine to whine. Great plumes of spray fanned either side of the boat and rearwards into the wake. They continued their journey for five minutes or so before T J eased back on the throttle and almost came to a halt.

"Why are we stopping?" shouted Sean.

"I need to continue my story. It's safer to tell you here rather than ashore." He turned to James. "I guess Sean has brought you up to date as to the reasons why I am here."

James nodded.

T J held the throttle in the forward position. It was enough to steer the boat slowly on the same course parallel with the coastline. They were about half a mile from shore. Sean noticed a few small white, pink and yellow painted houses behind the white sandy beaches. There were also some rather more grandiose dwellings. Offshore, several small fishing boats bobbed in the sea. Sean undid the buttons on his shirt. Great rivulets of sweat were already running down his chest and back. The speed of the boat and the wind on their bodies had kept them remarkably cool up until then. T J removed his cap and wiped his brow. His black hair glistened with sweat. He continued with his story, picking up where he left off from the night before.

"Marais has apparently been using Tanzania as a stop-off point for a multi-million-dollar syndicate before distributing drugs to other parts of East Africa. Kenya is the biggest market for the syndicate and it is centred on downtown Nairobi."

Sean threw James a sideways glance.

T J continued: "One of the ways the drugs are being smuggled is by using specially registered matatus that are driven up the coast from Dar, across the Kenyan border and into Mombasa. These matatus actually carry very few passengers. From Mombasa the drugs are redistributed into different vehicles and taken by road into the heart of Nairobi. Kirinyaga Crescent is the centre of the activity. It is conveniently placed en route to the Old Nation Terminus on Tom Mboya Street, a busy stop-off point for matatus on rural routes. Consignments of heroin, crack cocaine and marijuana are either distributed wholesale or sold by some of the dealers operating there directly to the end users. The dealers use small outlets under the guise of spare-parts dealerships for goods imported into Kenya."

"I've heard stories about the drugs trade but I didn't realise it was on such a large scale in Kenya," said Sean shaking his head.

"Surely the police know about these activities?" queried James.

"Of course they do but they do virtually nothing to combat it. Most of them are allegedly paid by the dealers to turn a blind eye. Some are not only taking bribes from the dealers but they are also taking bribes from the end users who often turn up in their expensive vehicles to buy their next fix. Most of the users are even sons and daughters of the rich and famous from the higher echelons of Kenyan society, both black and white. They go to Kirinyaga Crescent in the evenings to buy cocaine in particular. The dealers even deliver the drugs to customers in the upmarket and fashionable estates in Nairobi, like Kileleshwa, Runda, Hurlingham, Karen and Lavington."

Sean raised his eyes in recognition of the names.

"Many of the dealers are Congolese and from West African countries and they have adopted ingenious ways of attracting less attention employing disabled people who carry the drugs to the users while they remain in their cars. Onlookers are duped into thinking that they are on their usual begging missions. In fact they are delivering the drugs to their clients who drive away in their expensive cars within minutes of contact. The Congolese were the first to perfect this method in Kinshasa, the capital of Zaire."

"You certainly seem to have done your research. I also have experience of drug-running methods from my time spent in Colombia and it all adds up," agreed James.

"The rich are not the only users who visit Kirinyaga Crescent. The infamous Nairobi Street boys and men have also been sucked into this trade. When the police moved them on from the city-centre colonies that they used to hang out in they moved to Kirinyaga. It didn't take them long to start using the drugs available, a change from the glue-sniffing they were used to. The drugs the street boys also now peddle to pay for their new habit mostly includes crack cocaine in crystal form. It looks like little sugar cubes. Other drugs they peddle to the rich are mainly cocaine in powder form and sometimes heroin. Incredibly there is so much hard cash in the area that a major bank has even opened up a new branch allegedly to take advantage of it!" said T J smiling.

"This is all very interesting," James said, "but how do you want us to help you?"

"You can help me gather further information about the drugs syndicate and I in turn will help you with information about your casino scam. Victor Marais is the common denominator in all of these things. The Tanzanian government is desperate to find solid proof against him so they can arrest him and bring him to trial."

James went on to explain to T J about their project at the casino. He told him how Martin Donaldson and the other croupiers were arrested. How they were now languishing in prison and that they were all looking at long sentences.

"Although we and Martin are directly employed by Chidoli, Martin is in a deniable position as Chidoli would never admit publicly that he employed him. Martin is now in a very difficult situation," sighed James. "Not only that, we are not here to get involved in your drug-enforcement operations. We have another job to do."

T J remained silent.

James continued. "The only way of getting Martin out of prison is to organise an escape!"

"Hmm," pondered T J. "That's going to be very difficult without the possibility of casualties."

"We have the expertise to get him out, but thereafter it won't be easy to get him out of the country. The airport and the port will be closely watched and escape by road is difficult and slow."

"Never mind about Martin at this stage," interrupted Sean. "Isn't the purpose of the exercise to prove that Marais is ripping off the casino himself?"

"That's true but we still have to get Martin out," suggested James again, clearly worried about his friend and employee.

Sean had so far gathered information from croupiers at the casino that the Bahamas cups scam was really a minor irrelevance to the whole story. Apparently when Marais actually discovered the scam he was privately delighted because it took the emphasis away from his own operation, stealing from the casino himself and thus reducing his tax burden to the Tanzanian government.

"In fact I wouldn't be at all surprised if he was the one who set up the whole cups scam in the first place," said Sean as he removed his sunglasses and wiped away the drips of sweat that had formed on them.

"Hold on a moment, guys. My information from a very reliable source is that Marais didn't know about the cups scam. He is merely using it to his own advantage now," said T J.

“I’m sure Martin will soon find out who started the scam. I have every faith in his ability to do so,” responded James.

T J looked at his watch. “Come on, gentlemen. I have something to show you. I am sure we can all benefit from it,” he said mysteriously.

At that point he turned the boat towards the shore. “Hold tight, guys,” he yelled above the sound of the engine as he pushed the throttle forward. The nose of the boat lifted out of the water. James and Sean clutched the grab handles beside their seats as T J took the boat up to full speed. They travelled at that rate for the next twenty minutes or so before he eased back on the throttle again. By then they were in the inky blue water of Dar Es Salaam Bay.

§

“Wow!” exclaimed Sean as he spotted the sleek-looking boat with black tinted windows temporarily anchored up alongside a pontoon in Dar Es Salaam Bay. “I’ve never seen a boat like that before!!”

“Gentlemen, that happens to be the very latest in ultra-fast boats. The design comes from research and development carried out in the World Power Boat Championships over the last three years,” T J informed them.

“I’ve heard about it but I didn’t realise it was in general production,” added James, equally impressed by the style.

“It’s not,” countered T J. “Although initially it was designed to be sold as an ultra-fast military patrol craft, the first buyer of the Bora 20 happens to be a company registered in Mauritius. So far the military have been slow in responding to the potential.”

“Don’t tell me. Let me guess, it’s a Marais-owned company,” suggested Sean.

“You are absolutely right. And what’s more we have reason to believe it’s being used to transport heroin and cocaine from Zanzibar to Mombasa and Dar.”

One of the main trafficking routes for heroin was from the Far East via the Middle East to Zanzibar. Originally Zanzibar was one of the most important trading ports in the whole of East Africa. The security in Zanzibar was very lax and it made it easy for traffickers to land on the east coast in the dead of night. It was transported from there by small fast lightweight boats. The Bora 20 was powered by Turbomeca gas turbine engines giving 1,800 horsepower and capable of speeds of up to seventy-five knots. It has a closed cabin configuration for a crew of up to eight people. The aft deck has 7.62-millimetre general purpose machine guns fitted to the port and starboard sides and mounted on the roof was a 30-millimetre cannon. It had electric thrusters to operate at low speed without the main engines running.

"I don't suppose that the Kenyan or Tanzanian navies have any vessels that can outrun the Bora?" asked James, looking very serious.

"You are absolutely correct!" T J replied. "In a high-speed chase the only thing that can be used are helicopters and they are only good for tracking over relatively short distances."

"So once again, have you got any firm proof that Marais is involved in all these operations?" said Sean.

James interrupted. "Is there anything that he can be prosecuted for?" His voice was filled with frustration.

"Nothing definite yet but three months ago a small Cessna plane carrying fifty kilos of gold bars was intercepted on arrival at Wilson Airport in Nairobi."

Sean smiled. "Let me guess – the plane was registered to one of Marais's companies?"

T J shook his head. "Not quite. We did some research and discovered it was registered to a company owned by David Koech, the former head of CID in Nairobi."

The plane had arrived after midnight after the airport had closed. Undercover officers from the Drug Enforcement

Agency were acting as a result of a tip-off and had surrounded the airport. Their informant had told them that a shipment of cocaine was being brought in from West Africa via Zaire. When they searched the plane they were astonished to discover fifty kilos of gold onboard in a diplomatic bag. They subsequently handed it over to Customs and Excise officers.

"So was there any connection to Marais?" asked James.

"Not then, but after digging a little deeper we discovered that David Koech had purchased the company from Marais last year at a very favourable price. Apparently it was way below true market value."

James frowned again and shook his head. "So what happened to the gold?"

"Two days after it had been handed over to Customs and Excise a man purporting to be a senior diplomat from the South African High Commission based in Nairobi turned up and claimed it. He apparently held diplomatic immunity and the customs officers were left with no alternative but to hand over the gold to him."

"Was he actually a diplomat from the South African High Commission?" asked Sean.

James chipped in: "I don't get the connection with South Africa. I thought you said the gold came from West Africa via Zaire."

"On closer investigation it turned out he wasn't South African. Someone at the customs office had been bribed. The South Africans later issued denials of any involvement. We still aren't sure where the gold came from."

T J was clearly dejected with the latest turn of events.

"Africa!" exclaimed James, pursing his lips in annoyance.

"You say that but corruption is a human problem and not specific to Africa. Corruption is a two-way street and it would end almost immediately in Africa if the West didn't continue to fuel it," responded Sean. He was disappointed with his friend for blaming Africa, especially as he was of African origin.

According to T J some Flying Squad detectives based in Nairobi were openly involved with the drug traffickers in Kirinyaga Crescent. They visited the Crescent daily and collected their protection money from the dealers. They were the ones who were suspected of bribing someone in the customs office to collect the gold. They were the ones who were helping the drug trafficking to continue unabated.

"So again you are no nearer to getting Marais arrested and charged?"

"Not yet, but we will get there," replied T J sounding as optimistic as ever.

"On another note, T J, tell me how you can help us with Martin's escape from prison?" James asked.

T J pointed in the direction of the Bora 20. James and Sean turned towards it again as it bobbed up and down in the water alongside the pontoon. Sean looked quizzically at James. He in turn looked at T J enquiringly and then laughed. T J said nothing. James remained silent for a few moments. His face broke into a smile as it dawned on him what T J was suggesting.

"Are you saying you want me to hijack that vessel and use it as a getaway craft for Martin?" he laughed again. "You can't be serious!!"

"Oh yes I can!" At that he fired the engine into life again before he could hear James's response. He turned the boat north and headed back towards the Golden City.

15

FIVE DAYS LATER Martin and David Smith were exercising in the prison yard. During that time Martin had struck up a new rapport with David. He had slowly drawn him into his confidence. David knew that he was looking at another long prison sentence. After great deliberation he finally admitted to Martin that he had been caught up in the Palace Casino scam in South Africa back in 1985. He explained he had served four years in Mafeking Prison and had been released in 1989 and returned to London but vehemently protested his innocence.

Although he was clearly angry and bitter about his unjust incarceration his time there had taught him patience. He realised on his release that he would never be able to prove his innocence but he was determined that he would seek revenge on the people responsible for claiming he had been involved.

"There were many, many more people involved in the scam who were never caught," David said, in between a set of press-ups. "One in particular is now a multi-millionaire living in South East England and working for a blue-chip firm of merchant bankers!"

"Go on," said Martin, breathing heavily from the exertion of a set of squat thrusts.

Apparently several senior managers had been involved. Three or four of them left quietly after the Palace Casino scam had been uncovered. David explained about Tony Stanley's involvement and how he and his wife Lindsay had returned to London very soon after the managers' meeting with Marais in Mauritius. It was too coincidental that twelve croupiers had been arrested so soon afterwards. Martin and David completed their exercises and sat down. They inhaled deeply to recover their breath.

David suddenly announced: “My name is not David Smith. It is an alias. My real name is Chris Powell!”

Martin was taken aback by his sudden revelation.

Chris went on to explain about his time in Bophuthatswana. “I was nearly twenty kilos heavier prior to serving my time in Mafeking Prison. When I was released I was unrecognisable as the man who went in four years earlier. Since my release I maintained the fitness regime I started there. Most of the weight came off during a hunger strike that I began in the first few months inside. I was innocent and I wanted to draw attention to my plight. After two months I realised that the British press had lost interest in the case and no one, not even Amnesty International, who shared an initial interest, cared anymore. So I gave up and decided to knuckle down and serve my time without drawing further attention to myself.”

David went on to explain about the address book and how the names of the croupiers found their way into it and how it had entered Marais’s possession.

“I ran into Tony Stanley in London on my release. He had been one of the main players in the scam. He never liked me. He seemed to think for some reason that I had been having an affair with his wife Lindsay.”

“Had you?”

“No!!!” said David emphatically. “She had actually had a one-night stand with one of the other managers when Tony was away one weekend in Durban.”

“So why did he think it was you?”

“Lindsay had always been very friendly towards me and we got on very well. I thought she was too good for that bastard,” he said bitterly.

When Tony Stanley had returned from his weekend in Durban he began to hear various rumours about Lindsay's indiscretion. Several names had been mentioned, including David's.

"Tony put two and two together and made five. He came up with my name. He convinced himself that I was the person who had shagged Lindsay. He exacted revenge by including my name in the address book after the Yugoslav gangsters had sold it to him."

"How did you know it was Stanley who included your name?"

"Peter Archer visited me in Mafeking Prison while I was on remand before my trial and told me he had seen the address book in Alan Hudson's room before he disappeared back to the States. He assured me my name was not in it then!" His voice rose in anger.

"Why are you so sure it was Stanley who put your name in it and not somebody else? It could have been Hudson after Archer left his room."

"By chance I bumped into Stanley in London in the bar of the casino at the Mayfair International Hotel on my release. Initially he did not recognise me but I recognised him immediately. I had pictured his face in my head every day of the four and a half years I had spent in prison. The thought of meeting him again had driven me nearly mad. When I introduced myself, Stanley taunted me about my long sentence, which he said was revenge for the affair he'd accused me of having with his wife. He had laughed loudly."

"Wow, how did you feel about that?"

"I wanted to kill him for taking four years of my life away from me."

"After his revelations, I lost my temper and attacked him. I quickly wiped the sneering smile from Stanley's face. I broke his nose with my first punch, an arcing right hook. I managed to throw another flurry of punches that inflicted further serious damage to Stanley's face before some burly security guards intercepted and threw me out of the casino."

Chris's voice had become almost shrill. He breathed in and began to calm down before continuing.

"I never saw Stanley again. It was probably my good fortune that the bouncers intervened because I probably would have ended up killing him and doing another stretch."

"What happened to Tony's wife Lindsay?"

Apparently Lindsay left Tony about six months after their return to London. The money that Marais had paid him off with had turned his head. He began gambling heavily and womanising. It hadn't taken him long to spend the first £125,000. Within three days of his return to London he gave the two sets of accounts to Marais's lawyer and simultaneously received a banker's draft for the second payment of £125,000. Even back in 1986, £250,000 didn't go far unless it was invested wisely. Luxury foreign holidays and several top-of-the-range sports cars followed. Tony lived the high life for a while.

After Lindsay discovered his first affair with a page-three model, she threatened to leave him but forgave him because she felt guilty about her earlier affair at the Palace. Several affairs later and after a few severe drunken beatings by him she finally left him. She categorically denied she had had any affair with Chris and was mortified when she discovered Tony had falsely included Chris's name in Alan Hudson's address book. She realised that Tony had been responsible for getting an innocent man imprisoned. She was beside herself with guilt and knew she was powerless to do anything about it. She tried to get her father, who was a Labour MP, to pull a few strings to help get Chris released from Mafeking Prison, but as the crime had caused a very embarrassing diplomatic incident at the time he was unable even to arrange an appeal. Furthermore he didn't want to drag Lindsay's name and his family name through the press because of what Stanley, his son-in-law, had done. He had always hated him with a passion. He felt sorry for Chris Powell but felt there had been far worse miscarriages of justice and hoped he would survive prison.

When Tony eventually ran out of money he realised he had to start working again but soon found out that Marais had blocked his path to future employment in the gaming industry. He even contacted Marais in an effort to blackmail him financially and threatened him by saying he'd kept a photocopy of the accounts. Not long afterwards, Stanley took a severe beating when he answered his front door to a couple of strangers. He was last heard of working as a clerk in a small bookmaker's shop in the East End of London.

"I spent the next five years drifting from job to job. Although I don't have a criminal record in the UK, it was difficult to explain almost five years missing on a CV. I told prospective employers that I had spent some of the time travelling around Africa and working at a water-sports school, as a windsurf instructor in Kenya. I'm not sure that many of them believed me. One prospective employer even asked 'How do I know that you didn't spend those last five years in prison?'"

Chris chuckled, much to Martin's amusement.

"So what brought you back to Africa and to one of Marais's casinos of all places?"

"Unfinished business, I guess," said Chris philosophically. "It began to eat away at me that I was in a dead-end job in a telesales centre with little prospects. It was a job I hated with a passion. I heard Marais had set up a new casino operation in Tanzania and decided that the time had come to take my revenge on him."

Martin scratched his head. "Damned lice," he swore, "I can't wait to get out of here. This place is driving me nuts!"

Chris began scratching himself too. Conditions in the prison were not good. Most of the croupiers had contracted head and body lice. The food was appallingly bad. Meals consisted of porridge and tea for breakfast and mainly of ugali, a sort of maize cake, with cabbage and a watery soup pretending to be a stew, for dinner. Several of them had suffered diarrhoea and severe stomach upsets. Greening, from the High Commission, had persuaded the authorities to give them new blankets that were lice-free and managed to get them a concession of a shower with soap once a week. Archer and Mallett had gone on hunger strike in protest against the appalling conditions to try and gain sympathy from the British and Western press to publicise their plight more.

"I wish Archer and Mallett would stop their protest. The same thing happened when I was in Mafeking. I went on hunger strike with a couple of the other croupiers. All it did was to antagonise the government and the same thing has happened here."

"I agree with you. I have always felt that they would be better to keep a low profile and try and adjust to the conditions," interrupted Martin. Martin's military training and experiences when on covert operations had landed him in some conditions that were even more severe than the ones he found himself in at that moment. He had been toughened physically to endure some very torturous regimes.

"Exactly that," replied Chris. "A touch of déjà vu if you ask me," he said with quiet resignation in his voice.

"You still haven't explained how you ended up at the Golden City."

Chris had eventually left his job at the telesales centre. He cleared out his flat and put the few possessions he had into storage. His physical appearance had already changed dramatically. He had bleached his hair to put the finishing touches to the changes. Finally he changed his name to David Smith. Armed with a forged passport, he flew down to Dar Es Salaam and ended up at the Golden City.

After spending a few days relaxing and gambling at the tables, Chris had introduced himself to Peter Archer who initially did not recognise him. Archer feigned shock when Chris suggested running a Bahamas cups coup. He pretended he was not interested to begin with. At first he suggested he was going to inform Marais about the approach by Chris and have him thrown out of the casino and Tanzania. Greed however took over. The thought of ripping off another casino strongly appealed to Archer and eventually he relented and agreed to set up another coup. It wasn't long before he had recruited the other croupiers he needed. He had not wanted the American, John Daly, to be involved but Daly was very friendly with Matt Bradley, the Inspector. Bradley had insisted that Daly be allowed to join in. Archer did not like Daly being involved from day one. Daly was brash and loud. The sort of person who would boast about his exploits at the bar after a few drinks too many and draw attention to himself unnecessarily. He was also one of the first to change his spending habits after the money began to roll in. He even began to buy drinks at the bar. It was something completely out of character for him.

"Archer at least had the good sense to get the others to pool some of their takings and invest in two racehorses to run at the Nairobi meetings. It was a front for any outward signs of newfound wealth," continued Chris.

Martin got up quickly as he saw some of the other croupiers coming towards them.

"I think we will continue this conversation later," he said quietly to Chris. Chris nodded in agreement.

"One last thing though. Do any of the others know your true identity?" Martin asked Chris as he kicked a pebble across the yard.

"Not as far as I know! Archer swears he hasn't told a soul."

16

SEAN HAD BEEN in Dar over a week and had begun to worry about returning to Mombasa. He had telephoned Njeri every day to check how Achieng was and spoke to Achieng on each occasion. She showed no real signs of missing him. Typically, like most children, she was having a great time because she was able to play with Thomas and Grace but she did keep asking him when he was coming back. When he last called home, Njeri had begun to quiz him about what he was doing in Dar. She sensed that Sean was not telling her everything about his trip.

"So when are you coming back then?"

"Any day now," Sean lied, not knowing when the project would be finished.

"That means nothing!" Njeri retorted angrily. "Is it tomorrow, the next day or next week? The children are all back at school now. Achieng misses you even more now that she is in the school routine."

"I would have thought it was easier for you having them gone all day," replied Sean. His male logic took over.

Njeri paused. "Well yes, it is, but that doesn't help when Achieng has cried the last two mornings because you haven't been here to take her to school."

Sean swallowed hard. He was overcome by guilt.

"I'll do my best to be back by the weekend," he lied again. His feeling was made worse by memories of letting down his elder daughter, Louise, when she was younger. History was repeating itself. He hung up the phone but remained in his chair on the balcony overlooking the sea. He watched as a striking-looking fish eagle swooped on its prey, scooping up a large fish, which tried to twist and turn in the bird's distinctive orangey-red claws, but to no avail. The huge bird soared away to find a convenient place to devour it.

Sean collected his thoughts. Although he knew he was committed to helping James on the project he was anxious to get home as soon as possible. He picked up the phone again and asked the operator to call James at the Serengeti Hotel. The phone rang briefly and James answered.

"Sean, I'm glad you called. I am about to go to the gym for a workout. I'll meet you there and we can talk about the latest developments."

"I'll be there in ten minutes. I have some important information for you. I also need to talk to you about a couple of other things."

"Roger that," said James. He hung up. He guessed Sean wanted to talk to him about returning home. He sensed he was anxious to get back to Achieng but he was determined to make sure he stayed to complete the project. Friendship apart, he was calling in the favour for helping Sean track down Akinyi's killers. Besides which he needed to complete the project as quickly as possible. Another project was due to start in two weeks' time and his client wanted him to be personally involved in it. Although he employed good people there were certain projects that required his expertise. His next one was to kidnap a Russian scientist who was working for Saddam Hussein in Basra in southern Iraq. Intelligence reports had suggested he was prepared to defect to the West and provide full details of Saddam's alleged chemical weapons' stockpile. It was a highly dangerous mission and would certainly be the riskiest that he had undertaken since he had started his security firm. The SAS and US Special Forces could not be recruited to carry out the operation. The government had put the project out to tender and James had won the contract. Many regarded it as a suicide mission. James however thought the chances of success were good. Basra was close to the Kuwait border and he had worked out that with his own handpicked team of five others he would be able to complete the mission successfully. It was a deniable operation. If the Iraqis captured him or any of his team they were on their own. The British and US governments would deny any knowledge of them. The rewards were very, very good but for very, very high stakes. His and the lives of his men were at risk. He had been careful to recruit operatives who had no close family ties.

§

Sean arrived at the gym ten minutes after James, who was waiting in reception. They gave each other a high five as a way of greeting.

"Five minutes to talk before we get started on some serious training, my friend," laughed James.

"Before we start I need to bring you up to date with my investigations over the last few days."

Sean looked serious.

"Go ahead, we can step outside and talk."

James pointed to a coconut palm tree close to the gym entrance.

"Over there in the shade will do."

He ambled outside. Sean followed close behind. James sat down on a bench beneath the tree. Sean remained standing but lifted his foot onto the bench and rested his elbow across his knee. He hadn't been very successful with his gambling and was slightly down on his initial investment. His beginner's luck in Mombasa had simply been that, as James had quite rightly suggested.

However, he had been successful in managing to find out if anyone else was involved with the Bahamas cups coup. At first he came across a brick wall of silence from the croupiers working at the Golden City but very soon he managed to charm Dawn Turner, one of the female inspectors, who provided him with all sorts of information. She told him she was Peter Archer's girlfriend but she denied any involvement in the coup. According to Dawn no one else played any part other than those arrested. Peter Archer had very cleverly kept the numbers involved to a bare minimum. In normal circumstances the cups were more easily detectable than in the days of the Palace coup in South Africa. Dawn explained that the chips being paid out by the dealer from the bank should normally be spread on the table before being passed to the winner. When the coup was being operated at the Golden City this didn't happen, such was the arrogance of those involved, because they thought they would never get caught. However, because they only ever operated one table at a time with Chris Powell, as the gambler and a two or three dealer change with Inspector and Pit Boss on duty, no one outside their inner circle could interrupt the flow of higher denomination chips through the cups. Whenever there was a change of shift from outside their circle, Powell would leave the table shortly afterwards. He would return when the shift changed back to the staff involved in the coup. He was careful when he left and made sure there were enough gamblers at the table so attention wasn't attracted to him when he left or returned. In any given evening he was apparently laundering three or four thousand US dollars through the cashier in the group. The Tanzanian government had given special dispensation to Marais to operate in US dollars. It was a good way of bringing foreign investment and currency into the country. Marais also benefited from it because it was easier for him to launder dollars.

After Powell cashed up at the end of a night he would bank his share the next day and leave the balance at a safety deposit box at the Post Office on the complex. Peter Archer would turn up later with a duplicate key and remove the previous day's steal from the box. He subsequently distributed it amongst the other members, after first taking his share. Only Powell, Archer and Mallett, the cashier, knew exactly how much was being stolen. The others seemed readily to accept the shares given to them without question.

Sean lifted his elbow and removed his leg from the bench. He stretched his arms above his head.

"You've certainly been busy. What other gems have you uncovered?" asked James.

"There's a good deal more but mostly to do with Marais. I'm sure T J will be interested to hear about what I've found out."

According to Dawn Turner, it had long been rumoured that Marais was drug trafficking, smuggling gold and money laundering. It had been rumoured that, in addition to him operating a drugs drop-off and pick-up point off the east coast of Zanzibar, another foreign national, thought to be a German, was involved in the cartel. He had spent a number of years in Tanzania before moving to Kenya. She didn't know his name but apparently in 1994 he had purchased several beautiful islands in the Indian Ocean close to the Kenyan-Tanzanian border south of Mombasa. All of the islands had great natural beauty and were originally part of a marine park that belonged to the Kenya Wildlife Service. Apparently they had been allocated to a number of well-heeled people in Kenya, an assistant minister among them. They in turn had sold them on to the foreign national at vast profit. The title deeds were supposedly legitimate.

The foreign national planned to turn the islands into exclusive holiday resorts for the very rich and very famous. Benki, as the most attractive, was likely to be developed first on similar lines to Marais's Golden City. One of the unique features of that idyllic paradise was that in April and August a short-lived high tide engulfed the beaches making the island and any buildings on it look as if they were floating on water. Until the development started the islands were allegedly being used as a drop-off point for an international drugs trade mostly serving Kenya.

"Jesus, Sean, you've been busy. Are you sure Dawn Turner is genuine?"

"Well, after an initial reluctance she was the only one willing to talk freely to me. None of the others I spoke to seemed to know anything. Most of them expressed surprise at a coup being operated, let alone uncovered."

James stared at Sean. He expected Sean to ask next when they would be returning to Kenya. He pre-empted his question.

"With any luck we will be out of here soon. The trial date has been brought forward to the day after tomorrow."

"That's quick," responded Sean. He was surprised at the sudden change.

"Everyone has changed their pleas to guilty in the hope of more lenient sentences. I spoke to Mwingara earlier today and as there is no defence being offered, the Judge called for an immediate sitting of the court to pass down sentences."

"What about Martin?"

"I visited him yesterday and told him that, once sentenced, we will arrange his escape as soon as possible afterwards."

According to Mwingara it was highly unlikely that once they were sentenced the croupiers would be transferred to another prison. It was expected they would serve their time there, as it was close to the British High Commission and American Embassy in Dar. The High Commission and Embassy staff at least would be on hand to visit them from time to time. Greening was largely ineffectual but even he could at least keep a check on the health of the prisoners. Mwingara suggested that they would be sentenced to two to three years each, plus a substantial fine. He thought that, after all the fuss had died down and once they had paid their fines, the prisoners would be paroled in six to nine months and deported back to the UK and the USA respectively.

"If Mwingara is right and they have to serve six to nine months then we need to organise Martin's escape straightaway," said James with a hint of excitement in his voice.

"Why take the risk of an escape bid if he's likely to be out so quickly?" James looked serious for a moment.

"Six months is a long, long time in that hellhole. Not only that, I need him for my next operation, which starts in two weeks from now!"

"Sounds to me as though you need the excitement and adrenaline rush of all the action," replied Sean.

"Maybe I do but once they are sentenced we need to get our heads together with T J."

Sean looked at James carefully. "I am damned sure you know your modus operandi already," he remarked dryly.

A big smile appeared on James's face.

"Come on, time for a workout and then a few beers in the bar tonight. We've only got a day or two to finalise everything before the escape!"

Sean looked far from happy. "I don't want to put a dampener on the situation, James, but I think Marais and his security staff are on to me."

The smile left James's face as quickly as it had appeared. "What makes you think that?"

"Shortly after I spoke with Dawn Turner I was apprehended by André Joubert and a couple of his heavies on the way back to my room. He asked me to accompany him to Williams's office."

Sean turned pale at the memory.

"What happened then?"

"I felt so intimidated that I was left with little alternative but to go."

"Go on."

James remained calm.

"The walk to Williams's office gave me a chance to collect my thoughts. By the time I got there my heart was racing like never before but it gave me time to anticipate some difficult questions."

"What did Williams have to say for himself?"

"He asked me why I was at the Golden City and why I had been asking the staff so many questions."

James looked anxious for the first time. "What did you say?"

"I expressed my indignation at being brought to his office against my will and being asked such a stupid question. I told him I was here on holiday to gamble and that was it. I asked him if he asked all his guests such impertinent questions."

"Have you been too obvious in asking questions?"

Sean reddened. "Of course I haven't! Dawn Turner was the only person that I had a long conversation with."

"I asked you earlier if you thought she was genuine. What do you think now?"

Sean went on to explain that he wasn't sure whether she was setting him up or not. She had freely given him plenty of information. He felt that as Peter Archer's girlfriend she would be unlikely to be helping Marais.

"Maybe Archer is working for Marais and is double-crossing his fellow-croupiers!"

Sean looked horrified. "I'd never thought of that! If that is the case then we had better warn Martin as soon as possible not to get too friendly with Archer in prison."

James nodded his agreement.

"What was the end result with Williams?"

"Nothing really, but he made it abundantly clear that he'd be watching my every move."

"You're going to have to be very careful from now on. I think it's time you pretended to be a completely novice gambler."

"I think that's a stupid thing to do, if you don't mind me saying so."

James could see Sean was annoyed that he could even suggest he start to play the fool at this late stage.

"Sorry, mate, but you don't want to end up in the slammer like Martin, do you?"

Sean looked dejected.

"Come on, let's go and have that workout."

§

It was early evening. The sun had gone down. The light from the moon and those from the yachts were already reflecting on the water. Sean was sitting on the terrace of the bar, overlooking the marina. There was plenty of activity around the boats as they rocked gently to and fro in their moorings. The sweet smell of scent from the tropical flowers planted around the terrace permeated the air. A number of geckos scuttled around the pool area. They darted in and out amongst the vegetation. Sean was on his second beer as he waited for James and T J to arrive. He did a double take as he watched a beautiful black woman sauntering across the lower terrace towards him. A hush fell on the place as several drinkers stopped talking and turned and watched her. Her hips swung sexily as she walked. She was wearing a mini-skirt and halter top that pulled tightly across her ample bosom. As she tottered on her high-heeled, wedge espadrilles laced up her lower calves, she swung a small handbag with a long strap backwards and forwards. It almost scraped the ground as she did so. She continued walking towards Sean and as she got closer he realised he wasn't dreaming. It was Njeri Mwangi. She really was a stunningly beautiful woman and had become even more attractive as she got older. She had lost the innocence of youth. She climbed the three steps to the upper terrace and stopped short of his table. With legs astride, she placed her hands on her hips and stood in front of him. A look of defiance appeared on her face. She seemed to be prepared for Sean's reaction. A babble of voices struck up in the background as the other drinkers began to lose interest in her as they assumed she had found her man.

"Here I am, Sean!" she exclaimed confidently. Her big brown eyes seemed to grow larger as she said it.

Sean cleared his throat. "I can see that!" He was trying his best to stay calm. "What the hell are you doing here?" he hissed angrily, doing his best to keep his voice down. "You're meant to be at home looking after the children!"

"Akoth and Opiyo are looking after them." Njeri seemed as though she didn't have a care in the world.

"But I left you in charge."

"Don't talk to me like that. I'm not your lackey! I agreed to look after Achieng for a week! You didn't come back as promised. If I hadn't been around you would have left her with Akoth and Opiyo anyway." She was doing her best to deflect attention from her abandoned responsibilities.

Before Sean could respond, Njeri pulled up a chair and sat down opposite him.

"That gives you the right to leave them in charge without consulting me, does it?" replied Sean indignantly. He was becoming exasperated.

"Aren't you going to buy me a drink now I'm here?" asked Njeri, changing the subject, hoping at the same time to defuse Sean's anger. She knew she still had the ability to twist him around her little finger. Sean shook his head in frustration. He signalled for the waiter.

"A drink for madam, please," he said as the waiter arrived.

"Vodka and tonic with lots of ice and lemon," Njeri asked.

"So now you're here, you'd better tell me why you've come."

While Njeri waited for the waiter to return with her drink Sean rapped his fingers on the table. The waiter came back and placed her glass on a coaster before pouring the tonic into it. There was a faint popping sound as the tonic fizzled over the ice cubes.

"Assante sana, raffiki," Njeri addressed him in Swahili. At the same time she fluttered her eyelashes at him. The waiter looked embarrassed as he turned away.

"Still the flirt, Njeri," said Sean, with more than a hint of disapproval in his voice.

Njeri smiled and blew Sean a kiss in a provocative manner. Sean couldn't help breaking into laughter.

"Let me ask you again. What are you doing here?"

"I needed a holiday. Is that a good enough answer for you!" she said defiantly as she sipped her drink. "And I thought it was a good opportunity to see you on your own, now that MISS GREENE is back at work." She deliberately emphasised Miss Greene.

"What do you mean by that?" protested Sean defensively.

"She was probably here last week," Njeri suggested. She was deliberately goading Sean.

"Don't be so ridiculous! I'm here to work!" he retorted angrily. He stopped himself from getting up from the table and telling Njeri to piss off. Her petty jealousies in the past were one of the reasons why their relationship failed previously. She was continuing to play her little games.

"I do detect you *are* jealous." His voice sounded very cold.

Njeri bristled. "Why should I be jealous? If MISS GREENE is your new love interest what can I do? Mark my words though, Sean, one day you will be mine. We still have unfinished business!"

"What do you mean by that?" He fidgeted uneasily in his chair. He took another sip from his beer.

"So she *is* your love interest! That's why you don't give me an answer."

Sean looked at his watch. "James and T J will be here soon, so if you've got anything else sensible to say, let me know now."

He was becoming bored with what he viewed as Njeri's childishness. The pair sat in silence for a few minutes. Sean eventually spoke.

"Where are you staying?"

"That's a stupid question. Here of course," responded Njeri angrily.

"How can you afford to stay here...?"

Njeri interrupted before Sean could continue. "Why shouldn't I be able to afford it? I have a good business now. Of course I can afford it. If you must know I'm in room 434."

"But that is next to mine!"

Njeri smiled sweetly. "Perhaps I could pay you a visit later?" Her voice softened as she said it. "After lights out," she giggled.

Sean couldn't help laughing. "Really, Njeri, you are incorrigible!"

"So what business are you doing with James?"

"I can't tell you that but I don't want you to be around because it may get dangerous." Sean's manner was such that it indicated don't ask any more questions.

At that point James and T J arrived. James was surprised to see Njeri sitting with Sean. After Sean introduced T J to Njeri he said, "Njeri, we three guys have some business to discuss. So make yourself scarce for a while. I will see you later."

Njeri was about to speak but Sean put a finger to his lips. "No buts," he said firmly, "Be gone with you."

Njeri knew Sean was in one of his serious moods and made a hasty exit. She decided she would catch up with him later. She stood up from the table. As she walked away she deliberately swung her hips in an even more seductive manner than when she arrived. She knew full well all eyes would be on her again. Sean watched T J as he gazed after her. Sean chuckled as he watched Njeri. She was always the actress, he thought, as she sauntered away. Her flamboyant mode of dress drew added attention.

"She's got some body, that one, Sean!" exclaimed T J in admiration. "I see, Sean, that you've already attracted one of the local girls."

"Something like that!" he responded without trying to explain his friendship with Njeri.

T J persisted. "Is there something you should be telling us, Sean?"

"What the hell is she doing here?" asked James, turning to Sean.

"That's exactly what I asked her myself."

James raised his eyebrows as if to say he didn't really want to know the answer. "Gentlemen, it's time to discuss business," he said, changing the subject. He pulled his chair closer to the table.

In hushed tones, James explained to Sean that T J was going to put them through their paces the next day with an underwater scuba training session in the swimming pool behind the Bilicanas Hotel. It was a large pool that was often used for scuba training. As a former US Navy Seal T J was an expert. James had done scuba as part of his basic training for the Regiment, as the SAS was known. He had a PADI (Professional Association of Diving Instructors) diving certificate. Sean on the other hand was a mere novice by comparison. He had dived on several occasions but had never completed a PADI course. Generally he found it quite claustrophobic and his anxiety underwater caused him to breathe too hard. Secretly he hoped that James and T J didn't plan on diving too deep. Still, he was pleased that a morning's practice in the pool would help him overcome his fears. The practice would be followed by a short dive from the Go and Sea Diving Centre, situated south of the Msasani Slipway in Dar. It was typical of trained professionals to carry out as much training as possible before an operation. Furthermore both T J and James wanted to be certain that Sean was proficient enough to accompany them.

James further explained that the court case would start at 1000 hours in two days' time. The prisoners would be driven under armed guard from New Bagamoyo Prison to the central Police Station off Sokoine Drive in the centre of Dar. They finished their meeting and departed for bed for an early night in preparation for the next day's exercise.

17

HALF AN HOUR after Sean returned to his room there was a loud knock on his door. He looked at his watch. It was 2230 hours. He hadn't ordered room service. Housekeeping had already turned down his bed and two long mosquito nets had been drawn around it, completely enclosing it to protect him during the night. He was drying himself as he climbed out of the shower. There was another series of loud knocks on the door.

"Wait a moment," he called out in annoyance at the impatience of the person there. He pulled a towel around his waist. Then he looked through the spy hole in the door to check who it was. A dark figure filled his view. He released the catch on the door and turned the handle. Almost immediately Njeri entered the room, brushing past him quickly.

"I should have guessed it was you!" he said, irritated with her forthright manner.

"I've come to check that you called home and spoke to Achieng and Akoth."

"You've got a bloody cheek! You've got a nerve checking up on me!"

"Well, did you?" Njeri asked again as if to rub salt into the wound.

"Of course I did. Achieng was asleep when I phoned but I spoke to Akoth and Opiyo to check all was well."

"Can I have a drink?" Njeri walked to the mini-bar that was

located underneath the dressing table. Before Sean had time to respond Njeri had pulled half a bottle of champagne from the fridge. She slammed the door shut. It gave a dull thud.

"Open this for me." She handed him the bottle.

Sean was becoming annoyed with her attitude. He was tired and he had an early start in the morning. Clutching the champagne bottle in his right hand he raised his left one in a questioning motion.

"What's going on, Njeri? I haven't time for this. I've got an early start in the morning!"

"Don't be like that. I need to talk to you. It's very important."

"What's so important that it can't wait until tomorrow?"

Njeri flopped down on the settee and picked up the TV remote control and began flicking through the channels. Meanwhile, Sean slowly removed the gold foil from the neck of the champagne bottle and popped the cork. He tilted the bottle quickly and poured the frothy contents into a champagne flute. The liquid bubbled to the top before it settled. He handed her the glass and placed the bottle in the ice bucket. He looked at his watch.

"You've got half an hour maximum to tell me what you want, Njeri."

Njeri winked at him and smiled. "Come and sit here," she purred seductively and patted the seat beside her.

Sean shook his head. "I'll be back in a minute." He tugged at his towel and headed in the direction of the bathroom, picking up a pair of boxer shorts as he did so. Njeri leaned forward in her seat and caught a reflection of Sean in the mirror as the towel slipped from his body. It seemed to her that his body was more toned and in better condition than she had ever seen it. He pulled on his boxer shorts and returned to the sitting room. Njeri quickly sat back in her seat, her eyes averted from the mirror. He smiled as he realised that she must have caught a reflection of him.

"Okay, you have now got twenty-five minutes left to talk." He grabbed the remote control from her and switched off the television. "We don't need any distractions from that," he scolded her, as if a naughty child.

Njeri looked coyly at her glass. "I need a top up," she said, handing Sean her glass. She deliberately didn't want to face him when she started talking. Sean got up to fetch more champagne.

"Sean, I know you're probably still angry with me because of the way I behaved in England," she whispered in barely audible tones.

Sean frowned, wondering where her line of conversation was going to lead. He poured the remainder of the champagne into her glass and tipped the bottle upside down carelessly in the ice bucket. A little water splashed over the sides as he did so. He returned to his armchair opposite Njeri and handed her the glass.

"Thanks," she said quietly as she took another sip. She lowered her eyes and looked at the floor.

"This is very difficult for me, Sean, but I still love you," she suddenly blurted out. "No matter how much I have tried to get you out of my mind, I cannot." Her words tumbled out. "For the past eighteen months my heart has been aching for you."

Sean was somewhat taken aback. He coughed nervously and shifted uneasily in his chair. He was at a loss for words. He was never a great one for romantic conversation at the best of times.

"I beg you, Sean. Please give me one last chance. I promise I won't let you down this time. I have changed my ways. You may frown on me because I got involved in prostitution in Europe, but at least I saved some money and invested in a good business. I will never go back to my past way of life!"

Sean said nothing. He was momentarily overwhelmed with sadness for Njeri. He genuinely had a soft spot for her in spite of her fall into prostitution in England and then Germany. He could never understand why she had done it. She had been living with him in Richmond. Life was improving for her and she had tremendous opportunities to better her life after her struggles in Kenya. He felt it was not up to him to moralise and make a harsh judgement about her, though he was not sure he could ever forgive her for it.

"Give me one last chance, Sean. I beg you, please. We don't have to live together to start with. We can court each other as boyfriend and girlfriend. We can see what the future brings. Besides which Thomas and Grace need a father," she said almost as an afterthought.

Tears began to roll down her cheeks. She leant forward and buried her face in her hands. Sean inhaled deeply. He didn't know how to handle the situation. The sound of her sobbing filled the room. It was even noisier than the air-conditioning unit and the fan that whirred overhead. Sean stood up. He walked to the bathroom and picked up a box of tissues. As he returned to the sitting room Njeri had begun to recover her composure. The tracks of her tears had left lines on her cheeks where her mascara had run. He passed her some tissues and put the box down on the low table in front of her.

"Wipe your eyes," he said gently as he touched her shoulder, doing his best to try and reassure her.

His comment and touch brought another onset of tears. The tissues were soon soaked through. Njeri pulled some more from the box.

"Sometimes, Sean, you are so cold and harsh," she said between sobs. "You sit there and say almost nothing. You seem so cold...so distant...so hard-hearted," she said as if her heart was breaking.

Sean grimaced and swallowed hard. "Njeri, I cannot promise you anything. I have recently put my life back on track. I'm not ready to get into a relationship..."

She interrupted him. "Except of course with Miss Greene!" she retorted angrily.

"You didn't let me finish," he snapped back. "I was going to say with you or anyone else."

"So I suppose your fling with Miss Greene was simply that – a fling. I don't suppose she'll be too impressed with that!! Explain that to her when you next see her!" Her eyes flashed at Sean defiantly as she challenged him.

Sean looked sheepish. He paused for a moment. "Njeri, let me get this project out of the way first. When we get back to Mombasa we can talk about it over dinner one night."

Njeri eyed Sean carefully. She felt he was merely trying to placate her and simply playing for time.

"Njeri, I have to go to bed," he said as he looked at his watch again.

This brought on another flood of tears. "Sean...I need you...I need you to hold me...tonight!" she sobbed, fighting back the tears. "I don't want to sleep on my own," she wailed.

Sean wondered how he was going to get out of that one. Against his better judgement he relented. "Okay, Njeri," he replied, knowing she was not going to take no for an answer. He couldn't be sure whether they were genuine or whether she was shedding crocodile tears. "You can sleep here tonight but no funny business or you're straight through the door." He got up from his chair. "I'll get you a kanga, you can sleep in that."

Sean didn't notice Njeri smiling broadly as he turned away to get the kanga. She had implemented the first stage of her plan to win him back.

Soon after they had climbed into bed he turned out the light. He felt the warmth of her body as she snuggled up next to him. He was briefly tempted to make love to her but quickly dismissed the thought, even though the closeness and warmth of her body had aroused him. He shut his eyes and was soon overcome with tiredness.

§

The long rays of daylight that streamed through the gap where the curtains joined together awoke Sean. It was 0630 hours. He looked across at Njeri in the bed. She looked at peace with the world as she lay in a deep sleep. The white sheet covering her moved slowly up and down as she breathed gently beneath it. He didn't disturb her and slipped quietly from the bed.

After a quick shower he made his way down to the pool behind the Bilicanas. A hazy mist surrounded the complex. It had rained heavily during the night. Some low grey clouds were scattered across the sky. He enjoyed the cool morning breeze on his face as he strolled along. Another couple of hours and the temperature and humidity would begin to rise. The quietness of the morning was momentarily broken as a flock of crows skimmed across the tops of the coconut palms, cawing loudly as they flew. Their wings stilled as they swooped down onto a group of acacia trees that were splashed with scarlet flowers.

T J and James were already at the poolside checking over the diving equipment. They looked up from their work and acknowledged Sean by raising their hands. They continued their work in silence for a few more minutes. Sean did not disturb them but observed closely as they inspected and tested the regulators on the scuba tanks. Each harness had a set of two tanks fitted to it. Each had been filled with compressed air. Short hissing sounds exploded from the tanks as T J released the regulator valves. He did his best not to waste too much valuable air. Sean sat down cross-legged on the ground and leaned back on his elbows for support as he watched.

A short while later, having completed their checks, T J crouched down on his haunches and began to remind Sean of the basics of diving and the safety procedures. After a short induction Sean stood up and strapped a set of tanks to his back. He bent down and rinsed his mask and snorkel in the pool before fitting it over his face. He then pulled the mouthpiece to his lips. As he went through the motions, memories of what he had learned on his earlier training dives flooded back. He switched on the regulator and began to breathe as slowly as he could to start with, to adjust to the flow of air from the tanks. He gave T J a thumbs-up sign to confirm he was ready for his first practice dive in the pool. T J signalled his response. Sean bent down and picked up a set of flippers in his left hand. He sat down at the edge of the pool and tipped himself backwards into the water causing a huge splash and water to ripple over the sides. As he resurfaced he removed his mouthpiece, switched off his air supply temporarily and began to fit his flippers to his feet. At first he struggled awkwardly but soon had his flippers securely positioned. James and T J went through the same procedure, except they fitted their fins before entering the water.

Three hours later and after various practice dives and manoeuvres T J called a halt to the training. The three of them carefully packed up their equipment in readiness for the afternoon session. T J had arranged for their tanks to be refilled at the dive centre. Remmy, one of the staff, was on hand to transport the equipment back to the Msasani Slipway.

After a relaxing shower, a light brunch and a short rest the three headed in the Mitsubishi Pajero that T J had hired, to the Msasani Slipway on the edge of Msasani Bay on the north side of Dar. They arrived at 1400 hours.

"Now I have some good news, Sean. I don't plan to do any particularly deep diving."

It was not unusual for Special Forces to dive to depths of thirty metres and usually up to ten metres, but T J wasn't going to enlighten Sean. A smile appeared on Sean's face. Although he felt much more relaxed after being trained by T J he was still afraid of diving too deep. He knew scuba diving could be dangerous.

“How deep?” responded Sean, impatient to find out what T J planned next.

“Have a look at that!” T J pointed to a small craft moored up adjacent to the slipway.

“That is a Subskimmer. It is a unique Special Forces craft that combines the benefits of a mini-submarine with those of a rigid-hull inflatable,” he said proudly.

He went on to explain that the Subskimmer could travel up to 120 nautical miles at speeds of up to thirty-five knots. It could submerge at any time to operate as a mini-submarine or semi-submerge at speeds of up to four knots. In semi-submerge mode it could still be driven by the outboard motors with only the heads of the divers and snorkels visible. The craft remains virtually silent and is hardly visible to the naked eye. At night it is almost undetectable. In a fully submerged state it utilises the electric thrusters at speeds of up to three knots and depths of up to 100 metres. It can be left anchored to the seabed for extended periods. In the event of Special Forces personnel not coming back from their mission the control centre on the mother ship can activate the transponder fitted to the craft and recover it. All the Special Forces personnel carry a boat locator on their wrist so that when they return to the submerged craft they can find it with pinpoint accuracy.

“Let’s hope we don’t have to use it in fully submerged mode then,” laughed Sean nervously.

Remmy, who had earlier collected their equipment from the swimming pool, was on hand to assist them in preparing to board the Subskimmer. He smiled when he recognised the three of them, revealing a perfect set of white teeth. He was short and stocky with the build of a nightclub bouncer.

A small crowd had gathered around the Subskimmer. A babble of voices filled the air. It was a unique craft and almost new. It had not been seen in those parts before so it created a great deal of interest. Several people were talking animatedly about its merits, though most of them probably didn't understand or know about its full capabilities. T J was not about to enlighten them. Sean was concerned that the Subskimmer seemed to be drawing too much unnecessary attention to the three of them. However, neither James nor T J seemed to be perturbed. They simply went about the business of preparing themselves for their trip. This time they had organised wetsuits that were cut off at mid-thigh. They pulled them on and then fitted the harnesses with the twin tanks to their backs. Sean followed their lead. They then clipped a pair of flippers each to their belts so they could use them later if needed. Finally, Remmy handed them a knife each fitted into a scabbard. James and T J strapped them to their right calves.

"What's this for?" said Sean. A look of surprise appeared on his face.

"You never know when it might come in handy," replied James.

"There are a lot of sharks in the deep, bwana," interrupted Remmy, a slight smile appearing on his face as he watched Sean swallow hard.

Sean quickly strapped on the knife.

T J carried out a safety check on James and Sean to make sure all their equipment had been fitted correctly. He tested the regulators and made sure the tanks were full. James in turn checked over T J's harness. The two of them were consummate professionals. Meanwhile Remmy checked Sean's equipment.

T J was the first to climb aboard. The small crowd had stepped back to make a pathway to the craft for them. T J moved up the craft and crouched down to the left-hand side of the central control panel and then climbed across and straddled the seat behind the panel. James followed and placed himself to the right of the central buoyancy and trim tank, slightly behind T J. The Mark 2 version of the

Subskimmer allowed the driver to sit on the right-hand side and also had seats for all the divers when above the surface. These also folded down when submerged so that the divers could sit on them underwater. Meanwhile Remmy assisted in steadying the craft to the rear. Beads of sweat glistened on his dark skin and trickled from his forehead as he did so. The small gold earring in his left ear flashed brightly as the sunlight reflected off it.

The craft rocked as Sean climbed aboard and he positioned himself to the left of the buoyancy and trim tank adjacent to James. T J turned and gave the thumbs-up to Remmy. He began to slip the Subskimmer from the mooring. He unhooked the line and threw it to James who coiled it neatly, knotting the end and dropping it into the aft section in front of the waterproofed outboards. Remmy gave the craft a mighty push and T J fired the engines into life. The small crowd stepped back in surprise as the dull roar from the 150-horsepower Yamaha twin-prop engine silenced their conversations.

T J eased the craft slowly into Msasani Bay and turned northwards towards Bongoyo Island, which is located about seven kilometres north of Dar. They were beyond the Msasani peninsula when they saw the ferryboat returning from Bongoyo. T J raised his arm in acknowledgement as the crew waved at them.

18

MARAIS, WILLIAMS AND Joubert were deep in conversation in Marais's office. Two hours earlier Marais had been informed that all the croupiers and David Smith had changed their pleas to guilty. He was mightily relieved. It would at least take any attention away from him. The insurance company would be forced to accept that he was not involved and they would have to pay out. All the rumours regarding his involvement and the suggestion that he had set up the Bahamas cups scam would at last be laid to rest. The Tanzanian government would be off his back, at least for the time being, and he could get on with all his other business interests without any undue fear of being caught.

The sentencing of the nine was due to take place the next day. As there was no case to answer as far as he was concerned he had no intention of attending court and facing the media circus of the Western press who would be in attendance. Instead he had arranged for David Williams to go.

Once he knew the details of the sentences he planned to have a staff meeting. There he would inform all the staff of the results and make it abundantly clear to them what would happen to any of them who stole from his casino in the future.

Several minutes after the start of the meeting there was a loud knock on the door. Marais looked up and yelled out "Come in!" The door was opened by Jappie Mulder and in strode Pieter Coetzee, the general manager of the Bilicanas Hotel. Marais had been expecting him. Mulder closed the door quietly behind him. Once again Coetzee was immaculately dressed. He appeared to be trying to walk even taller than he normally did. His chest barrelled out in front of him. He hesitated and half-bowed as he neared Marais's desk. Marais pointed to him to sit down. Coetzee raised his right hand in acknowledgement of Williams and Joubert. Tufts of black curly hair on the back of his hand contrasted sharply with the cuff of the immaculately pressed white shirt he wore.

"Gentlemen," he said gruffly as he sat down. His face remained deadpan. "What information have you got for me, Pieter?"

Coetzee sat bolt upright in his chair. He was doing his best to look important.

"I have been keeping a watchful eye on Mr Cameron and his Kaffir friend Mr Annan. Although they are both staying at different hotels on the complex they appear to be very friendly."

"What do you know about Delport, the American?"

"I'm not sure, sir, but the three of them have met for drinks on more than one occasion. What's more, yesterday morning Delport seemed to be giving the other two lessons in scuba diving in the swimming pool behind the Bilicanas."

"And what's wrong with that?" queried Marais.

"As guests on the complex don't you think if they needed scuba lessons they would have organised it with Dieter Hartmann who operates the diving school here?"

"A good point, but if they're already trained they wouldn't need lessons," Marais said sarcastically. He turned to Joubert. "And what have you to report?"

Joubert went on to tell them that during the last few days Cameron, Annan and Delport had been playing the tables.

"Cameron has been asking many questions about the coup. Delport was overheard in the bar remarking loudly about it in front of other guests."

"More important, Annan has been to the New Bagamoyo Prison to visit the nine arrested," said Williams.

"Oh really!" exclaimed Marais. "Tell me more."

Williams went on to explain that Annan was apparently a legal expert and seemed to be acting for the British High Commission in conjunction with one of the croupiers, Martin Donaldson.

"Why is he acting for Donaldson only and not any of the others?"

"I'm not certain it's only Donaldson he is acting for, but he spent the longest amount of time interviewing him. Furthermore Donaldson is the only British croupier who has a different lawyer to the others."

Marais looked puzzled.

At this point Joubert continued with his report. He explained that after lunch he had followed the three to the Go and Sea Dive Centre. Once there they all climbed aboard a strange-looking craft. Joubert was referring to the Subskimmer. He explained that he had never seen anything like it before and that they had all been wearing wetsuits. Each of them was carrying a bag.

Marais interrupted. "What happened then?"

"They disappeared out to sea and returned some four hours later, shortly before nightfall."

"What!" Marais exploded. "You mean you didn't follow them!"

Joubert looked flustered. He didn't like it when his boss put him under pressure and was relieved when Williams intervened: "My orders were to follow them at a discreet distance. If André had followed them out to sea they might have recognised him from the casino and their suspicions would have immediately been aroused. I told him to wait for their return."

"Hmm," mumbled Marais, looking deep in thought.

There was an unhealthy silence for a few minutes as Williams, Joubert and Coetzee glanced at each other nervously. Marais's moods were unpredictable. He asked again, "Do any of you know anything about Delport?"

Coetzee and Joubert remained silent. They were both hoping that Williams would speak again as they glanced furtively at him in anticipation.

Williams realised that the other two were going to say nothing. So he began to explain what he knew. Delport had never stayed at the complex before but was an enthusiastic gambler who visited the casino most weekends.

"Where does he work?"

"When he checked in at the Bilicanas this time he put down his occupation as an IT manager at the American Embassy in Dar."

"Have you checked that?"

"Yes, indeed they confirmed that, but..."

Marais interrupted but realised Williams had something further to say. "Go on."

"I'm not entirely convinced about his occupation. Whenever I've seen him here I always get the feeling his behaviour is all a big act."

"What makes you think that?"

"Years of experience and a hunch I have about him."

Williams flicked a fly away from his ear as he finished speaking. Marais stood up.

"Gentlemen, I think the time has come to pay closer attention to our three guests." He almost snarled. "If they are poking their noses into business that doesn't concern them we will have to do something very serious about it." There was an icy resolve in his voice. He looked across at Williams.

"David, I want five minutes of your time alone."

19

IT WAS NOT long before they landed on the beach on the southwest side of Bongoyo Island. As they came into the shallow waters T J signalled James and Sean to jump out shortly before they hit the coral white sand. He eased the bow on to the shore and James grabbed the rope and pulled it round so that he could tie it to the stump of a palm tree close to the shore.

Once the craft was firmly fixed T J moved back behind the buoyancy and trim tank and opened the aft storage box, producing several water bottles and three small rucksacks. He threw a bottle and a rucksack each to Sean and James. He gulped some water down before replacing the cap securely. He pulled the strap around his neck and let the bottle dangle in front of him. He threw his rucksack over his right shoulder. The sun was by now very hot so T J pointed to a clump of trees set back from the beach.

"Let's go and sit over there in the shade and I can run through the escape plan."

The beach was almost deserted except for a few fishermen about 100 metres away who had laid out their morning catch to dry in the sun. After their initial interest in the arrival of the strange-looking craft and the three muzungu occupants they returned to the task of inspecting their nets carefully for tears in preparation for the next day's fishing.

The three of them reached the shade beneath the palm tree and removed their harnesses and leaned the oxygen tanks upright against each other in the sand. They unclipped their flippers from their belts and sat down on the sand. James was the first to speak.

"T J, tell me why you have the use of the Subskimmer?"

T J smiled. "I have contacts at the US Embassy in Dar. It has recently been tested by a Special Forces team of Navy Seals based at the US Navy compound up in Bahrain."

After good test reports it had been loaned out to the East and Southern African Drug Enforcement Agencies whom T J was working for. T J's boss was the Military Attaché at the US Embassy in Dar and had arranged to use it for three months. It was delivered by a giant USAF C5 plane to Dar and offloaded, where it was taken to the Msasani Slipway for storage.

"I'm no expert," interrupted Sean, "but how do you explain why the Subskimmer is at the Go and Sea Dive Centre? Surely it would be based at a military location?"

"As you can see there is no military identification on the boat. As far as any local interest is concerned it can only ever be used as a surface craft. Nobody here is aware of its true capabilities."

In addition to T J and his Drug Enforcement Department, the US Embassy were using it on a part-time basis in conjunction with a non-governmental organisation, Tanzanaid, to deliver medical supplies to Pemba, Zanzibar and the other small groups of islands in the archipelago. A couple of doctors from the US Marine Corps would sometimes accompany the deliveries and provide free medical aid to the people living on the islands. T J was often employed as the driver so that he could become accustomed to handling the craft.

T J described his plan for arranging Martin's escape. On Thursday night, under cover of darkness, the three of them would pick up the Subskimmer from its mooring at Msasani. From there, they would travel up the coast to where the Bora 20 was regularly housed at an old sisal warehouse at the water's edge near an inlet of the Mbezi Creek. This is where the operation would start to become dangerous. Marais's men, who guarded the Bora 20 at all times of the day and night, were heavily armed. However, T J had operated surveillance on the warehouse for the last three months. When the Bora wasn't used for drug-running or smuggling at night, the number of guards was reduced to four. There were three shift changes during the night. The first was at 2000 hours followed by a change every four hours.

The plan was to arrive shortly after the change of shift at 0400 hours and steal the Bora 20. Once they overpowered the four guards it would give them nearly four hours before the morning watch arrived. T J would take charge of the Bora with Sean. James would be left to handle the Subskimmer on his own. They would then travel in convoy fifty kilometres up the coast and moor the Bora in readiness for Martin's arrival.

Sean listened carefully but became more and more worried and confused as T J laid out his plan. He looked over at James quizzically, who looked equally perplexed. James wondered to himself why T J was so keen to get involved in an escape bid from prison. If he was caught his job could be in jeopardy.

"What are you looking so worried about?" T J could see the concerned look on both their faces.

"It's all very well telling us all this but how are you going to get Martin out to the Bora? He's hardly going to be walking out of the main gate!" Sean said with a hint of sarcasm.

"This is where we use the element of surprise. I am in the fortunate position of having several options at my disposal." A glint appeared in his eyes. Sean could see now that he also had that same look of excitement and expectation that James had when an operation was about to begin. The Special Forces obviously attracted similar types to carry out their work.

"Once convicted, we assume that the nine will remain in New Bagamoyo Prison. If they aren't transferred to another prison it is likely that within a day they will be issued with prison uniforms and assigned to one of the work parties that leave the prison every day to work on one of the prison farms."

"Surely they won't be assigned to a work party straightaway?" questioned Sean.

James looked pensive.

"It is possible that they won't all be put in a work party."

"And if they are not, where will they be?" asked Sean.

"They could be assigned to the kitchens or the laundry," responded T J.

"So okay, let us assume they are in a work party. What happens next?"

"We have a Black Hawk helicopter at our disposal!" T J exclaimed.

"Isn't that the type that was used in the Somali engagement in the early 'nineties?" asked Sean.

"Sure is!" responded T J. "It handles well. It is very versatile and can fly low at treetop level. It is very powerful and can airlift a lot of troops."

Sean raised his eyebrows. He took another swig of water. He was sweating heavily and losing a lot of fluid because of the humidity. The sea breeze was not strong enough to help cool him down.

The prisoners at New Bagamoyo Prison were normally woken at 0500 hours. After a breakfast of porridge and tea they cleaned out their cells. Then the prisoners allocated to the farm work parties had their ankles chained together. The chains were long enough to allow them to walk in a shuffling manner but it was impossible to run. Once the prisoners were chained they were transported by lorry to the prison farms in the surrounding fields. They normally arrived at the fields at 0700 hours. It was hard work in the scorching sun with very little chance of a break except at midday for half an hour for lunch.

T J continued: "We are going to fly in and land in the field and pull Martin out. The whole operation will be over in minutes."

"That doesn't add up to me," said Sean. He was beginning to feel even more sceptical about the operation. "First of all the helicopter is likely to be recognised. There can't be many Black Hawk helicopters in this area. It must be obvious it belongs to the US Army."

"The chopper will not carry any markings."

"Even so, who else would have a Black Hawk?" reiterated Sean. "Aren't you forgetting something else?"

"What might that be?" asked James, becoming impatient with his friend's scepticism.

"The guards must surely be armed."

James nodded his head.

"They are not going to stand idly by as Martin jumps into a helicopter," said Sean shaking his head.

"Not in normal circumstances, but don't forget it will be armed with a machine gun far more powerful than the AK 47s the guards will be carrying."

"So my next question is, who is going to be flying the Black Hawk and what will my role be?"

T J went on to explain that he was originally trained at Fort Rucker in Alabama as a helicopter pilot specialising in Black Hawks. Thereafter he had served in the US Navy Seals before his retirement. James would join him on the Black Hawk and operate the machine gun. Sean's role was to stay with the Subskimmer on Bongoyo Island. After picking Martin up, T J would fly the helicopter to where the Bora was moored up. He would then hand the Black Hawk over to a US Navy pilot who would be waiting for them there. The pilot would return to the embassy in Dar where the Black Hawk was normally parked up. From there they would take Martin across to Zanzibar in the Bora where he would hide up for a few days at a remote villa on the east coast near

Pwani Mchangani. They would then return to meet Sean at Bongoyo and hide the Bora as best they could before they returned to Msasani in the Subskimmer, supposedly having been out on a diving trip.

James was not revealing his fears to Sean that the plan was fraught with danger. First of all Martin may not be assigned to a work party. In which case the whole operation would be a complete failure before it started and they would have to re-think the escape plan. Secondly any one of them could be shot at the point of rescue. The first part of the operation, when they had to overpower Marais's guards and hijack the Bora, was also critical. He was at a loss to understand why they needed to steal the Bora 20 in the first place. Any mistakes and failure to overpower the guards would mean they could be arrested or even killed in the process. He was more than satisfied with the use of the Subskimmer and felt it was all they needed to transport Martin to Pwani Mchangani on the east coast of Zanzibar.

James eyed T J carefully.

"I don't agree with your plan to hijack the Bora 20. We don't need it. We've already got the Subskimmer. What the hell do we need the Bora for? It will alert Marais to start searching for it. We will already have enough problems escaping from the Tanzanian Police and Army who sure as hell will want to recapture Martin."

Sean could see that James was positively bristling with anger. It was unusual for James to display such emotion openly.

"Hey, chill out, man!" exclaimed T J, opening his arms out with the palms of his hands turned up in a gesture of submission. "Do you want me to help you with Martin's escape or not? Without me you've got no chance of getting him out."

T J had a point and James knew it. There was no other way of helping Martin to escape. Not at such short notice anyway.

T J obviously had his own reasons for stealing the Bora 20 and James knew full well he was not about to divulge them.

James resigned himself to go along with T J's plan but he was far from happy about it. He kicked the sand in front of him in disgust.

"Come on then, you'd better start training us on this craft. If I'm to be left in charge of it I'm going to need to know how to operate it."

T J swallowed hard. He needed James on his side, not against him.

"Come on, guys, let's go then," he said trying to sound as relaxed as possible. He picked up his equipment and headed back to the Subskimmer. For the next three hours T J tested the Subskimmer to the maximum. He taught James and Sean all they needed to know about operating the craft on their own.

20

MARTIN AND CHRIS Powell were deep in conversation in the prison compound. In less than twenty-four hours their fates would be sealed. It was three o'clock in the afternoon. The Sergeant Officer had already informed them that they would be woken the next morning as normal at 0500 hours and then taken direct to the courthouse at the Central Police Station on Sokoine Avenue for sentencing. Their court appearance was timed for 1000 hours.

"I don't understand why we are being taken so early to court. It's only a one-hour drive, maybe an hour and a half at the most," questioned Martin.

"If my experience in South Africa is anything to go by it's a way of humiliating us. There we were chained in pairs around the ankles and then handcuffed together. We were kept like that on the journey to and from the court all the time we were awaiting sentencing," replied Chris. He winced at the thought.

"Tell me about your time in Mafeking. At least it might give me an idea about what to expect here. It looks like we're going to be here for some time," Martin remarked with sad resignation in his voice.

"Not if I can help it!" exclaimed Chris with a mischievous glint in his eye.

"What do you mean by that?"

"I'll go into that later but first of all let me tell you about Mafeking. It's not something I ever thought I would have to remind myself of or even have to recite my experiences to anyone again, but I guess it will never leave me." He swallowed hard and inhaled deeply before touching the corner of his left eye as if he was wiping away a tear.

The compound was full of prisoners stretching their legs after the cramped confines of their cells. The other croupiers were huddled in two separate groups on the far side of the compound. Martin Bradley, Daly, Peter Porter and Steve Vickers were lounging against the far wall talking animatedly. Archer, Mallet and Jeremy Lascelles were crouched down on their haunches, deep in conversation.

Chris began a résumé of his time in Mafeking. It had been a great shock to him when he was arrested. He had vehemently protested his innocence and found it doubly difficult to deal with his unjust incarceration once he'd been sentenced. One of the saving graces in Mafeking was that at least he served it with colleagues from the Palace. He was sure one or more of them had implicated him and had added his name to the list in Alan Hudson's address book. Peter Archer, who also worked at the Palace at the time, visited Chris on several occasions and it was he who suggested that Tony Stanley was actually the man responsible for putting his name in the book. He certainly had the opportunity when he purchased it from the Yugoslav gangsters who had stolen it from Alan Hudson's room in the hotel in Johannesburg.

Once Archer had suggested Stanley was the main culprit it made Chris's life much easier to bear in Mafeking with the other croupiers. He carried a mental picture of Stanley's face and waited for the day he would meet up with him again to exact his revenge. It wasn't long before he got himself allocated a job in the prison kitchens. There he managed to steal small quantities of the prison officers' food, the quality of which was much better than that of the prisoners.

After spending eleven months working in the kitchens he managed to get himself transferred to the prison gardens and vegetable plots during the summer months, with a white South African, Jon Vorster, who himself was serving three years for fraud. Duties there were fairly light and most days were spent watering the plots with a hose. The most arduous task was weeding with a hoe. The one big advantage of working outside in the summer was at least they had fresh air and the sun on their back most days. Even better, he was housed in the low-risk, low-security compound. Conditions there were much better than in the high-security part of the prison, which was home to the real hard core criminals, murderers and rapists.

Two of the other croupiers convicted with Chris had the misfortune of spending eight months in the high-security section. To avoid the risk of being raped in prison they both managed to persuade the prison authorities to let them serve their time there in solitary confinement. Conditions though in the solitary cells were diabolical by comparison even with the high-security section. The cells were about six feet by six feet, with no windows and a grimy stone cold floor to sleep on. Sanitary conditions consisted of two buckets that were only emptied once a day. They were given two blankets for bedding. Exercise amounted to only fifteen minutes a day in the exercise yard. The remainder of their time was spent locked up in almost semi-darkness. When they were eventually released back to the low-risk compound the two of them had completely changed, both physically and mentally. They were almost unrecognisable as the two men that went in.

Chris had been lucky to befriend Jon Vorster. He had already served a year of his sentence and knew the prison system very well. He was a typical out-and-out conman but a very likeable rogue in the long-held traditions of suave smooth-talking conmen with silver tongues. Vorster was involved in almost every conceivable money-making operation possible. He managed to buy and sell cigarettes and food with ease. He even arranged to provide bhang to those who were inclined to smoke it. He always had plenty of food from his connections in the kitchens. Chris and Vorster had befriended several of the prison guards who turned a blind eye to their activities in exchange for regular supplies of cigarettes and a few rand.

Vorster was a great practical joker and on more than one occasion he created havoc and great hilarity with one or more of his pranks. The most memorable was when he sabotaged the prison lawnmower used to cut the grass in the Prison Governor's garden and the bowling green, the Sergeant Officer's pride and joy. Sergeant Officer Wiese was an Afrikaner obsessed with bowls. He organised inter-prison challenge matches between prison officers. On one occasion the Mafeking officers reached the final. On the eve of that event Wiese instructed one of the prisoners to cut the grass on the green in preparation for the game the next day. The grass was normally kept immaculately short and it resembled the smooth surface of a billiard table. It was Wiese's pride and joy. Unbeknown to the Tswana prisoner given the task of preparing the grass for the final, Vorster had reset the roller cutting blades on the lawnmower so that the right-hand-side was set lower than the left-hand-side. The unsuspecting prisoner diligently went about his work without realising he had cut the green with channels and ridges of grass that reduced it to an unplayable mess. The right-hand channels had almost all the grass torn from their roots. Wiese went absolutely ballistic when he saw the damage. The final was cancelled and subsequently awarded to the opposition. Wiese was apoplectic with rage and suspected Vorster and Chris were the main culprits but had no specific proof. There were other light-hearted moments during Chris's time in Mafeking, but they certainly didn't outweigh the grind of prison life.

Sleeping with forty prisoners in a cell designed for only twenty was also a particularly uncomfortable experience, not least with the threat of rape. Although the white prisoners managed to stick together for self-protection it was always a risk at any time. During what was still the apartheid era in South Africa the white man was feared by black prisoners, even in the confines of prison, where they were all equal. As far as Chris was aware none of the others had suffered the pain and humiliation of rape. Homosexuality though was rife and the worst thing at night was to hear the sounds of male sex in the same cell. The worst offender in Chris's cell was Derek Julius, the gambler who had been working the Bahamas cups in conjunction with Alan Hudson. Julius had a penchant for the young African prisoners in the cell and often bedded them in clear view of everyone else. Chris was appalled by this and kept his distance from Julius, the only one of his fellow-detainees whom he disliked intensely.

"So what are the things that you most remember from your time in Mafeking?" asked Martin.

Chris paused. "I was almost permanently bored. I have never experienced boredom like it and most of all, time. I never wore a watch inside and to this day I still don't. I measured the time of day by watching the sun. It was a trick one of the Tswana prisoners taught me."

"Was there anything else?"

"Yes. The smell," Chris stated emphatically. He winced as he said it. "The smell that was always in my nostrils was that of unwashed human bodies. The body odour of forty sweating men in a cell was sometimes almost too much to endure. Mixed with the smell of raw sewage it's a smell that I've relived occasionally since my release. I've even experienced it on a cold clear day in London for no apparent reason."

At that moment voices were raised on the other side of the compound. The other croupiers were now all huddled together. Some of them were shouting at each other. From what Chris and Martin could hear they were arguing about the court case the next day. Daly, Bradley and Vickers were the most vociferous. Chris turned his attention back to Martin's last question.

"I know someone on the outside here in Dar Es Salaam who could possibly get me out of here sooner than you think," continued Chris.

Martin looked astonished. "Tell me more."

Martin was barely able to contain his excitement at the thought of escaping. He had planned to talk to James about a possible escape plan when he saw him next before the court case at the Central Police Station. He could see that Chris seemed a little wary of revealing any plan to him. They hadn't known each other long. Martin himself was also reluctant to reveal to Chris that he was actually at the Golden City working undercover for Chidoli.

"Forgive me if I don't tell you everything at the moment but I need a chance to talk to that person first. I'll be seeing him before the case tomorrow. I'll tell you the outcome when we're brought back here after sentencing, as we are likely to be."

"Fair enough, I believe that we can both help each other."

Martin smiled. Chris looked hard at him and offered his hand. They shook.

"Until tomorrow then," replied Chris. He too didn't want to reveal to Martin his other reason for being at the Golden City.

21

IT WAS PAST seven o'clock in the evening by the time Sean, James and T J returned to their hotels. Sean was dog-tired. He desperately wanted to talk to James alone but hadn't had a chance because T J never strayed from their sides. He could see something was troubling James as he appeared to be more agitated than he had ever seen him before. Sean went over and over in his mind T J's plan to hijack the Bora 20 and even with his inexperience of all things military the plan seemed fatally flawed on several counts. In particular, like James, Sean didn't understand why they needed the Bora when they already had the Subskimmer at their disposal. It was one thing to sabotage the Bora or put it out of action but to steal it seemed ridiculous to Sean. It was not an easy thing to hide. They would be very conspicuous if they travelled anywhere in it. Marais's company had owned it for nearly a year. It would be too much of a coincidence for there to be a second craft of the same make purchased by someone else in the area.

T J drove firstly towards the Serengeti Hotel where James was staying, and Sean saw his chance to stay and talk to James. As the latter climbed out of the rear of the big four-wheel-drive he slung his kitbag over his shoulder and headed for reception. Sean, who was in the front passenger seat, turned to T J and said, "Thanks for the lift. I need to collect something from James's room. I'll make my own way back to the hotel."

Before T J had a chance to reply Sean grabbed his kitbag from the back seat and was out of the car in a flash. He slammed the door behind him.

"Maybe I'll see you later for dinner," he shouted through the closed window of the passenger door. T J waved in acknowledgement. He had a look of surprise on his face. Sean had caught him completely unawares.

Sean trotted after James and caught up with him, as he was about to go through the big revolving glass doors at the entrance to the hotel. As they both appeared on the other side in reception James said, "What was that all about?"

Sean chuckled momentarily, remembering the look of surprise registered on T J's face.

"I need five minutes of your time."

James pointed to some low-level settees situated on the edge of reception in an area leading to one of the bars. It was a busy area with many people walking to and from the bar. It would not be easy for anyone to overhear their conversation there. Before Sean began to talk a waiter appeared and asked them politely if they would like a drink. James waved him away.

"No thanks, we won't be stopping long."

Sean went on to express his fears about the hijacking of the Bora 20. He needed to hear James's expert opinion of what they should do. James listened intently. He was very calculated in his methods and planning. Although he liked to hear a second opinion he would ultimately make his own decision.

"I tend to agree with you, Sean. Unfortunately we've got ourselves involved with T J a little too deeply and for the time being there's not much we can do about it."

"You mean he's our only chance at the moment of helping Martin to escape."

James nodded. He explained that once Martin was free they could re-assess the situation. The current project would grind quickly to a halt. Chidoli would not be pleased that so far James had been unable to get any concrete evidence against Marais. Marais himself was ecstatic that all the croupiers had changed their pleas to guilty and from the next day they would all be serving long sentences, including Chris Powell, who would be starting his second term of imprisonment as a result of stealing from one of Marais's casinos. Marais would certainly be making it well known to the rest of his staff who Chris Powell was. The insurance company would be forced to pay out Marais's claimed losses. The only saving grace was that James would be ready in good time for his next project in Iraq. Chidoli's was the first project so far that James had failed to complete successfully since he had formed the company. To say he was disappointed would be to put it mildly. Somehow he had to retrieve the situation and turn the tables on Marais. He would still get his fee from Chidoli for the work he had completed but his professional pride was at stake and his expertise had been questioned. T J's knowledge of Marais's gold- and drug-running exploits could yet save the day for James.

"T J's okay but he's a little too gung-ho for my liking," said James eventually.

"So you won't need my services after tomorrow."

He was partly relieved that he would be going back to Mombasa the day afterwards but he felt deflated by their failure to complete the project to Chidoli's satisfaction. The current project had been a change from the mundanity of the life he was currently leading in Mombasa. He too craved excitement. He reflected on his time in Germany with James and, although it had been dangerous and at times life-threatening, he had enjoyed the adrenaline rush that it had given him. He hadn't experienced that since his days as an international rugby player. As a sportsman at the top of his game, particularly in such a physically aggressive game as rugby, he liked to push himself to his absolute limits. He enjoyed living on the edge. Now however he had taken on responsibilities for Achieng that he hadn't previously as a father. Although he had financially always supported his eldest daughter, Louise, and had seen her as often as he could because of his divorce, he had never had that day-to-day responsibility with Louise that he now had with Achieng. He was especially sad because it had taken the death of Akinyi to give him that responsibility.

He enjoyed his work in Mombasa but it did not have the cut and thrust of the life that James led. Neither did he have James's military experience. His knowledge of security matters was almost non-existent. However, he felt strongly that he had other qualities that James could use in his business. He wondered briefly whether he should ask James about the possibility of joining him on a semi-permanent or full-time basis. After all Africa was a continent that had ongoing opportunities for James and his kind. He was torn between his loyalties and commitment to Achieng but it was a question that had been nagging at him in the days since James's arrival.

While Sean was lost in his own thoughts James replied. "I at least need you until the day after tomorrow when we spring Martin from prison. After that maybe you can hang around for a couple more days. We could help T J have one last shot at Marais before we go."

"Sure, I don't mind."

Sean had now come to terms with the fact that Akoth and Opiyo were looking after Achieng. He had arranged for them to contact his brother John in Edinburgh should anything untoward happen to him. James seemed relieved that Sean would be around to help.

"I'm off for an early night. Another evening with T J will be too much to bear," he laughed loudly. His comment relaxed him.

"My sentiments entirely," Sean agreed.

22

It was 0730 hours when the two prison vans carrying the prisoners from New Bagamoyo Prison arrived at the Central Police Station, flanked by an armed escort. Martin was chained and handcuffed to Chris Powell, as were the rest of the croupiers who were chained in pairs in the first van. The prisoners in the second van were a mixture of Tanzanians who had been held on remand at New Bagamoyo. They were up for preliminary court hearings. Most of them had been held for relatively minor offences. Some expected to be released after paying small fines, others would be bailed if they or their families managed to scrape enough money together. Otherwise it would be back to New Bagamoyo.

It was uncomfortable being chained up and particularly difficult to alight from the van, which made it a slow process for everyone to climb down. Even at 7.30 a.m. it was very humid in Dar. The journey on the bumpy roads from New Bagamoyo had been tortuous. There was no air conditioning in the van and the only two small windows that opened were set high up close to the roof. Two prison officers had been allocated to sit in the back of the van that the croupiers were in. Their presence served no real purpose other than to make everyone more squashed and uncomfortable than they otherwise would have been. Even the prison officers realised it was unnecessary for them to travel in the back of the van with the prisoners. All it did was to create resentment on both sides.

The inside of the van was almost completely dark and as they alighted the prisoners did their best to shield their eyes from the contrasting glare of the sun. After being held for about fifteen minutes next to the vans they were then marched in line to the cells beneath the police station to await their fate. By this time they were all very dehydrated. Peter Archer requested that one of the prison guards fetch them some water. His request was refused. On entry to the station their handcuffs and leg chains were removed. They were then herded into a windowless cell to join approximately twelve other prisoners. The look of surprise and amazement on the faces of the Tanzanian prisoners at the arrival of so many white ones was a sight to behold. The guards departed and locked the cell door behind them.

Peter Archer again requested water. As he was leaving one of the guards pointed to a rusting tap on the wall. The new arrivals all gazed in the direction of the tap and then glanced furtively at each other. There was a sudden rush. Daly was the first to get there and he hastily turned the tap on. He let a steady flow of water pour into his cupped hands. At first he splashed it onto his face and neck, wasting a lot in the process. He repeated this process several times before he stuck his mouth under the tap and gulped heartily to try and quench his thirst.

"Hurry up," shouted Lascelles from the back of the queue. A few of the others murmured their agreement. Daly took a final gulp and one by one they took it in turns to drink. As Martin took his turn he initially recoiled at the salty taste and the grittiness of the water. He drank his fill and wiped his lips with the back of his hand. When they had all had a chance to drink Archer was the first to break the silence.

"Do you think we'll get a chance to see our lawyers before we appear in court?"

"I sure hope so," drawled Daly.

"Jacob Mwingara and Mr Annan said we'll be able to see them for a few minutes," added Martin.

"Let's hope so. I want to see that High Commission fellow. What's his name?" piped up Lascelles.

"Greening," someone said.

"Jonathan Greening," Mallett agreed.

"Yes, I want to speak to him as soon as possible," said Lascelles in his crisp clear public-school accent. "I'm going to tell him in no uncertain terms that he's to start getting someone heavy in the British government to intervene and get us released immediately."

Some of the croupiers laughed. Lascelles was clearly annoyed at the others laughing at him.

"Mark my words. A splodge of wonga, of the kind that will get us out of here in no time, is what I suggest."

There was more laughter.

"Where do you propose we get a splodge of wonga from, of the kind that gets us out of here?" replied Archer in annoyance as he mimicked Lascelles.

"It all seems a little late for that," Daly interrupted. "We're stuck in this fucking hellhole for a good time longer," he commented acidly.

"I'm going to get Greening to contact my local MP. My father is a close friend of his and I'm sure a word in the right place will get us out of here," Lascelles said pompously.

"Do as you like," Powell said, "but my advice to you all is to keep your heads down, stay out of trouble and with any luck we could be out on appeal in six to nine months' time." He glanced at Archer.

"What do you know!" shouted Daly.

"Shut up, all of you," Archer ordered them. "There's no point arguing amongst ourselves. That will get us nowhere."

A deathly hush fell on the place. Tempers were frayed. Everyone was anxious to know their fate. Although they all secretly harboured the thought that they would be released with suspended sentences, deep down they all knew they would end up back in New Bagamoyo Prison. The Tanzanian government was clear on their stance on corruption and they were determined that the Golden City

Nine, as the press had dubbed them, would be serving long sentences. There would definitely be no leniency afforded to the white European prisoners.

§

At nine o'clock a senior police officer appeared at the door to their cell and announced that the prisoners would be allowed fifteen minutes to see their lawyers and representatives from the British High Commission and the American Embassy, prior to appearing before the Judge. The nine filed out of the cell slowly. The Tanzanian prisoners watched them with mild amusement. Martin was in the middle of the line of prisoners and Chris directly behind him. They were led up a flight of stairs. At the top they reached a long windowless corridor that was lit by bare bulbs hanging from the ceiling. The walls were painted in two colours, the bottom half dark green and the top a dirty cream colour. It was typical of the decoration in a government building. Cracked grey linoleum tiles covered the floor. One by one the prisoners were led into separate rooms. Inside each one was a police guard. A couple of the croupiers shared the same lawyers so they went into the room together.

Martin entered his room. Mwingara and James were already seated at a small square table. They both got up and shook hands and sat down again. Martin pulled up a chair.

"Am I glad to see you, James," he whispered.

Mwingara turned to the policeman who was standing to attention in the room and said, "You can leave us now."

The policeman stamped his feet and saluted. He marched out of the room, closing the door behind him. He remained directly outside and peered straight through the porthole in the centre of the door.

After a brief discussion lasting less than five minutes Mwingara got up and left the room. He had previously arranged with James that he could spend some time with

Martin on his own. Mwingara had already outlined to Martin what would happen once the sentences were passed. The previous day he had attended a meeting with all the other lawyers and the Judge who had suggested to them that the sentences would be an average of five years per man. When he heard the news Martin shut his eyes and swallowed hard. The grim prospect of any amount of time beyond the last three weeks spent in custody was too much to bear. Although he had spent weeks on end on surveillance in places like Northern Ireland or in the jungles of South America during his time in the Regiment he always knew then that it was never long before he'd be returning home. His current situation though was completely different. This time he'd lost his freedom.

"James, for Christ sakes you have got to get me out of here."

"Don't worry, I'm working on that."

Martin looked puzzled by James's cheerfulness.

"Go on, tell me more!"

James looked towards the door. The policeman's face was still positioned at the porthole, his big brown eyes staring at them through the glass. James could not be sure that the room wasn't bugged. He carefully put one of his fingers to his lips pretending he was wiping them. He lowered his voice almost to a whisper and began tapping the fingers of both hands on the table. Martin followed suit. They were creating a background noise that would help drown their hushed tones in case the room was bugged. The most obvious place for a concealed microphone was under the tabletop. Before Martin arrived James had already run his hands beneath the table to check for any offending equipment. He had found nothing. Even so he wasn't taking any chances. He explained to Martin that Mwingara had told him that on the morning after their return to prison they would most likely be assigned to work parties on the prison farms.

"By all accounts you'll be in one of the farm work parties."

"I could be in the prison kitchens though. What will happen then?" replied Martin anxiously.

"If that happens we'll have to put plan B into action," responded James.

"And what is plan B?" Martin raised his eyebrows.

"I don't know yet!" exclaimed James.

Martin looked serious again.

"If I'm in a work party on one of the prison farms what do you plan to do, James?"

"In a moment. All I will say is if you're in a work party be prepared for any eventuality the day after tomorrow."

James explained how Sean had met T J and his involvement in a prospective escape attempt.

"We have a Black Hawk helicopter at our disposal. T J is an expert pilot and trained at Fort Rucker in Alabama."

Martin had heard of Fort Rucker and the reputation of the pilots who trained there. He nodded his head in admiration.

"Go on."

"On your first morning on the work party T J and I are going to fly in and pick you up from the field. From there we are going to fly to the coast and meet Sean who will be waiting with a couple of boats. T J will hand the helicopter over to a US Navy pilot who will return to Dar. T J will then take you across to the east coast of Zanzibar where you will hide for a few days in a safe house. Thereafter we'll pick you up and get you back to Kenya."

Martin relaxed. It all sounded so easy.

"It all hinges on whether I'm in a work party or not."

"You had better make sure you are!"

James had no idea what plan B would be if Martin wasn't in the work party. He slipped a roll of money, which was tightly wrapped in polythene, under the table to Martin.

"That should get you in to a work party I'm sure," said James.

Martin slipped the roll of money into his pocket. Somehow he had to hide it away before the inevitable search back at New Bagamoyo. James looked at his watch. They had a couple of minutes left before the interview was over.

"Before you go I need to tell you about David Smith, the gambler," whispered Martin.

He looked across at the door. The policeman was actually looking away for the first time. He appeared to have lost interest temporarily. There was some shouting and raised voices in the corridor outside that had distracted his attention.

Martin explained how he had got to know David very well and how his name was actually Chris Powell. James listened carefully. He first wanted to know whether Martin had got any further information about Chris. When Martin finished speaking James told him that he too knew about Chris and his time in Mafeking.

"How the hell do you know about that?" said Martin, raising his voice.

"Chidoli told me and what's more Marais apparently knew all about him as well. It's a good thing Chris has pleaded guilty because Marais was all set to reveal his true identity to the Judge to make sure that he was imprisoned for a very long time."

At this point the policeman knocked on the door and opened it. Their time was up. James stood up and Martin grabbed his right wrist and whispered, "Chris will be coming with us when you arrive with the helicopter."

"No chance!" James hissed back.

Martin remembered his last conversation with Chris at the prison.

"James, you have to listen to me. Before we came here Chris told me he was working for someone who might be able to help us."

Before they could continue their conversation the policeman was in the room.

“This way, sir,” he beckoned to James as he held the door open for him.

Martin waited for the policeman to tell him what to do next. As he went through the door James turned slightly and mouthed a big no silently to Martin. Martin stiffened but he had already decided Chris would be coming with him.

Ten minutes later Martin and the others were taken from the interview rooms and marched in single file into the courtroom.

23

TJ HAD changed his earlier plans to visit Marais's warehouse at 0400 hours. The three of them were sitting in the Subskimmer waiting patiently for the moment Sean and James would break into the warehouse after the shift change, to steal the Bora 20.

The floodlight mounted on the roof of the warehouse blazed a metre-wide corridor of light that stretched across the water for over 200 metres in the direction of the Subskimmer. The water trapped within the spread of light rippled gently and seemed to make the light look like it was moving from left to right, creating a series of moving stepping stones. The rest of the water was in total darkness.

Beneath the floodlight a series of coloured lights were set in descending order down a flight of steps to the lower level. Some seemed to burn brighter than others. In the centre of the sea wall beneath the lower level there were two large wooden doors partly covering an archway. Sean assumed this was the entrance from the sea that led into the lower depths of the warehouse. He strained his eyes as he peered across the water in the hope of seeing some sign of activity near the warehouse. Some of the other warehouses to the left and right were bathed in light whilst others were almost in complete darkness.

Further back and to the left-hand side yellow headlights mixed with the red of brake lights on the road as vehicles passed by. It was nearly midnight and, even though they were only about 600 metres away, he couldn't hear the sound of the engines as the vehicles passed by to the left and looped out of sight behind the warehouse along the main road. Straight ahead of him there appeared to be a junction going north. It was lit by three sets of overhead streetlights soaring five metres into the air. Other than the faint sound of a generator tirelessly whirring away in the distance, not another sound disturbed the night air.

Sean's mouth was dry with expectation. T J mumbled occasionally to James as they crouched down behind the central control panel. He was careful not to let the sound of his voice carry across the water. He was giving James last-minute instructions as they planned their assault on the warehouse. The Subskimmer bobbed slowly up and down in the water. T J had deliberately set anchor twenty metres behind and fractionally to the left of a thirty-foot dhow anchored in the bay. It helped to act as a barrier between them and obscuring them from the warehouse. They were all wearing full wetsuits with hoods pulled over their heads and black diving shoes on their feet. Their faces were smeared with black camouflage cream that seemed to be attracting an increasing number of mosquitoes to Sean's face. As they waited patiently Sean was getting more and more nervous. He was bursting for a piss and was doing all he could to take his mind off it. T J had earlier issued them with Heckler and Koch MP5 machine pistols that he had obtained from the armoury at the American Embassy in Dar. James and T J were of course experts in their use whilst Sean did his best to remember what to do from his time at Hereford with James. James had earlier given him a quick reminder how to flick the safety catch on and off and also how to reload. He still wasn't confident about using it.

Shortly before midnight T J and James turned to Sean and whispered a set of instructions.

"You stay here with the Subskimmer. T J and I will be back as soon as we can. The guards will be changing any time now."

Sean nodded. The time was now 23.59.

Ten minutes later T J and James slipped over the side and into the water. Sean watched them closely. His heart was pumping. Within a few metres they had disappeared underwater to make their way across the bay to the warehouse.

Before he left, James gave Sean his set of night-vision goggles. Sean peered across the water and could make out a couple of figures walking along the sea wall to the front of the warehouse. He assumed they were two of the guards for the new shift. They must have been doing preliminary checks, thought Sean, before settling down inside for the next few hours until the next shift change at four o'clock. They carried what looked like rifles slung over their shoulders and had flashlights, which they occasionally used to inspect for any sign of life in the water below the sea wall.

After completing their checks they disappeared back inside the building. Moments later Sean made out the figures of James and T J as they climbed out of the water to the right-hand side of the sea wall adjacent to the slipway directly below the warehouse.

Once they reached the top of the slipway they quickly removed their scuba tanks from their backs and hid them among some steel containers that were stacked up in the corner of the small yard to the right of the main building. They then proceeded to remove their MP5 machine pistols from their waterproof black bin liners. They also removed the condoms they had pulled over the muzzles for extra protection. Within a matter of seconds the two of them had disappeared out of sight.

Sean froze momentarily as he suddenly sensed movement in the water about fifteen metres to his left. He crouched down lower in the Subskimmer and peered over the top of the central control panel. He hardly dared to move but he was curious to know what had disturbed him like that. He soon realised the cause for his concern was a small two-man fishing boat. The two fishermen onboard were using paddles and were heading slowly to the shore. They didn't seem to have noticed the Subskimmer in the dark. Sean's heart missed a beat and he breathed a sigh of relief as they continued on their way, seemingly oblivious of his presence, as they disappeared into the night.

Meanwhile T J and James had climbed the set of steps to the right. At the top and straight ahead of them was a door marked "Staff". They ran towards it and both fell flat against the wall either side of the door. T J pulled a knife from the scabbard on his calf. He crept forward. With his left hand he gingerly grabbed the door handle and levered it slowly downwards. Surprisingly the door was not locked and they were both immediately inside.

Once inside there was a short corridor that led to a flight of seven stone steps. A single electric light bulb lit the corridor. There was a distinctly damp smell that filled the air. James sniffed. T J signalled to him to climb the stairs first. T J then replaced the knife in the scabbard. Both of them had their MP5s at the ready. It was at that moment that T J produced two silencers from a plastic bag that was strapped to his waist. He handed one to James and promptly fitted his to the end of his MP5. James followed suit. They slid the safety catches. James looked distinctly uneasy about the use of silencers. In his experience silencers would only be used if he or any of his Special Forces colleagues intended to use them to kill someone.

At the top of the stairs James peered through a large crack in the wooden door panel. It was big enough to give him a reasonably clear view of what was on the other side. The sound of what seemed to be a sports commentary came from a television that was at the far left-hand side of the room. The TV was angled so that James couldn't see the screen but he detected the differing images of flickering light. The four guards were stretched out in armchairs opposite the TV. They were smoking and drinking tea or coffee from large mugs. They had abandoned their rifles, which were leaning against one of the walls in a pile. Again James was overcome by a feeling of uneasiness. It was highly unusual for armed guards to put aside their weapons in such a way. He was surprised that Marais was not employing more professionally trained guards. He expected that some at least of Marais's employees would be former South African Special Forces personnel. If they were, there would be no chance of them treating their weapons in such a cavalier manner. Either that or they would at least be carrying other weapons. If not a knife each, they would certainly be armed with a pistol of some sort.

Other than the armchairs and a low-level coffee table the room was sparsely finished. The guards seemed to have settled themselves in for the night. James pushed his right eye against the crack in the door. There looked to be full-height walls to his left and straight ahead and to the right there was a low-level wall. James assumed it overlooked the warehouse below. It was there that he expected to find the Bora 20.

T J signalled James to descend the steps and to report what he had seen. They huddled together in the middle of the corridor facing the door. They had their guns at the ready. James mentioned his unease about the weapons.

"We will simply walk in and tie them up," whispered T J.

James couldn't believe what he was hearing. Either T J was supremely confident in his own ability or he was bluffing. Furthermore he must have been very confident in James as his partner. He knew James had been with Special Forces but he had no idea about his abilities in close-quarter combat. He was taking too many things for granted.

"Hold on a moment, there are four of them in there," James hissed.

"No problem," replied T J. "We've got these, remember," he said as he waved the MP5 in the air flippantly. He pulled his diving suit hood up over his head and stroked his moustache with his left hand.

Before James had a chance to respond T J was up the steps in a flash. James reacted automatically and followed him. At the top T J grabbed the door handle with his left hand and marched in. James was at his shoulder.

The look of surprise on the faces of the four guards was a sight to behold. The two seated on the left-hand side of the room were black. They didn't seem to be armed. They stood up immediately and raised their hands above their heads as they saw T J and James brandishing their MP5s at them.

The two white men to the right however made no effort to raise their hands to surrender. In a split second the bigger of the two sprang up from his armchair and in one flowing motion dived across towards the low-level wall. As he did so he spun head over heels and somersaulted on his hands. He landed feet first on the top of the low wall before disappearing below.

Meanwhile the second of the two pulled a pistol that had been wedged between his thigh and the inside of the armchair he was sitting in. In one sweeping motion he aimed the gun at T J.

Before the man had a chance to fire T J reacted and pressed the trigger of his MP5. The pistol flew from the man's grasp and he arched forwards clutching his wrist. T J's first volley of shots was followed by another silent burst of fire that thudded into the man's body. The force of the bullets rocked the man back on his feet and he spun round. A look of absolute shock registered on his face as he tumbled to his left. Blood spurted violently from a gaping wound in his chest.

Seconds later T J callously turned and aimed a volley of shots at the two black men. The shots hit them almost simultaneously in their knees. They screamed out in pain and fell forwards onto the floor.

James was almost frozen to the spot. He hadn't expected for a minute that T J would shoot the two who had raised their hands in surrender. He shook his head in disbelief.

"What the hell did you do that for?" he shouted.

Something inside his head told him he couldn't stay rooted to the spot any longer. He leapt towards the two black men who were writhing in agony on the floor. He patted their bodies down with his free hand to check they didn't have any concealed weapons. After a fruitless search he examined the wounds in their knees. By now they were crying out in pain. There was virtually nothing he could do for them. He had no medical supplies on him. Blood was oozing from their wounds and great ripples of blood were flowing across the wooden floor. He glanced feverishly around the room desperately searching for something to try and stem the flow of blood. His eyes fell on a pile of towels at the sink in the corner. He quickly grabbed them. He had another quick look around and found a small bundle of blue nylon rope on the far side of the room. He rushed over and grabbed it and returned to the two men. He pushed his gun into his diving belt and one by one he pressed the towels onto the wounds to try and stem the flow of blood. There didn't seem to be any damage to their main arteries. He looked at their shattered knees.

"Keep pressure on here until medical help arrives. If the wounds keep bleeding heavily then apply this rope tightly around your legs above your knees. It will act as a tourniquet. Make sure you release it every twenty minutes or so. That way it won't cut off the blood supply for too long to your lower legs."

They both nodded, fear etched across their faces as they moaned in pain.

James thought that they would probably survive but it

would be unlikely they would ever walk again without the aid of sticks. After he had done the best he could for the two men he went towards the white man who by now was motionless on the floor. James felt his neck for a pulse. Blood trickled from his mouth. The man was dead.

T J was long gone in pursuit of the first white man who had vaulted the wall. James's concentration was broken by the sound of gunfire. He pulled his gun from his belt and headed for the low wall.

Peering over the top of it, he could see the Bora 20 bobbing on the water below in the centre of the warehouse. Moments later he heard the roar of the engine as it burst into life. He watched as he saw T J make a desperate lunge in a vain bid to leap onboard. The Bora shot forward in the water in the middle of the warehouse and aimed directly for the two wooden doors that filled half of the entrance to the bay. There must have been a remote control on them because they parted almost miraculously as the Bora squeezed through the gap between them. T J meanwhile had bounced off the side of the Bora and ended up in the water disappearing under the surface. He resurfaced and swam three strokes to the sidewall and hauled himself up back onto dry land.

"Bastard!" he shouted after the Bora.

Outside in the bay Sean was amazed to see the Bora 20 appear at breakneck speed and disappear off into the night.

24

SEVERAL DAILY NEWSPAPERS were spread across Chidoli's desk. The Golden City Nine were front-page news. Staring out were photographs of Chris Powell, Peter Archer, Matt Bradley and Tom Mallett. They had been highlighted as the leaders of the casino scam. On the inside pages were photographs of the other five, John Daly, Peter Porter, Steve Vickers, Jeremy Lascelles and Martin Donaldson. The front-page headliners had each been sentenced to five years with additional fines of 200,000 Tanzanian shillings, or a further two years each in prison in lieu of the fines. The other five had received sentences of four years each with fines of 150,000 Tanzanian shillings or a further year in prison. Chidoli pointed at the newspapers.

"Gentlemen, it looks like we only have a partially successful result."

James and Sean remained in their chairs and nodded their agreement. So far James had remained silent and had let Chidoli do all the talking. Chidoli continued:

"We still have a situation where Marais is free to carry out his drug-running operation."

At that point James sat upright in his chair.

"Edward, we are still in the process of gathering evidence against Marais."

He went on to explain their contact with T J Delport and their visit the previous night to the warehouse.

"It was there we uncovered a huge cache of arms. There were rifles, machine guns, mortars and RPGs, hundreds of thousands of rounds of ammunition and no end of explosives!"

Chidoli's face registered a look of surprise mixed with shock. "What were you doing at the warehouse?"

James paused. "I was acting on a tip-off that Marais was storing drugs there."

Chidoli looked at James curiously. He wasn't quite sure why James was now also investigating Marais's drug-running connections. He decided not to pursue the subject for the time being.

"What do you think he's planning to do with all the weapons?"

"I can't be sure but there are enough there to start a small war. It certainly is far more weaponry than he needs to arm his guards at the casino."

"Does anyone else know you visited the warehouse last night?"

James cleared his throat. "Unfortunately, Edward, things didn't quite go according to plan."

James looked embarrassed but went on to explain the sequence of events at the warehouse the previous night. He omitted to tell Chidoli about their original plan to steal the Bora 20. Chidoli groaned.

"Marais will realise someone has been snooping around for something more than a simple robbery. None of the local gangsters would take a risk by trying to rob one of Marais's warehouses. That will surely make him become even more careful now."

"There is more than a very good chance that he will arrange for the weapons to be transferred to a safer storage facility, if he hasn't already done so," replied James.

"There is also another more pressing matter to deal with," Sean interrupted.

"And what might that be?" responded Chidoli as he eyed them both suspiciously.

"Matters have begun to spiral out of control. T J killed one and seriously wounded two other guards."

"What!" Chidoli responded. "I'll get on to Matthew Kalinga, the Chief of Police, right now. I'll get him to put the warehouse under surveillance. I'll check with the local hospitals whether anyone has been admitted with gunshot wounds. It won't take too long to find that out."

James looked at his watch. It was now 10.30 a.m. The guards would have been discovered at 4.00 a.m. when the shift changed. In all probability if Marais had been informed of the break-in he would have arranged to move the weapons immediately.

Chidoli picked up the phone. He was soon explaining the situation to Kalinga and asked him to put the warehouse under twenty-four-hour surveillance. Chidoli himself was doubtful that the weapons would still be there but it wouldn't hurt to have the warehouse watched for a few days. He asked him also to contact the local hospitals. He put the phone down.

"Edward, there is not much more we can do here. I'll be around for a couple more days in the hope that I can investigate Marais's drug running," said James.

He wasn't about to reveal to Chidoli that they had planned to help Martin escape from prison the next morning. He still needed T J's help with the escape bid. Somehow he hoped Martin had uncovered further information about Marais's activities from Chris Powell or any of the other croupiers. Now that they had all been sentenced and hadn't received suspended sentences they would be working out ways they might get themselves released from prison by passing on information to the Tanzanian government. If any of them had any extra information about Marais's illegal business empire they might be able to broker a deal for an early release back to the UK.

"Let us hope that something radical happens in the next few days. I will give you forty-eight hours and then I'm going to report everything you've told me to the President himself.

We will meet again before you go." Chidoli smiled nervously as he said it. He had a suspicion that James was not revealing all his plans. If Marais had nothing to hide he would react vociferously to one of his guards being killed and two wounded. A major diplomatic scandal would ensue if it was proven that Chidoli himself had employed someone to investigate his own business partner, Marais, with the blessing of the Tanzanian government.

Furthermore one of his employees had become embroiled in a US-led raid on Marais's warehouse. If however Marais was involved in drug running and, as it was now being suggested, arms dealing, he would cover up the raid on the warehouse and deal with it in his own way.

James's arrival hadn't exactly produced the results he'd expected. Chidoli, himself, was convinced Marais had something to do with setting up the scam in the first place. He was also convinced that he had made false claims from the insurance company about the scale of losses the casino had incurred as a result of the scam.

§

The sequence of events at the warehouse the previous night had unnerved Sean. When James explained to him on their journey back to the Msasani Slipway what exactly had happened he couldn't quite believe what he was hearing. T J had dragged them all into a bleak situation. They were now accessories to the possible charge of manslaughter if not murder. Although he had considered the idea of asking James for a full-time job once the project was complete he realised then he didn't want to live a life like James's and the likes of T J.

He was soon back at the Bilicanas Hotel and standing on the balcony overlooking the harbour area below. Njeri had already checked out and had taken the midday flight back to Mombasa via Nairobi. He was angry with himself that he had even contemplated the thought of joining James full time. It was one thing for him to have chased around Germany with him looking for Akinyi's killers but putting his life in danger on a regular basis didn't make much sense to him now. It was true that his life in Mombasa lacked some of the spark he craved for but risking his life on operations like the one he was currently on was also risking the chance that Achieng might end up growing up without a father. He was angry also with men like Marais who operated as though they were above the law. Although Marais had set up the Golden City in Tanzania he was also developing his business interests in Kenya. If things were to go wrong for him in Tanzania, Kenya offered him the chance of an escape route. It would be easy for him to bribe well-connected people in the Kenyan government with little fear of being arrested or extradited back to Tanzania.

Sean loved living in Kenya and now treated it as his home. He had even become a Kenyan citizen. He was angry with the existing regime in Kenya because it had allegedly blatantly robbed billions of shillings from the country. While a certain group of people were living in the lap of luxury, millions of their countrymen were going regularly without food and could barely clothe themselves. Unemployment was high. The roads were in a dreadful condition and the whole infrastructure of the country was in danger of total collapse.

As much as Sean and other Kenyans like him, both black and white, did their best to run legitimate businesses they were constantly struggling. He remembered Akinyi's words that the only way forward in Kenya was to fight the problems from within and not rely on foreign aid that, invariably, was hijacked by greedy politicians to line their own pockets. If that meant not accepting donor aid for a time then in the long term it would help get people to change their attitude to asking for handouts. Some of the politicians who were accepting aid on behalf of Kenya were no more than criminal beggars in her view.

Sean knew that one of the root causes and most unreported problems of Kenya was in fact capital flight for a huge number of reasons. In the first instance it was for the servicing of government debt to donor countries. Almost eighty per cent of the donor aid in any one year that came into the country flowed out in the very same year. Most was used to fund loans given to politicians who in turn took out further loans back in the countries it originated from in the first place. This scheme of a back-to-back loan gives borrowers the chance to accumulate private assets abroad. There was active complicity between the donors and the government. Allied to this were exemptions from taxes and duties on the services and goods provided.

Thirdly there was a huge flow of domestic capital funnelled overseas. For example, in the hotel and tourism industry that Sean worked in, vast profits were taken overseas by the owners. What made matters worse was that many workers in that industry were not even paid, or were very poorly paid and relied only on tips from guests to survive. The advent of all-inclusive holidays in some resorts meant that some staff working in the hotels couldn't even rely on tips to survive. Added to that many staff had to provide sexual favours in return for getting a job in the first place and then on an ongoing basis simply to hold down a job. He felt at a loss to know what to do but it was not something he was directly responsible for.

Another major problem was the awarding of contracts to foreign companies by donors, when a local company was perfectly able to service the same contracts, often at lower rates.

It was all very well the West accusing countries like Kenya of mass corruption but the truth of the matter was that, since independence, the West had actually assisted in fuelling the problem of corruption with the offer of bribes in return for lucrative business contracts. It was a problem that had escalated out of control. More so when supplies were double invoiced or orders placed with European companies, paid for out of government coffers and not even delivered. Few people knew it but "bribe money" was actually a legitimate tax-deductible item in the UK.

Sean clutched the handrail tightly as he looked over the balcony. He was suddenly overcome with a feeling of powerlessness. He felt obliged to continue to help James in return for James helping him find Akinyi's killers. He vowed this would be his last project. He would be back in Mombasa in another two or three more days. Once there he would take stock of his life again. He had to consider seriously whether he wanted to renew a romance with Njeri or develop his relationship with Nikki. He turned from the balcony. It was now after one o'clock. Achieng would be home from school. He went into his room and dialled his home number. He felt a lump in his throat as Achieng answered the phone.

25

DAYLIGHT WAS BREAKING as Sean, James and T J arrived at the Msasani slipway to collect the Subskimmer. They now had to carry out their plan for the escape without the aid of the Bora. It would slow them down but they had to deal with the situation as it now was. At such an early hour the traffic had been very light and it only took them twenty-five minutes from their hotel. In spite of the sequence of events the night before T J didn't seem to have a care in the world and insisted that he wouldn't talk to James about what had happened until after the escape attempt was over.

During the journey T J gave them a briefing for the day ahead. On arrival at Msasani they were met by Remmy, who had prepared the Subskimmer. They changed into full wetsuits and loaded the Subskimmer with the equipment they needed and were soon on their way. They headed northwards up the coastline to an almost deserted stretch of beach, which T J had reconnoitred earlier. It was approximately ten kilometres north of New Bagamoyo Prison. T J brought two extra diving suits with him. Sean assumed he had selected two different sizes because he wasn't certain of Martin's exact size. He had already arranged for the villa in Zanzibar to be stocked with food and several changes of clothes for Martin's stay.

A short time later they arrived at their destination. T J set anchor twenty metres from the shore and they swam to the beach. Once ashore they walked across the sand and sought out the shade of some coconut palms. The soles of their wet diving shoes were soon covered with dry sand. Once they reached the trees the ground became firmer but it was scattered with loose twigs and dead palm leaves that crunched beneath their feet. Within another fifty metres or so they reached a clearing. It was here that T J had arranged to meet the US Navy pilot with the Black Hawk. They stood beneath the trees at the edge of the clearing and waited. Another ten minutes and the pilot would be arriving at the scheduled time.

The sky was full of clouds and it wasn't long before the heavens opened. The heavy rain beating down on the big palm leaves created an avalanche of sound. The trees offered some protection from the rain but great puddles of water soon began to form all around them. Less than five minutes later the rain stopped abruptly. It coincided with the whirring sound of a helicopter hovering overhead. The three of them crouched down in a huddle to avoid the downdraught from the helicopter. Moments later the pilot brought the big machine to earth. T J and James ran over as the pilot cut the engine. He peered out of the window and gave T J the thumbs-up sign. James and T J climbed aboard and moments later T J was in the cockpit taking over the controls from the pilot. James meanwhile checked over the machine gun that had been mounted at the door opening. The pilot alighted and five minutes later the helicopter was back in the air. The pilot joined Sean under the trees at the edge of the clearing. They watched with interest as T J turned the big black machine and set course towards the prison farm next to New Bagamoyo.

The previous day T J had checked with a contact in the prison which of the croupiers had been allocated jobs in the farm work parties. Luckily Martin had been included along with all the other croupiers except for Lascelles and Mallett, who had been assigned jobs in the prison kitchens. Daly had managed to get himself transferred to the prison infirmary claiming he was suffering from a stomach disorder.

Within minutes T J had flown the helicopter down along the coast to the prison farm. He sighted the prison fields after focussing on the eight watchtowers about a kilometre away in the background. He flew in low, clearing the tops of the trees scattered around the area to the edges of the fields and headed directly towards the prison. After his initial low-flying sortie he buzzed low over the watchtowers and turned eastwards back out across the Indian Ocean. He turned north again and circled around for the second time and swooped back towards the prison farm.

By this time all the prisoners and guards in the working parties had been alerted to the huge Black Hawk that seemed to appear from nowhere. They all gazed open-mouthed as the huge metal bird appeared again and this time hovered slowly over the top of the fields.

Martin, who had earlier alerted Chris that an escape bid was going to be made that morning had quickly surveyed the area after T J's first swoop overhead to try and select the most likely place that he would land. He estimated a position approximately fifty metres to the north side of the working party. All the prisoners were chained at the ankles in pairs and Chris was Martin's partner. There was a buzz of conversation from the prisoners that was soon drowned out by the noise of the helicopter as it returned again minutes later. Martin and Chris had done their best to move closer to the area that Martin had selected without drawing too much attention to themselves and their movement. They were now only twenty metres away from the area he had pinpointed. Progress had been fairly slow as the heavy chain hampered their movements. At the same time they had to look as if they were still tilling the field with their hoes. There were about 100 prisoners in the group scattered across an area approximately half a mile square.

Six guards had been allocated to watch the working party. Four of them had sought refuge in the shade behind the prison vans parked at the edge of the fields, close to the roadside. They were lounging around smoking and chatting while the other two guards had taken up positions beyond the prisoners and approximately 150 metres away from the road and the other four guards. The routes to the north and the south of the guards were unguarded.

Chris and Martin in the meantime were checking T J's progress in the helicopter, as he appeared again from the north. He hovered lower and lower, as he drew closer and closer to them. Martin momentarily glanced at Peter Archer who was studying the movements of the Black Hawk. Huge clouds of dust flew up causing the prisoners to shield their eyes. Martin watched as the helicopter came almost to a stop, only feet above the ground. It rolled slightly from side to side in the way helicopters do. The big rotor blades whirred feverishly above. Martin turned again to Archer and watched with mild amusement as he could see on Archer's face the realisation of what was about to happen. Martin lifted the chain linking his left ankle to Chris's right one and gave it a tug. The pair of them then scrambled as quickly as they could towards the helicopter. The guards in the meantime had been very slow to react. It was as if they were in a trance as they looked on in disbelief.

James stood firmly behind the machine gun mounted in the doorway opening and trained it on the two guards closest to him. The four guards near the prison vans posed no immediate threat to him. Twenty seconds later Martin had swung himself up onto the floor of the helicopter to the left of James. He felt a huge wrench backwards on his left ankle as he felt Chris's full weight behind him. Chris was still on the ground. Martin twisted his body over and grabbed the chain with his right hand. The earlier force of Chris's weight against the chain forced the chain to tear into the skin on his ankle and rip harshly into the bone. He screamed out in pain. He clenched his teeth to dull the pain and dropping his left arm down he clutched at Chris's right arm as Chris made a concerted effort to jump onboard. Martin gave an almighty tug and Chris tumbled in on top of him, knocking the breath out of him. At that very moment T J revved the engine into action and the helicopter twisted into the air. Inside Martin and Chris rolled out of the tangled mess they were in and plunged further into the depths of the helicopter. While all this was going on not a shot had been fired. Chris and Martin sat up and gasped for breath. Moments later they broke into fits of laughter.

In the fields below pandemonium had broken out. The two guards closest to the work party were frantically running around trying to bring order back to the prisoners. The Tanzanian prisoners were cheering loudly and waving at the helicopter as it disappeared into the distance. Archer, Porter, Vickers and Bradley were screaming in unison, "You bastards! What about us!"

The four guards near to the prison vans had taken an age to realise what had happened before their eyes. In their moment of realisation they pulled their rifles up to their shoulders and fired a volley of shots pointlessly after the retreating helicopter. Their efforts were too little and far too late. They would have a lot of explaining to do on their return to prison.

§

Sean had spent the last twenty minutes or so chatting to the US Navy pilot who had introduced himself as David Rogers. He was a thin wiry man with sandy-coloured hair and a weather-beaten face that looked as if he had spent too long in the sun. He had spent the last three years on attachment at the US Embassy in Dar. He was dressed in civilian clothes.

Meanwhile back on the helicopter Martin introduced James to Chris.

"I thought I told you not to bring anyone else with you," said James curtly.

Martin could see he was annoyed. Chris pulled at the chain that bound them at the ankles.

"There's not much we could do about this, is there?" He laughed loudly. "I'm only too glad to be out of that hellhole of a prison!"

"Hi, Chris, it's good to see you!" T J yelled from the cockpit.

James and Martin looked at each other in bewilderment.

"You mean you guys know each other?" asked James. He had a puzzled look on his face.

"We sure do!" drawled T J.

Martin shrugged his shoulders. He looked at James as if to say it was news to him as well.

"You had better cut that chain off. There are some bolt cutters somewhere in the back there," T J shouted above the noise of the engine.

Martin and Chris began searching around and eventually came across a big set of steel bolt cutters.

"I think you owe us an explanation, T J, don't you?" James shouted back.

"I'll explain later. There will be time enough for that when we get to Zanzibar. As soon as we get this thing back on terra firma," T J drawled.

He turned back towards his console to concentrate on his flying. Moments later they were above the clearing behind the beach. The rotors of the helicopter slowed and finally whirred to a halt as T J switched off the engine on hitting the land beneath them.

James by then had cut the chain from Martin and Chris's ankles. He examined Martin's. Blood was seeping slowly from a deep wound that stretched all around the inside of the ankle. Small pieces of skin and flesh were hanging off where the chain had cut in. He glanced at Chris's ankle. Other than a slight swelling and bruising the skin hadn't been broken. T J was swiftly out of his seat. He jumped down to the ground. James shouted at David Rogers.

"Have you got a Medipack on board?"

"Yes, it's in the cockpit. I'll get it," he said as he climbed back onboard.

T J shouted, "Hurry up, we don't have much time."

He threw a diving suit at Chris who promptly pulled it on after removing his prison uniform. It was a perfect fit. T J already knew his size. Martin's on the other hand was fractionally too big for him. It was a blessing in disguise because it didn't fit too tightly over his damaged ankle. After he pulled on his suit he carefully rolled up the left leg so that James could treat his wound. David Rogers appeared with the Medipack and handed it to James. James broke it open and expertly cleaned and dressed the wound, finally unrolling the leg of the wetsuit and covering the bandage with it. Martin followed that by carefully pulling on his left diving shoe so that it too fitted snugly over the outside of the legging. Chris and T J had already disappeared back down to the beach and were swimming swiftly out to the Subskimmer to prepare for the trip to Pwani Mchangani on the east coast of Zanzibar.

Ten minutes later David Rogers was ready to go. He had removed the machine gun from the mounting and had stored it safely back in the storage box. After checking the flight management system he fired the engine into life. The big rotor whirred into action and David was soon in the air for the journey back to the US Embassy in Dar. As he turned out to sea he buzzed over the top of the Subskimmer and gave T J the thumbs-up sign as he flew past. T J acknowledged him with a wave and carried on with his safety checks. Chris and T J then pulled on their scuba tanks and were joined by Sean, Martin and James who had swum across from the beach. They in turn pulled on their scuba tanks. T J lifted the anchor and pointed the Subskimmer in the direction of Zanzibar. Within fifty metres they were in fully submerged mode for the journey underwater.

26

NEWS OF THE prison breakout had already been relayed to Marais in his office. He was raging. He was more convinced than ever that James, Sean and T J were responsible. The news had followed the report of the break-in at the warehouse and he was not best pleased. Neither he nor David Williams could understand why nothing seemed to have been stolen. Marais was very unimpressed that two of his security guards had been hospitalised and one killed. The two white guards were former South African Special Forces soldiers and he had expected more from them than to suffer the ignominy of coming off second best. The two wounded guards were former soldiers in the Tanzanian Army and their level of training could not be compared to that of their Special Forces colleagues.

However he was at least pleased that Dannie Burger had managed to escape with the Bora 20 intact. It was his actions that had saved the lives of the two wounded guards. If he hadn't escaped in the Bora and returned to the Golden City where he had informed Williams what had happened the two guards would more than likely have bled to death.

Williams could only guess at why the warehouse had been targeted. He could only suggest that whoever had visited the warehouse the previous night were indeed highly trained Special Forces experts themselves and very good ones at that.

"What the hell's going on, David?" Marais screamed. He thumped his fist down on his desk.

It was now more than an hour since the escape and it was over ten hours since the break-in, which Burger reported had occurred shortly after their arrival on duty at midnight. If he hadn't escaped, it wouldn't have been discovered until the new guards arrived for their shift change at 0400 hours. As it was, it was nearly 3.00 a.m. before an ambulance arrived to get his wounded colleagues to hospital. The body of the dead guard was taken out to sea and fed to the sharks and his disappearance simply put down to another unexplained disappearance in Africa. When Burger informed Williams of the break-in they both returned immediately to the warehouse. After a thorough search of the premises there was no sign of anything missing. All the weapons were still in place.

Williams made the decision not to inform Marais what had happened until their morning meeting at 10.00 a.m. By the time he arrived at Marais's office he had been up all night and looked tired and drained. The wrinkles on his forehead and the crows' feet around his eyes looked more prominent than normal.

"I'm at a loss to know why the warehouse was broken into. Nothing was missing, sir. I assure you," replied Williams. He expected to be on the receiving end of one of Marais's tirades at any moment.

"Now I'm told that Chris Powell and the other one, Donaldson, have escaped. That's twice now that bastard Powell has ripped me off! Once in Mafeking and now he rips me off here." His voice boomed as he spat out the words. He thumped his fists down again on the desk. This time he repeated it five or six times.

"What I don't understand, sir, is why it was only Powell and Donaldson who escaped. The Black Hawk helicopter is big enough to have fitted all the other croupiers in."

"It's fucking obvious, isn't it? That fucker Powell must know something about my operation here and at Benki Island." He raged again. "You'd better find out and find out fast or you'll be looking for another job." He stabbed his finger in the air in Williams's direction.

Williams swallowed hard. He was exhausted. At that precise moment he really didn't care if he lost his job or not. He felt like telling Marais he could stuff his job but he knew he would never get another in the casino industry again. Marais would make certain of that.

"I take it you haven't informed the police yet," Marais continued with a sneer.

"No, sir, I was waiting until we had managed to move the weapons somewhere else."

"At least you used your brain on that score!" Marais sneered again. "Come on, tell me what you know about Donaldson."

"I don't have much information on Donaldson. He's only been here a short time. It can only be because the two of them were chained together that Donaldson ended up getting the chance to go with Powell."

Marais's eyes were bulging. "Why the fuck was Donaldson the first to get to the helicopter then?" he shouted, waving the report that had already been faxed to him by the Prison Governor. It gave a detailed breakdown of what exactly had happened according to early eyewitness reports from the guards who had been in the field at the time.

"I'll do my best, sir, to find out exactly what's been going on." His face reddened with embarrassment at having missed something so obvious on reading the report.

Marais stood up and leaned forward with both hands on his desk. His face ended up not far from Williams's, who was seated the other side.

"You had better do better than that!" he snarled.

At that moment André Joubert came into the room. He watched quietly as David Williams was berated by Marais and waited patiently for him to finish.

"The arms have now been removed from the warehouse, sir," Joubert said in his thick Afrikaans accent.

Marais had earlier ordered the arms to be removed to

another secret and secure location in Dar. There were not enough storage facilities on Benki Island to take them there. The place still had to be developed. Some small buildings had been erected to house the drug shipments that were temporarily stored there before being removed to Kenya. Marais had considered the option of moving the guns to Benki but there were enough to fill a forty-foot container. It would be too difficult to make a shipment that big without attracting too much attention. He desperately needed to get the arms out of Tanzania.

"I hope you've doubled the guard then. There are more than both your jobs at stake if those weapons are discovered by the police."

Williams looked at Joubert whose nervous tic to his left eye twitched more than normal when he was put under pressure. He cleared his throat.

"The guard has been doubled, sir. I have also arranged for the shifts to be changed every two hours. The guards have also been issued with satellite phones so they are in constant contact with our office back here."

Marais's rage had subsided slightly.

"Will that be all, sir?" Williams asked. Tiredness was etched all over his face. He desperately needed some sleep and he couldn't wait to get out of Marais's office. Unusually for Marais he softened.

"Get out!" his voice quaked.

27

THE SUBSKIMMER SLOWLY emerged from the water. They were approximately one mile off the east coast of Zanzibar, close to Pwani Mchangani. The only things visible to an onlooker were the heads and snorkels of the divers. Here the waves were quite big and the craft bobbed up and down in the water. In the distance were long sweeping beaches of white sand with a background of trees. It was typical of an island or shoreline setting on the east coast of Africa. There were no boats near them as they semi-emerged. About half a mile nearer to the shore there were some fishermen going about their business in small fishing boats.

T J guided the Subskimmer closer to the shore into water that was about six metres deep and anchored it to the seabed. He would return to collect it later after first setting the boat locator on his wrist, which would enable him to find it with pinpoint accuracy.

The five of them swam underwater and eventually emerged in the shallows. The group of fishermen observed them as they appeared and after initial interest returned to their fishing.

T J and the others removed their flippers, snorkels and masks. They kept their scuba tanks on their backs and trudged off along the beach walking north for 200 metres then turning to the west towards a small villa in the trees. At the gate T J was greeted by a tall, well-built askari armed with an AK 47 rifle.

"Habari, bwana," he said with a smile.

He saluted as the others trooped past him behind T J. Once they reached the veranda they were met by the houseboy who offered them bottles of water. They then began to remove their scuba tanks. T J pulled his wetsuit down and tied the top half around his waist. The others followed his lead, except for Martin, who completely removed his suit and slumped down on a chair on the veranda. His ankle was beginning to give him serious pain. He lifted it and removed the bandage. It revealed a bloody mess. The skin around the wound looked very white and shrivelled. It was typical of the condition of a wound that has been exposed for too long in water. James had a quick look at it and asked the houseboy for some warm water and antiseptic lotion. He returned five minutes later and James cleaned and dried the wound.

"Some fresh air on it for a while will do it the world of good. You can bandage it later."

James turned back to T J.

"And now I think you have some serious explaining to do!"

He was still very angry with T J for killing one guard and wounding two others. He wiped some sweat away from his brow. There was no breeze. The branches of the palm trees that surrounded them were motionless. It was a very, very hot day. A mixture of spice scents filled the air.

"I guess I do."

T J wiped his moustache with the back of his left hand and sat down. James, Sean and Chris pulled up some chairs on the veranda. They all drank vigorously from the water bottles to quench their thirst. Dege, the houseboy, returned with a tray of sandwiches and fruit. He placed it on the table in front of them. They all grabbed a pile each and began to eat ravenously, particularly Martin and Chris, who had not had the luxury of sandwiches for a few weeks. They ate in silence. T J was the first to finish.

"Gentlemen, we are all here for a common cause."

Sean glanced at James. They both knew why they and Martin were in Dar and knew partly why T J was there.

However the two of them were puzzled by any other involvement that Chris might have other than setting up the cups scam at the Golden City.

T J went on to explain again why he was working in Dar and operating in conjunction with the Tanzanian government to try and combat the increase in drug trafficking in Tanzania and East Africa.

Prior to leaving London, Chris had seen an advert in the Africa Centre in King Street, near Covent Garden, for someone to work as a courier to deliver documents to Tanzania. As he planned to go there anyway he was intrigued, so he replied to it. Unbeknown to Chris it turned out it had been placed by T J's department from the American Embassy in London. Chris called the number advertised and arranged to meet T J at the Post House Hotel at Heathrow Airport. T J interviewed several potential candidates including Chris. He shortlisted the interviewees to two and after a second interview he selected Chris. Chris fitted the criteria of the person T J was looking for. He was the right age and single, with no commitments. T J eventually explained the full nature of the job was not as a courier as originally advertised but actually to work undercover in the Golden City to find out anything he could about Marais's alleged involvement in a drugs cartel. Chris's first reaction was to turn down the job. His original reason for going to the Golden City was to set up another gambling coup and he did not want anything to interfere with that. Furthermore he was far from being a detective or private investigator.

Before the interview, Chris had provided T J with his personal details and background. However he did not mention the time he had spent in Mafeking Prison but had included the fact that he had previously worked at the Palace Casino. Chris had no criminal record in the UK but T J was not satisfied with his explanation of the gap years during his time spent in Mafeking. Chris told him he had been managing a water-sports school in Kenya during that time. After delving deeper T J ran a check with his contacts in Kenya and there was no record of Chris having worked at the water-sports school he had mentioned. T J ran further checks in Bophuthatswana and soon discovered that Chris had been arrested in connection with the Bahamas cups scam, been convicted and served time in Mafeking.

T J revealed his findings to Chris at their second interview and asked Chris for an explanation. Chris denied any involvement in the coup and once again vehemently protested his innocence. He offered to take a polygraph test, to prove his innocence. He explained that it was something he had offered to do in Bophuthatswana but Marais had refused him the chance, even though it was a test that was used from time to time on staff in casinos. It was not always conclusive and apparently only ninety-seven per cent successful. People had been known to pass it who had later admitted guilt. T J had arranged for Chris to take a test a couple of days later. He was tested several times by an expert who asked a variety of questions specifically designed to prove someone's guilt or innocence. Chris's test results showed that he appeared to be innocent.

Once T J had the results he confirmed the offer of the job and agreed to pay him US$5,000 up front and a further US$5,000 upon successful completion of his task. Even if he was not able to get conclusive proof about Marais's involvement in the drugs cartel he would still be paid. Chris mulled it over and decided he had nothing to lose. He did not reveal to T J his plan to rip-off the casino. That was his revenge on Marais and the US$10,000 would be a bonus. He accepted the job. T J summed up:

"Chris made regular contact with me once he arrived at the Golden City but after his arrest I've had no contact."

T J looked annoyed when he mentioned Chris's

imprisonment. He never suspected that Chris was the mastermind behind the latest casino scam. His plans lay in tatters and not only that, he had already parted with $5,000. He was anxious to know if Chris had uncovered anything further about Marais's drug involvement. Everyone turned and looked at Chris expectantly and he in his turn looked acutely embarrassed.

"Listen, guys, I had my reasons for setting up the latest coup. I cannot deny I was involved. T J has already told you about what happened to me in Bophuthatswana. The polygraph also confirmed my innocence!"

T J was particularly annoyed that he had found himself assisting in Chris's escape. He was a convicted prisoner in Tanzania who had pleaded guilty to the charges laid against him. T J now had the possibility that should the Tanzanian authorities find out that he had been involved, he could be charged with aiding and abetting. It was an offence that could land him in prison and his career in ruins. The Tanzanian authorities were unlikely to divulge his involvement with their new drug enforcement agency. Added to that, the killing and wounding of the guards would land him in serious trouble.

Chris began to reveal details about his further investigations about Marais. It had been rumoured that a German national had purchased Benki and several other islands in the archipelago. Dawn Turner, Peter Archer's girlfriend, had even mentioned this to Sean. However, according to Chris, the German was actually a lawyer working for Marais. It was Marais himself who had purchased the islands under an assumed name.

Ten years earlier, Chris had served his time in Mafeking Prison with Marcus Corry, one of the ringleaders. As one of the chief cashiers at the Palace, Corry had very good access to the main offices. On one occasion on the night shift he had become rather bored and had begun looking through the filing cabinets in the office to pass time. There was nothing much of interest in the unlocked ones but he was overcome with curiosity about those that were locked. After several fruitless searches for the keys he got lucky one night and discovered a set that had been left underneath some paperwork in an intray on the casino bank manager's desk. The manager in question was alleged to be another one of the instigators of the Palace scam. He had been arrested by David Williams and his security officers on Marais's instructions and brought to Marais for questioning. He was fully prepared when the time came and had deliberately practised for that eventuality. When Marais accused him outright of being one of the main perpetrators he put on a very convincing act. He gave the impression he was mortally offended by Marais's suggestion he was involved. He shouted and gesticulated. He complained that he had started working for Diamond and Marais at the opening of the Palace in 1981 and that he had always been a loyal and trusted servant of the company. It was obviously a very convincing performance because Marais seemed to be completely taken in. Marais released him without getting the Bophuthatswana Police to prefer charges.

"What the cashier found in the locked filing cabinet made interesting reading," Chris continued, as he grabbed everyone's attention even more.

It seemed that Marais had established an intricate web of companies in many African countries. In particular his main companies were based in Zimbabwe and Kenya, where he had connections in very high political circles. One of the major shareholders of one of his companies was Robert Browne, a millionaire industrialist and a British Labour MP. At the time he was a household name in the UK and was a high-profile member of the shadow cabinet, as shadow Minister for Overseas Trade and Development.

Other major shareholders included several high-ranking

politicians in the Zimbabwe and Kenya governments. One of them, Charles Bett, was one of the most powerful and feared men in Kenya. He was a close associate of the President and his rise to the top had been rapid since the failed military coup in Kenya in 1982. He was known as Mr Big in Kenya, not least for his towering six-foot-six height.

"According to Corry, he found another set of keys in the filing cabinet that turned out to be duplicates to some safety deposit boxes held in the casino bank vault. After a couple of attempts at gaining access to the vaults on his own, Corry eventually managed to open some of the safety deposit boxes."

By now everyone was listening even more intently.

"Some of the deposit boxes contained cash, diamonds and an assortment of other jewellery. Most interesting of all were documents that appeared to be full records of Marais's companies."

"Did they reveal anything illegal?" James asked.

"Not at first but on closer investigation one set of accounts were for an import/export company based in Nairobi. Those accounts revealed that Marais and Bett were siphoning a massive amount of money from the Kenyan exchequer. The records clearly implicated Bett as a major player alongside Marais."

"How did they manage that?" asked Sean, who was particularly interested in the Kenyan connection. Sean knew if any of this information were to be divulged it could bring down the current Kenyan government.

"Charles Bett was receiving compensation from the Kenyan government for *not* exporting goods from Kenya!"

Sean looked at Chris in disbelief.

"You mean to tell me that this has been going on in Kenya since the mid 'eighties!

"Wait a minute," interrupted T J. He saw this information as an opportunity to bring Marais's empire crashing down around him. Sean and James watched T J with interest as they could see he was obviously weighing up the options now open to him.

"Could we find Marcus Corry and persuade him to testify against Marais in court?" he said, addressing his question directly to Chris.

"I should think there is absolutely no chance of that happening!"

§

Chris had a very good idea where Corry was now living and working in the South East of England. He was not about to divulge that information to T J or anyone else. He knew damn well that, considering Corry's newfound status, he would never entertain the idea of publicly revealing that part of his former life. He knew Corry would never resurrect his past and that he might have been involved in the original Bahamas cups scam at the Palace Casino.

Secondly Chris himself didn't want to reveal his own involvement, which would surely come out. Most important of all he also knew his own life would be at risk. It would not only be Marais who would be after him but also Bett, who was even more powerful. It would be easy for Marais to arrange a hit man to kill him and even easier for Bett. He shivered at the thought. At this point Sean interrupted.

"Can you explain exactly what Bett's company were not exporting?"

Chris looked at Sean.

"Diamonds!"

"Diamonds!" Sean repeated. "But Kenya doesn't have a diamond-mining industry! How the hell does he get compensation for not exporting diamonds when there aren't any diamond mines in Kenya in the first place?"

Sean felt anger welling up inside him. The others laughed in disbelief at what they had heard. There was a moment of silence as they all looked at each other. James sniffed the air.

"What's that smell?" He sniffed again and leant forward towards Martin and Chris who were seated opposite him on the other side of the table. He did a double take as he caught a stronger whiff. A look of disgust registered on his face.

"That stench is coming from you two! By god I've smelt some things during my time in the Army but that smell is right up there with the worst of them. T J, the sooner this meeting is over the better!"

He laughed and quickly returned to his original seat. It was now midday and the sun was at its hottest. Chris and Martin had dried out since their arrival at the villa and, not having had a proper shower for weeks, their body odour had begun to percolate.

"Am I hearing right?" said James. "Sean, are you sure that Kenya doesn't produce diamonds?"

"Sean is right," said Chris. "With Bett's help, Marais smuggled in a consignment of uncut diamonds from South Africa. Once they were in Nairobi they employed a diamond dealer from Amsterdam who cut and polished them. They then exported them at vast profit. That was the birth of the Kenyan diamond industry. Bett then persuaded his boss to issue a compensation initiative for not exporting any more diamonds from Kenya. His boss was easily persuaded for a twenty-per-cent cut."

"That's too far-fetched to be believable. You wouldn't read about it in a book!" James was disgusted at hearing another crazy tale of African corruption.

"If that information was released people would die laughing at the absurdity of it."

"Who was Bett's boss anyway?" asked T J.

Sean gave them a knowing look.

"There aren't many men more powerful than Bett in Kenya." Sean almost spat the words out.

The current regime in Kenya had institutionalised official corruption in Kenya. The chances of bringing investigations and prosecutions for corruption were absolutely zero. Ordinary Kenyans had totally lost confidence in it ending. The problem in Kenya and indeed other parts of Africa was that it had always been ruled, and still was, by elites who sought their own group self-interest rather than that of the country as a whole. It didn't matter whether the ruling class was black or white. It was one of the greatest of African tragedies, probably even more than the problem of poverty, Aids and inequality.

Ordinary Kenyans were waiting for a change and it couldn't come soon enough. The policy of those in power was often to buy the silence or acquiescence of whistle-blowers and critics by appointing them to positions of power. The most zealous supporters of anti-corruption had little or no chance of applying to the courts to prosecute the perpetrators. The Attorney General, on instructions from above, simply used a *nolle prosequi* to stop any local magistrate encouraging any case brought before them on the grounds of corruption.

T J quickly realised that they had reached an impasse. They had no conclusive evidence against Marais regarding his drug-smuggling exploits and there was next to no chance of him getting caught in possession of drugs of any description. He was too clever for that. All his businesses seemed legitimate on the surface and it would be very hard to prosecute him without conclusive proof. The latest revelations regarding Bett made no difference. Bett was a law unto himself. Even if they could persuade anyone to take the risk of testifying against Bett and Marais the chances of getting them to court were slim indeed. It would be almost impossible to give anyone twenty-four-hour protection without the help of the police. It was a well-known fact that the Police Department in Kenya would need disbanding and completely re-establishing before it could operate with impartiality.

In Tanzania however there was a chance of successfully prosecuting Marais if the right witnesses could provide sufficient evidence. However if Marais thought for a minute that was the case he would simply leave Tanzania and move to Kenya where Bett would offer him protection and immunity. Bett would welcome him with open arms because they could both pursue and further their business interests.

James reflected quietly on his current situation. He had been brought initially by Chidoli to sort out the problems at the Golden City. In a very short space of time he had got himself and Sean involved with T J and all that came with it. Marais's involvement was high on the agenda. On top of that there was the gun-running or drugs dealing. Now to cap it all was the latest revelation about the diamond compensation scam in Kenya. They all seemed to be inextricably linked with Marais's web of companies. Somehow he had to come up with a solution to break them down. It was certainly turning out to be his biggest challenge to date.

"I don't see an immediate solution to any of our problems. On our return to Dar I think we should arrange a meeting with Chidoli to discuss how we can proceed from here," suggested James.

"I agree," said T J. "Chris and Martin can stay here for a few more days and then we will sort out how we are going to get them out of the country."

"I'll give Chidoli a call as soon as we return to Dar. He may have a few helpful ideas," responded James. "In the meantime can you explain why you callously wounded two guards and killed another?"

"I have nothing to say on the matter. It was just one of those things."

Sean thought about pursuing the subject but thought better of it. It didn't seem as though T J was going to offer any form of explanation. Chris and Martin got up.

"I've been dreaming of a hot shower ever since I ended up

at New Bagamoyo Prison. Perhaps I'll get rid of that smell at last," said Martin, addressing his comment to James in particular. They all laughed but T J and Sean were both mightily relieved that Martin and Chris were going to be out of range. The smell had become almost unbearable.

"By the way, Martin," James paused, "and you, Chris, for that matter, make sure you stay within the vicinity of this villa. Whatever you do don't draw attention to yourselves."

It was definitely a command as far as James was concerned. There was a luxury hotel complex two miles north of the villa. James knew all about Martin's nocturnal habits and his taste for the high life. They couldn't afford for him to be seen outside and he knew if Martin got wind of some action he would be there in no time.

T J and Sean saw this as a moment to pick up their scuba tanks and head for the beach. James followed shortly afterwards.

"No problem, boss," Martin called after him. "Trust me!"

28

AT THE SAME time as Marais was conducting his meeting with Williams, Matthew Kalinga, the Chief of Police, was reporting the latest developments to Chidoli on the phone. When the two policemen assigned to watch the warehouse reported the arrival of two seventeen-ton vehicles with several armed guards on board they asked Kalinga for immediate back-up. Kalinga despatched four more policemen immediately. Two hours after their arrival the big wooden doors of the warehouse were flung open and the two trucks emerged. They pulled away slowly and travelled across the city, closely followed by the two policemen in a pick-up truck. Half an hour later they pulled up at another warehouse close to the airport. The roller shutter door was opened swiftly and they disappeared inside.

After Chidoli put down the phone he spent the next hour desperately trying to contact James. He left several messages at James's hotel asking that he contact him urgently on his return. When James picked those up at reception he called Sean immediately. He did not want T J at the meeting so he swore Sean to secrecy in case he bumped into him at his hotel.

One hour later they were in Chidoli's office on Sokoine Drive. This time Chidoli had been joined by Henry Murundi, the Tanzanian High Commissioner from London. James was very surprised to see Murundi there. After introducing Sean to Murundi everyone sat down around Chidoli's desk.

"I've being trying to contact you all morning. Where have you been?" Chidoli sounded very irritated.

"We've been diving off Bongoyo Island," Sean answered.

James gave him a glare as if to say "Shut up, let me do the talking". He was about to say something in response himself but thought better of it. Chidoli continued.

"There have been a number of developments. Firstly there has been a well-executed escape by helicopter from one of the prison farms near New Bagamoyo. By strange coincidence, James, your colleague Martin, and Chris Powell, were the only two involved."

"Oh really!" James feigned mild surprise at the news. Out of the corner of his eye he could sense that Murundi was scrutinising him carefully.

"Are you sure you had nothing to do with the escape?"

"As Sean said earlier, we were diving." James remained emotionless as he waited for Chidoli's reaction to his denial.

Murundi lit one of his big cigars. He inhaled deeply, drawing the smoke into his lungs, and blew out a long plume. A strong smell filled the air. Chidoli's office wasn't big. The small ceiling fan that whirred overhead moved the smoke around the room. Chidoli got up from his desk and went across to open the two windows. The noise of the city traffic filled the room as he sat down again and took up where he left off.

"Mr Murundi is here because of some major developments involving our friend Marais."

All eyes turned to Murundi who was puffing vigorously on his cigar. He flicked some ash into the ashtray on Chidoli's desk. He began to talk animatedly.

Two weeks previously he had been contacted by MI6 in London. They had warned him of the prospect of a forthcoming coup attempt in Kenya. It was expected to take place at any time in the near future. They had then contacted the Pentagon in Washington to arrange a meeting with officials from the American Defence Department, MI6 and Murundi at the Tanzanian High Commission. MI6 had been tipped off that Charles Bett planned to overthrow the Kenyan government, who had been blamed for a catalogue of human-rights abuses. The irony was that Bett was a central figure himself in some of those very same abuses.

Victor Marais was alleged to be one of the major backers of the coup. If it was successful his reward would be the chance to establish even bigger business interests in Kenya. MI6 contacted Tanzanian officials because Marais was currently a resident in Tanzania. MI6 had also heard similar rumours through other diplomatic channels.

The US State Department in Washington were very concerned about the situation. Any further unrest in East Africa following from the debacle in Somalia would be very difficult to handle. Kenya was strategically very important in East Africa. If Charles Bett was installed as the new President of Kenya relations with Britain and the United States would end up at an all-time low.

Bett was known to be anti-British and anti-American. He had studied economics at Sussex University in the 'sixties, which in those days was a left-wing hotbed of post-imperial guilt. He blamed British imperialists for leaving a terrible legacy to a continent divided by race, colour, religion and culture. He chose to ignore the tyrannies and one-party dictatorships that followed independence. He also chose to forget that, prior even to being colonised in the nineteenth century, Africa, like many other places around the world, was already divided by race, colour, religion and culture.

"Already the British and American navies are running a joint military exercise in the waters off the Kenya and Tanzania borders in case the coup goes ahead," explained Murundi.

"That probably explains the huge cache of arms we discovered at Marais's warehouse the other night," suggested James.

"What can be done about Marais?"

It worried Sean that a coup was about to take place in Kenya. He was very concerned that he was not at home with Achieng.

"Since my meeting with officials from the Africa section of the Pentagon and MI6, we met with a British businessman, John Roberts, who was a well-known arms dealer in the region. He admitted he had supplied large consignments of arms to Marais. He has proof of several payments from Marais."

"Is he prepared to testify to that?" asked Sean anxiously.

Murundi went on to explain that Marais had only paid for sixty per cent of the latest arms shipment. He had reneged on the final payment. Roberts was very, very angry. In return for immunity from prosecution he had agreed to testify at any forthcoming trial. He was now under a police protection scheme and living in a safe house under a twenty-four-hour armed guard in the South East of England.

James smiled. He looked across at Chidoli who had a serious look on his face but it soon broke into a smile. He rubbed his hands together.

"It looks like our friend Marais is in serious trouble."

He was already dreaming of running the Golden City himself. Regardless of Marais's whereabouts he was still the major shareholder. However, there was always the possibility his assets could be seized by the Tanzanian government if it was proven he was involved in criminal activities. Chidoli would bide his time and when the opportunity arose he would make his move to become the major shareholder. In the meantime he had to make sure the Golden City operated in the usual way. Murundi took a final drag on his cigar and stubbed it out in the ashtray.

"It's early days yet but a warrant will be issued for Marais's arrest. His arrest will coincide with a raid on the warehouse where the arms are currently being stored."

Chidoli confirmed that the warehouse was still under surveillance.

"And what about Marais's drugs connection? What can be done about that?" James knew T J did not want to miss out on a successful prosecution against Marais. It would be real kudos for his department if Marais was convicted.

"At the moment I would say not much, but I am sure that once Marais is arrested there will be many of his employees who might take the risk of providing evidence against him," replied Murundi.

Sean looked mightily relieved. If Marais was arrested and the arms seized, the coup in Kenya could not possibly take place and his immediate concerns for Achieng's safety would cease.

"If the coup doesn't go ahead what will happen to Bett?" asked Sean. He looked at James.

"In my experience of such things, the Kenyan authorities will receive a tip-off about Bett's involvement. I don't think he will have much chance of long-term survival given the Kenyan government's alleged record of torture and political killings," replied James cynically.

"I think the time has come for me to arrange a meeting with Marais," declared Chidoli. "He is under pressure right now and he might make a mistake he will regret later. He has to get rid of the arms quickly and he has to make sure that no one can claim he has any connection with Benki Island as a drugs haven and drop-off point."

"It strikes me that the sooner the Kenyan powers are tipped off about the planned military coup the better," interrupted Sean. "Bett will undoubtedly deny any involvement to save his own skin and he will surely implicate Marais and accuse one of his own political rivals in Kenya of being involved."

"If that happens you can rest assured that Marais will flee Tanzania in haste," responded James.

Murundi lit another cigar. He inhaled and blew circles of smoke into the air. He was deep in thought. He smiled.

"May I suggest, Edward, that you arrange your meeting with Marais but on this occasion I think Matthew Kalinga, the Chief of Police, should accompany you on the pretext that he is investigating allegations of drug-smuggling against Marais."

"That's a good idea and at the same time he can mention he has heard whispers about a military coup in Kenya linked to Marais's gun-running activities."

James's devious mind was working overtime. He was excited at the prospect of the outcome of the meeting. It would definitely force Marais to make a move. They all nodded their agreement. Murundi stood up.

"Edward, I will leave everything in your capable hands. I look forward to hearing the outcome of your meeting with Marais. Now, if you don't mind, gentlemen, I am off to lunch with the President."

With that announcement he turned on his heels and left the room.

James saw that as a chance for him and Sean to leave. He was determined to see T J so that he could confront him again about the shootings. There was no time like the present.

"Good luck, Edward," he said as he shook hands with Chidoli. "Please let me know when you need us next."

Chidoli shook hands with Sean. As they left the room Chidoli picked up the phone and dialled Matthew Kalinga's number.

§

Chidoli met with Matthew Kalinga at the Central Police Station prior to their meeting with Marais. Kalinga was a tall studious-looking man who wore black horn-rimmed spectacles. His dark hair was flecked with grey. He wore it quite long and it looked rather unkempt for a man in his position. It made him look older than his fifty-five years and like anything but a policeman. He would not have looked out of place if he had been a university lecturer.

However, he had been a career policeman ever since he graduated from university with a degree in political science in the early 'seventies after completing his studies at Moscow University. He was one of three exceptionally bright students who had been awarded a scholarship after the Arusha Declaration in 1967, which committed Tanzania to a policy of socialism and self-reliance. He was one of Julius Nyrere's protégés and whilst he was educated by socialist principles, he welcomed the arrival of multi-party politics in the early 'nineties after the fall of communism in Europe. He was one of the men at the forefront of the development of his country since the new government had come to power and had a reputation for being a strongly principled and fair-minded man. He had a calm aura about him and was highly respected as a man who wouldn't take bribes.

Kalinga normally only wore his policeman's uniform on state occasions. His usual mode of dress was a dark suit with a white shirt and tie. However, he had deliberately dressed in his ceremonial uniform for effect because he knew he would be paying Marais a visit. His black shoes were highly polished.

The two men spent half an hour together. Chidoli briefed him regarding the current situation with Marais. He told Kalinga about the most recent revelations regarding Marais's business empire and his shady dealings. Kalinga had already been informed about the potential military coup in Kenya and the alleged connection with the arms cache at Marais's warehouse.

Politically Kenya and Tanzania had been members of the East African Community along with Uganda, but that had broken up in 1977. A long dispute followed with Kenya and the border was closed for six years. Since then, relations had improved, and they were currently re-establishing a Tripartite Commission for East African Cooperation.

Kalinga had to be very careful to avert any diplomatic

incident with Kenya. If it was confirmed that a military coup was about to take place in Kenya that emanated from and with the backing of a current Tanzanian resident, albeit a South African by birth, then the whole Tripartite Commission could break down with disastrous economic consequences for Tanzania in particular. Kalinga and Chidoli spent the next twenty minutes hatching a plan as to how they would confront Marais.

Two hours later Matthew Kalinga was driven at high speed in an unmarked police car with blacked-out windows to the Golden City. His driver, Khaled, and two of his most senior Flying Squad officers, were in the car with him. Behind them, in a marked police Range Rover, with sirens blaring and blue lights flashing, were four heavily armed policemen.

The two vehicles screeched to a tyre-smoking halt at the main gate of the Golden City complex. Kalinga's driver waved an identity pass at the guards on duty and shouted an instruction in Swahili. The guards promptly lifted the barrier and Khaled gunned the engine of the big Mercedes and tore off up the drive with tyres squealing, at a speed that was very abnormal for vehicles arriving at the Golden City. The Range Rover followed closely behind.

As they passed through the barrier the guard in the small office picked up his phone and dialled Marais's office to forewarn him of the police arrival. Several guests out for a leisurely stroll on the neatly manicured lawns looked up in astonishment as they saw the two police vehicles flash by. The wailing sirens broke the tranquillity and calm of the early afternoon.

Moments later the cars screeched to a halt once again. The officers in the Range Rover jumped out immediately and took up their positions two metres apart from each other on the main steps leading up to reception. Their guns were cradled in their arms across their chests. Their fingers wrapped around the triggers. They were quickly followed by the two Flying Squad officers from Kalinga's car. Kalinga then jumped out. Moments later Pieter Coetzee appeared at the top of the steps. He waited in anticipation as Kalinga climbed up the steps to meet him.

"What is the meaning of this unexpected intrusion?" Coetzee was barely able to contain his anger.

"You have no right to charge in to my hotel like this and disturb my guests in this way!"

He rubbed his hands together nervously. He was not used to dealing with a black man in a position of such power. It was patently obvious to anyone watching the stand-off at the top of the steps that Coetzee didn't like having to restrain himself and defer to him. The only one he pretended to respect was Chidoli.

Kalinga stopped. He towered over Coetzee.

"Mr Coetzee, at the moment you are a guest in my country. Until you receive your resident permit please be very careful not to upset me. I do not take kindly to men like you speaking to me in such a manner. Tell Mr Marais and Mr Chidoli I am here to see them."

He remained calm and composed. He sensed this irritated Coetzee even more. Coetzee sighed. He turned on his heels.

"Follow me," he mumbled as he led the way.

Kalinga followed him, his gold-topped swagger stick tucked firmly under his left arm. He was flanked by the two Flying Squad officers. The armed police remained on the steps. Coetzee led them through reception, through a set of double doors on the far side and across a marbled terrace. The afternoon heat hit them as they noticed a considerable change in temperature from the comfort of the hotel air conditioning. Within minutes they reached the entrance to an office complex. Two uniformed security guards stood either side of a set of double doors. They saluted Coetzee and nodded to Kalinga. They both knew very well who he was. The guards pulled open a door each and ushered the four men through. Coetzee still led the way.

A young black woman was sitting at a low-level reception desk. She looked up from her work. She forced a half-smile when she saw Coetzee. Her smile turned to an inquisitive frown as her gaze fell on the three men following him. She shuffled a set of papers on her desk and was about to say something when Marais appeared through a door behind her.

"Mr Kalinga, this is indeed a pleasant surprise!" Marais demonstrated an unexpected exuberance for his visitors. "Welcome, gentlemen, please come into my office and make yourselves comfortable."

As they walked into the office Marais turned to the young woman behind the desk. "Esther, get these gentlemen some tea and coffee."

He turned to Coetzee. "That will be all, Pieter," he said dismissively, much to Coetzee's acute disappointment that on this occasion he was not to be invited into the inner sanctum. He was longing to know why Kalinga had made such a dramatic entrance. He nodded uncomfortably.

After issuing his instructions, Marais went into his office. Edward Chidoli was already seated at a large conference table. He feigned surprise at Kalinga's arrival. He stood up and offered Kalinga and the two policemen a seat each. They all made a display of shaking hands and sat down in silence. Marais remained standing.

Marais did his best to look calm. His body language however portrayed a different picture. His shoulders were tensed up and his fists clenched at his sides. He had met Kalinga on previous occasions but it was the first time he had paid a visit to the Golden City in what appeared to be in an official capacity.

"Mr Kalinga, what brings you to the Golden City and in such a noisy fashion?" asked Marais with a hint of sarcasm. He stuck his hands in his pockets.

"Mr Marais, we have received some very serious allegations about you!"

"Oh!" said Marais, turning his face slightly sideways away from Kalinga to avoid his stare. He continued, "Please explain these allegations to me. I am very intrigued."

"Mr Marais, we have received an allegation that you have stockpiled a huge shipment of arms."

Marais raised his eyebrows. "And where did you get that ridiculous piece of information from?"

Kalinga could sense that Marais was doing his best to appear calm but Kalinga could see the anger rising inside him. A red rash began to appear around his neck.

"We have received a tip-off from very reliable sources." He stood up. "I want to see you at the Central Police Station tomorrow morning at ten o'clock. I have some questions to ask you there."

Marais took his hands out of his pockets.

"Mr Kalinga, you have come all this way to ask me to attend a meeting at your office tomorrow morning. Why the hell can't you ask me your questions right now?" He raised his voice for the first time.

Kalinga smiled because he knew he had Marais rattled. He walked round from the other side of the table. The two other policemen stood up.

"And what happens if I don't come? You have no proof and no right to ask me any questions. I have done nothing wrong!"

Kalinga lowered his eyes and said with quiet determination, "Mr Marais, it will be in your best interests to attend voluntarily and I suggest you bring a lawyer with you." He began to walk from the room followed closely by his two colleagues.

"Huh, you can't make me come. Why aren't you spending your time trying to recapture the croupiers who escaped from prison instead of hassling me?" replied Marais aggressively.

Kalinga ignored his comment and turned as he was about to walk through the door.

“Mr Marais, you will force me to issue a warrant for your arrest.”

He left the room. Marais stood there speechless before he turned on Chidoli.

“You knew that bastard was coming today, didn’t you!”

Chidoli shrugged his shoulders and before he had a chance to respond Marais stormed from the room and slammed the door behind him. As he swept hastily through reception Chidoli heard him shouting.

“Esther, get hold of Williams right now. I want him in my office immediately.”

29

JAMES AND SEAN spent most of the morning trying to contact T J. After a fruitless search James discovered that he had checked out of the Bilicanas Hotel earlier. He had told one of the receptionists he was returning to Dar. James telephoned the US Embassy and asked to speak to T J but the switchboard operator told him that T J was on leave and wasn't expected back at work for another week.

James was growing frustrated at his failure to track T J down and more to the point he was very annoyed that T J hadn't let him know his plans. Along with the incident at the warehouse and T J shooting the three guards James was becoming increasingly disillusioned that he had ever got involved with him in the first place. He was at a loss to know where he might be.

After a great deal of thought and imagining what he himself might do in the current situation he telephoned the Go and Sea Dive Centre on the offchance that T J might be there. No one had seen him since their last visit. The Subskimmer was still moored up.

James was even more frustrated that he was unable to contact Martin at the villa hideaway on Zanzibar. Landline communications were very poor in Tanzania, even worse than they were in Kenya, and according to T J the villa had no direct telephone line anyway.

They originally planned to collect Martin and Chris the next day, so, as they were now at a loose end, James decided to bring it forward by one day. They could at least do that without T J's help. The police were still looking for the two escaped prisoners but they realised in all probability they would have been long gone from Tanzania. The escape looked too well organised and planned for them to remain in Dar with the risk of being captured. The local media had covered the story but as yet the international press hadn't descended on Dar on the scent of another good news story about the already controversial Golden City complex run by Marais. Some of the British and American national newspapers covered the recent trial but usually with local correspondents. The few staff journalists had returned to their own countries immediately after the verdicts were announced.

When Marais had originally opened the Golden City there was a great deal of criticism in the international press about him setting up a South African apartheid-style fiefdom in yet another African country. In James's estimation it wouldn't be long before the international press got a tip-off about the latest situation at the Golden City and the subsequent prison escape.

James hastily hired a car from the car-hire company at reception and shortly before midday they were on their way to the Go and Sea Dive Centre to collect the Subskimmer. Neither James nor Sean was expert in handling the craft but James felt sure that between the two of them they could make the trip across the water without too much difficulty.

Once at the dive centre they could check the weather reports. James reckoned that if the worst came to the worst they could hire Remmy for a few hours to take them across to Zanzibar. He at least was familiar with the shipping lanes and channels. A big tip would be enough for Remmy to keep his mouth shut about their journey and who was at the other end of it.

The original intention was to collect Martin and Chris and take them in the Subskimmer along the Pemba Channel and into Kenyan waters, where they would be dropped off at Shimoni on the mainland peninsula opposite Wasini Island.

The stretch of water from the Pemba Channel to Shimoni is one of the world's best stretches of sea for hunting big-game fish. Tiger sharks weighing up to half a ton and marlin up to a quarter of a ton have often been seen in those waters, so James knew there was a risk that they and the Subskimmer could be battered or attacked by them.

The Tanzanian island of Pemba is smaller than Zanzibar and separated by about fifty kilometres of water. Shimoni is only about a further fifty kilometres from Pemba. In total the journey would take only about three to four hours.

Once they reached Shimoni, they would be met by Opiyo, Sean's handyman. He would then drive Martin and Chris back up the coast road to Mombasa in Sean's Land Rover Discovery, and they would take a flight from Mombasa via Air Kenya back to Wilson Airport in Nairobi. Once in Nairobi and after sorting out new passports with the help of some of James's connections at the High Commission, they would have a choice of flights back to Europe.

By coincidence James and Sean left for Dar almost at the same time as Kalinga was being driven up the coast road to meet Marais at the Golden City. Their paths crossed on the journey but neither Sean nor James paid much attention to the police Range Rover as it sped past in the opposite direction. They were all too busy with their own thoughts.

They reached Msasani an hour later after battling through the lunchtime traffic.

Fortunately Remmy was on duty and it didn't take long for James to convince him that they had T J's permission to use the Subskimmer for the afternoon. The temperature was up around thirty-seven degrees centigrade and Sean was looking forward to the welcome relief of the blustery winds once they were out at sea.

After half an hour of preparations and checking the weather reports for the area they were ready to go. James had decided it wasn't necessary to take Remmy with them. None of the weather reports indicated inclement weather.

§

The villa where Martin and Chris were staying was set back from the beach and half hidden from view in amongst a variety of palm, acacia and casuarina trees. The exact location was between Pwani Mchangani and Matemwe and it boasted some of the finest sandy beaches on Zanzibar. James could make out the position of the villa by the location of an exceptionally tall coconut palm that towered above the rest over the compound.

They had travelled part of the way from Dar fully submerged and it was low tide when the Subskimmer resurfaced at least one and a half kilometres from the beach. After setting anchor, James and Sean had to make a twenty-minute trek across the sand to the shoreline. It was typical of so many beaches in Zanzibar that were subject to large tidal fluctuations. The sun was burning hot and they were both parched by the time they arrived. They had drained the small water bottles they carried around their necks within ten minutes of leaving the Subskimmer.

There was no sign of life as they neared the villa. James couldn't see the askari on duty. He became increasingly concerned the closer he got to the compound. An eerie silence filled the air. They carried no weapons with them. James whispered to Sean to hang back while he went up to the small gate leading from the beach. It was swinging on its hinges in the breeze making a gentle creaking sound as it did so. He pushed carefully past it and waved to Sean to follow him. Sean deliberately closed the gate behind him.

The terrace area was empty and the sliding door to the front of the villa closed. Strangely none of the other windows were open. The place looked completely deserted. Stranger still was the lack of cooking smells to fill the air. Knowing Martin as he did and having spent nearly a month in prison with a minimum of rations, James knew that if Martin was around he would be getting Dege to cook him all sorts of gourmet delights.

James crept up to the sliding door and tried to open it. It was locked. He turned and gave Sean a quizzical look. Sean shrugged. James then turned and followed the narrow pathway from the terrace round to the back of the building. He tried the kitchen door. It was locked. He peered through the small window to the side of the door. He could see nothing untoward. The kitchen appeared to be immaculately clean and nothing seemed out of place.

"I don't know what the hell's going on here," James said quietly as he turned to Sean.

"Me neither, but I reckon we need to break in."

James nodded in agreement. He looked around for something to break the window with. A short-handled garden hoe was lying alongside a rusting watering can. He picked up the hoe which was one that had the metal part fixed at a right-angle to the handle. He held it in both hands and made a stab at the window. The glass cracked and he took another full-forced swing. This time he turned his face away. As he did so the glass shattered. Most of it fell inwards except for a few small shards that flew in all directions. Sean ducked as some flew towards him, raising his hands upwards to protect his face. James continued to hack away at the glass around the wooden frame until he had a completely clear opening to climb through.

"Wait here a moment, Sean."

James picked up the coir doormat that lay in front of the back door and dropped it through the window onto the kitchen floor inside on top of the pile of broken glass. With that he grabbed the top part of the window frame on the inside with the palms of both hands turned outwards. He then swung his legs forwards into the opening and balancing both feet on the window ledge, dropped onto the kitchen floor. He landed directly onto the mat, which protected his feet from the pile of broken glass. He was still only wearing his thin rubber diving shoes.

Once inside he looked around for a key to the back door. After a fruitless search, he signalled for Sean to follow his lead. Sean duly jumped up in the same fashion and was inside within seconds.

They moved swiftly through the kitchen and dining room and had a quick look at the main living room that opened onto the terrace through sliding doors. The whole place seemed immaculately clean. Nothing was out of place. So far there was no evidence of anything untoward. All was quiet except for the background hum from the fridge/freezer in the kitchen. It was stiflingly hot inside. There was no air conditioning and none of the windows was open. It gave the place a smell of unpleasant staleness. They shuffled across from the living room and into the hallway. In front of them was a stairway.

James put his index finger to his lips and pointed up the stairs, suggesting that Sean should lead the way. Sean nodded. At that moment Sean's heart sank. Now he was in the front line. Up till then James had been his shield and protector. His whole perspective changed. He felt an adrenaline rush, swallowed hard and without thinking, he ran up the stairs, two at a time.

At the top he breathed hard. James was close behind and pushed past him. They crept along the corridor. James reached the first bedroom and carefully pushed the already half-open door with his left foot. As the door swung back on its hinges James was inside in one sweeping motion. The room was empty other than a bed and chest of drawers.

Sean remained in the corridor. He was waiting for James to make his next move. Moments later he reappeared in the corridor. He moved forward slowly, careful to slide along the wall to the left-hand side, in preparation for entering the next room that lay to his right. This time the door was closed. Sean stepped forward and tried turning the handle slowly but the door was locked.

Before James could whisper an instruction, Sean took a step backwards and then suddenly sprang forward and kicked hard against the door. The flat of his right foot landed inches away from the handle and door lever. The door felt the full force of his near ninety-five-kilo weight and the door lining gave way. The wood splintered all around it and the door burst inwards to the right, initially with a resounding crash and then with a weak backwards and forwards motion as it hit the wall behind it.

"Sean, don't go in there!" hissed James.

Before James had finished his sentence Sean was inside.

"Come quickly, James."

James responded immediately and followed Sean into the room. There in front of them and seated on the floor were Dege and the askari tied together, back-to-back, with their feet stretched out in front of them. Their ankles were bound with rope. Both their mouths were covered with black duct tape. Their eyes were bulging in a mixture of relief at the sight of their rescuers and fear, not being certain whether James and Sean were friend or foe, even though they both recognised them from their visit to the villa with T J a couple of days earlier. Sweat dripped from their faces.

James ripped the duct tape away from their mouths in one sweeping motion. As he did so the glue from the tape pulled at the skin and hair on their faces and they cried out in pain. The pain and fear on their faces changed to a look of elation as they realised James was there to help and end their misery.

James began to untie the ropes around their midriffs and then unknotted the ropes that bound their hands tightly behind their backs. Sean set about the task of untying the knots on the ropes around their feet. Within a few minutes they were free. James and Sean then helped them to stand up. They had obviously been there a long time because their legs buckled under them as their muscles had stiffened from sitting in one position for so long. After massaging their muscles and stretching their arms and legs they were in a fit state to make a move.

"Sean, next time consult me first before you charge into a room like that. How did you know that door wasn't booby-trapped?"

Sean looked at him with astonishment. It suddenly dawned on him that his inexperience could have got them both killed, if the door had been booby-trapped. He shivered at the thought of it.

"Sean, help get them downstairs whilst I check out the rest of the top floor." James left the room. He didn't want Sean stumbling into another potential disaster.

"Yes, boss," Sean said sheepishly.

Sean led the way back downstairs. Dege headed straight for the kitchen and pulled a pitcher of cold water from the fridge. Without a thought for the askari he poured half the water into his mouth but managed to spill the other half of it down himself and splash it onto the floor in the process. He looked extremely satisfied with himself. He then filled the pitcher from the tap at the sink and handed it to the askari to take his turn to quench his thirst. He was more careful not to waste any but drained it within seconds.

Sean meanwhile was going around the villa and opening as many downstairs windows as possible. The askari found the key to the doors from the living room. He turned the key in the lock and slid one of the double doors back.

The air had cooled slightly outside as it began to rain. At first a sprinkling of water covered the terrace before it turned to a deluge as the clouds burst from the heavens above them. James reappeared.

"There's no one or nothing else to worry about upstairs."

Sean knew from their previous visit that neither Dege's nor the askari's English was good. He began to speak slowly and clearly.

"Can you explain what happened and why you were tied up? What happened to Martin and Chris?"

Between the two of them they explained that Martin and Chris had eaten well the previous night, before retiring to bed at about 9.30 p.m. They had risen early, shortly before sun up at sixish and after going for a swim they ate a full breakfast.

After breakfast they had spent half an hour or so putting together their black diving suits and scuba equipment. They packed the few belongings they had and a change of clothes into a holdall and seemed ready to go.

"Bwana, I think they waiting Mr T J come back," said the askari, in broken English. He looked as though he was scared to give the full version of what happened. Sean sensed his fear.

"Don't worry, askari, we know it is not your fault they have gone," Sean said to reassure him. James looked at Sean and nodded.

The askari continued. Unbeknown to him, Martin and Chris had already overpowered Dege inside the villa and tied him up before depositing him in the bedroom.

"Bwana, I guarding outside. Mr Chris he come talk me. He give me cigarette."

Apparently the next thing the askari knew was feeling the sharpness of the blade of a panga or machete that was held tightly across his neck by Martin, who had crept up behind him. He dropped his AK 47 rifle and within moments his hands were tied behind his back before he was marched upstairs to the bedroom that Dege was being held in. There he was bound at the ankles and tied to Dege. He estimated they had been there for nearly six hours.

James looked at Sean again. They were both mystified why Martin and Chris had behaved in such a way. Without passports their movement would be limited. T J had only left them a small amount of cash. It hadn't been enough to buy air tickets and there was no way they could have flown out of

Zanzibar's airport anyway. The police would still be on the lookout for the two escaped prisoners from the mainland. Tourism was still at a low level in Zanzibar and most of those tourists were with package-tour companies. Two lone white men arriving at the airport would be too obvious not to be checked thoroughly by security and immigration. There had to be another way for them to leave the island.

"Dege, does this villa have a boat?" asked James.

"Yes, Mr James. Boat anchored in the sea. Me show you. This way, bwana."

He led the way to the beach. The rain had eased off and the sun was appearing again from behind the clouds. At the gate he was about to point out the place where he expected to see the boat. The tide was still out and other than three small wooden dhows that lay sideways on the sand there were no other boats in sight. He looked shocked.

"Mr James, the boat not there now!" he shouted hoarsely. He pointed to the place between the dhows where the boat was normally anchored.

"It looks like everything is disappearing around here!" Sean exclaimed. "First of all T J does a disappearing trick, then Martin and Chris and now the boat!" He laughed half-heartedly at his weak joke. "The next thing we'll be hearing is that Marais has done a runner!"

James didn't appreciate Sean's humour. They had now wasted the best part of an afternoon and they still had to get back to Dar.

"Askari, did you have any other weapons other than the AK 47?"

The askari looked sheepish. "One Browning pistol." He looked terrified that James was going to admonish him for losing his guns.

"Come on, Sean, we need to make a move. We need to get back to Dar as soon as possible. We need to see Edward Chidoli and Kalinga as a matter of urgency."

He wasn't about to reveal to them his involvement in the escape and now he had to deal with Martin and Chris's disappearance. He wondered whether T J had been involved in their disappearance from Zanzibar. He didn't like being taken for a fool. At that moment he felt nothing but contempt for T J.

§

Sean and James jogtrotted back across the sand to the Subskimmer. Once on board Sean pulled in the anchor as James quickly fired the engines into life. There was a throaty roar as the big outboards created a bubbling mass of water around them.

Moments later they were on their way. James soon had the 1,600-kilogram craft up to almost maximum surface speed of thirty-five knots. The engines whined as James sliced the craft through the big waves. Sean clung on to the central control panel to James's left acting as the lookout and spotter. Great plumes of spray reared up in their wake. Occasionally, as the craft slowed and lurched, when it bounced across a bigger wave, Sean was hit by a torrent of water as it splashed up over the side. As it cascaded down his face the salt stung his eyes and he could taste it on his lips.

The noise of the engines and the wind on their faces made it virtually impossible to hear each other as they shouted in a vain attempt to communicate. Their words were lost in the wind. James was determined to get back to Dar as quickly as possible. There would be time later to plan their next move.

Eventually they arrived in Msasani Bay. James slowed the Subskimmer to about three knots. His arm muscles were almost fit to burst as he released the tension of his hands on the steering wheel. He stretched his arms out in turn and flexed his fingers and wrists. Sean simultaneously released his grip on the grab-handle and followed James's example.

He rolled his head in a circular motion above his shoulders, first to his left and then slowly to his right. He waved when he spotted Remmy who was waiting patiently at the slipway.

As James was concentrating on steering the Subskimmer back to their mooring Sean looked up and saw the sleek Bora 20 as it gathered speed, heading in the direction from which they had come. The black tinted windows hid the identity of the passengers onboard.

"Look, James, the Bora 20!"

Sean pointed in the direction of the fast-disappearing craft. James was momentarily distracted and it caused him to bang the Subskimmer into the mooring. He looked up quickly before returning his attention to the task in hand. He had done his best not to damage the craft on the journey even though he was far from being an expert sailor.

"Oh shit!" He noticed he had hit the side of the gimballed steering thruster on the starboard side.

After the Subskimmer finally came to a halt James gave the steering thruster a cursory glance. He then ran his hand around the gimbals. There didn't seem to be anything bent and he decided the damage was only superficial. By the time he had finished his examinations the Bora 20 had disappeared out to sea.

"Come on, Sean, let's move it!"

James grabbed his bag from the storage box and turned to Remmy.

"Remmy, check and see if there is any damage to the thrusters and then give the boat a clean down."

Remmy nodded nervously.

"And if you see Mr T J, tell him I want him to contact me urgently."

He snarled his instruction, such was his anger about T J that Remmy was taken aback. He had previously been struck by James's laid-back manner.

"Yes sir, Mr James. If he comes I will tell him," he responded timidly.

James slipped twenty dollars into his palm and winked.

"Assante sana, bwana." Remmy thanked James with a big smile.

Sean by now had grabbed his own kitbag and the two of them marched off up the slipway to their hire car, leaving Remmy shaking his head in bemusement. He had no idea why James seemed so angry with T J. He decided it was not his business and returned to the task of inspecting the gimbals that housed the thruster.

During their journey back to the Golden City James and Sean discussed their next move. Both of them were equally at a loss as to what to do next. Eventually they decided to sit things out for another twenty-four hours in the hope that Marais made his next move. At that stage they were not aware of Matthew Kalinga's earlier meeting with Marais. Additionally they were at a loss to know where Chris and Martin had disappeared to. They wondered whether T J had any connection with their disappearance. He had admitted he was well connected to Chris, having employed him originally in London to go undercover at the Golden City.

James was at a loss to know why Martin might have got involved with Chris and T J. Of course there was a strong possibility he had uncovered something about Marais, Chris and T J, and he was only going along to see what transpired next. The other alternative was that T J had turned up and released Chris and Martin but had later managed to dispose of Martin once they were out to sea in the boat. The permutations were endless. Furthermore the askari's AK 47 and Browning pistol had disappeared with them.

If there were no major developments in the next twenty-four hours James and Sean agreed there was little point in hanging around any longer in Tanzania and that they would both return to Kenya.

30

MATTHEW KALINGA ARRIVED at the Central Police Station bright and early the next morning in anticipation of his interview with Marais at 10.30 a.m. Marais failed to appear at the given time and by noon there was still no sign of him. Kalinga was disappointed but not surprised. His non-arrival was not unexpected. Kalinga himself had set noon as a deadline and he had already planned his next move.

He knew Marais had more than one way of exiting the country, other than the obvious flight from Dar Es Salaam. Even so he had sent a team of police officers to the airport earlier that day on the off chance he would be arrogant enough to try and take a flight from the main airport. They had issued photographs of Marais to all the airline check-in staff, security guards and immigration officers. If Marais turned up the instruction was to arrest him immediately.

Kalinga had set up a plan to raid the warehouse near the airport where Marais's arms cache was still being stored. The warehouse had remained under constant surveillance since Marais had moved the arms there. None of the trucks had left and very few people had arrived or left the warehouse. Those that had were followed and their movements monitored. When the time came to raid the warehouse they would be picked up simultaneously by squads of police for questioning.

Shortly before five o'clock in the afternoon the armed police surrounding the warehouse received a call from Kalinga to go in and arrest all those on the premises and seize the arms. The police were supported by a Special

Forces squad of Tanzanian troops who sealed off all the roads leading to and from the warehouse with roadblocks.

When the police moved in, those inside were handcuffed and taken to the Central Police Station under armed escort to be interviewed and charged. Within half an hour of the warehouse raid Kalinga ordered a squad of ten officers waiting one kilometre outside the Golden City to move in and arrest David Williams. He was brought back to Dar to be personally interviewed by Kalinga.

After an initial interview he was taken to the police cells and held overnight for further questioning in the morning. Kalinga thought a night in the cells might encourage Williams to agree to testify against Marais. It was clear that Marais had now left Tanzania and it would be very unlikely that he would ever return except if he was extradited from another country and brought back to face trial.

Williams knew all about the arms being held at the warehouse. After the break-in he had visited the original warehouse where they were stored. It was on his instructions that they were moved. Several of the guards who were arrested were prepared to testify to that.

Kalinga decided that he would present the facts to Williams the next morning and that he had been tipped off by MI6 and the Pentagon about the intended coup in Kenya. Kalinga knew that Williams would quickly realise he would end up as the sacrificial lamb. He only had one option and that would be to agree to testify against Marais in return for immunity from prosecution himself or at least a plea bargain, with a promise of only a suspended sentence.

Kalinga's next move was to announce a press conference for the next morning at 11.00 a.m. He invited all the local press, international correspondents and representatives from the American Embassy and the British, South African and Kenyan High Commissions. Once his plans were in place he left his office at 2100 hours and drove up to the Golden City to meet with Chidoli. James and Sean were also invited to attend.

Edward Chidoli was all smiles after Matthew Kalinga explained to him the latest situation regarding Williams's arrest. It was obvious Marais had fled the country. It seemed the Golden City would now be Chidoli's sole responsibility unless of course Marais somehow managed to avoid prosecution.

"James, it seems now your work is finished here. Although I must say the turn of events is not entirely down to you. I am sure your final invoice will reflect that!"

James shifted slightly in his chair. He knew what Chidoli was suggesting.

"Of course, I won't charge you for the time Martin spent in prison!"

Everyone laughed.

"Now you mention Martin, have you heard from him since his escape?" asked Kalinga.

"Not a word. I'm at a loss to know where he is."

James didn't want to expand on any further explanations about Martin's disappearance.

"My intelligence sources tell me that your friend Delport has not reported back to the American Embassy. Do you know anything of his whereabouts?"

James looked at Chidoli and back to Kalinga.

"I've absolutely no idea where he is. The last I saw of him was when we went diving off Bongoyo Island."

"It would be a good idea if you and Sean came to the press conference tomorrow," interrupted Chidoli, as if to stop Kalinga asking any further questions.

They both nodded their agreement.

"I have one more question before you go, James," said Chidoli. His tone had changed and he had a more serious look on his face.

"What might that be?" asked James, frowning.

"I am going to have to sack Williams. He is very much Marais's man and with the threat of prosecution hanging over him I can't possibly keep him employed at the Golden City."

"Do you want someone to replace him?"

"Yes, James. Would you consider the position as Head of Security for yourself? I can pay you a good salary and the lifestyle you would enjoy would be second to none here. Your family could move here with you."

James's response was quick. It was almost as if he was prepared for the question.

"Edward, I am very flattered but I have too much at stake with my own business. I could however recommend someone who would be eminently suitable for the job and they would come with impeccable references. Would you like me to fax you their details in the next few days?"

"That's a great shame, James, but please fax me those details. I can always arrange an interview with him." He turned to Sean with a smile. "I don't suppose you would like to be Head of Security on a temporary basis until I can find a permanent candidate?"

Sean looked taken aback. He smiled in response.

"Edward, I too am very flattered but I am not a security specialist. I would not be able to provide you with the expertise of someone like James. We will be gone straight after the press conference. I need to get back to Mombasa. I also have another business to run. Do you know anything more about Marais's drug-running involvement? Will anything come of that?" he asked changing the subject.

"Now we have got him implicated in the coup plot in Kenya, any charges likely to arise in connection with his drugs cartel will be held on file for the future," said Kalinga.

"So he's got away with it!" said Sean in disgust. He was greatly disturbed by the rise in drug-associated crime problems in Kenya. He wanted somehow to cut off Marais's drug running into Kenya, even if it was only temporary. He already had his own plan as to how he would do that. He would speak to James about it on their return journey to Mombasa.

"Only if the coup charges don't stick will we pursue the drugs cartel. One thing at a time," responded Kalinga.

"Gentlemen, I think we've covered all we can here tonight," said Chidoli. "We will see each other at the press conference tomorrow. Some of us have got families to go home to."

Sean nodded his agreement. He couldn't wait to see Achieng again. It had now been nearly three weeks since he had seen her.

§

Williams looked tired and drained when he shuffled into the interview room at 7.00 a.m., flanked by two armed policemen. He had spent a sleepless night in one of the cells with twenty other prisoners. His eyes were red and bloodshot.

Kalinga was already seated in a wooden chair behind a long brown trestle table. He didn't stand up when Williams entered but beckoned to him to sit down in the chair opposite him. The two policemen stood behind him as he sat down.

"I want a lawyer."

"All in good time, but first let me tell you about your boss Mr Marais and the latest developments regarding him."

Kalinga had a deadpan expression on his face. He spoke totally without emotion.

By the time Kalinga had explained to Williams about the information he had received on the planned coup in Kenya, Williams looked a broken man. What little colour he had in his face when he arrived was now totally drained from it. He looked ashen and at least ten years older. He knew he was staring at a prison sentence of at least five years. He wrung his hands in despair as Kalinga observed him across the table.

"If I was to help you with your investigations, where would I stand then?" Williams spoke in a hushed whisper. He couldn't bring himself to come right out and ask for immunity from prosecution. He wanted Kalinga to make the offer.

"I cannot make any promises but I can speak to my superiors and ask them if we can broker a deal. I am sure you don't want to spend the next five years of your life in one of our prisons."

Williams shook his head and bit his lip. Kalinga could see he was doing all he could to contain his emotions.

"I am prepared to make a statement but first I want my lawyer present."

"Okay."

Kalinga pushed a telephone across the table. Williams picked up the receiver and dialled his lawyer's number. Kalinga stood up and left the room.

Half an hour later Williams's lawyer arrived. He spent twenty minutes on his own with him, preparing a statement. When it was completed he asked one of the policemen waiting outside to contact Kalinga.

Within twenty minutes of his return Kalinga had offered Williams immunity from prosecution. He had already spoken to the President and the Attorney General who had given any deal their blessing.

Williams signed his handwritten statement and his lawyer acted as his witness. He also signed a document to the effect that he had made the statement voluntarily and had not signed under duress. He passed it to Kalinga who looked very pleased indeed.

"Thank you, Mr Williams. I would be grateful if you would wait here for a few more minutes while I get a copy typed up for you to sign."

Williams nodded his agreement before leaning his elbows on the table and clutching his head in his hands. He was visibly shaking as Kalinga stood up and left the room. He returned ten minutes later with the statement typed in duplicate, by which time Williams had regained his composure. He signed the statement and Kalinga passed his lawyer a copy.

"Thank you again, Mr Williams. You are free to go. However I have retained your passport. Please therefore do not attempt to leave the country. You must report to the Central Police Station once a week until such time as there is a trial. In the meantime I will arrange for one of my officers to protect you. He will not be far from you. You are now a marked man. When Marais finds out you are acting as a witness for the prosecution your life will be in grave danger."

Williams nodded. He whispered a hoarse "Thank you" as he stood and walked slowly from the room.

At 11.00 a.m. Kalinga arrived at the press conference to address the gathered throng of journalists and High Commission staff. As he walked up to the dais, flashbulbs were going off and there was a buzz of anticipation around the room. The sound of voices filled the air. A multitude of different languages mixed.

Kalinga tapped the microphone that curled back towards him on the front of the lectern. The loud knocking that echoed through the PA system captured people's attention. A hush fell over the room. Kalinga read from a statement he had prepared earlier:

"Ladies and gentlemen, earlier today I issued a warrant for the arrest of Victor Marais, the Chairman and Managing Director of the Golden City Casino resort. The warrant has been issued in connection with an alleged coup plot that was due to take place in Kenya in the next few days. Yesterday evening a team of police raided a warehouse near to the airport and seized a huge cache of arms. The warehouse is owned by a company registered in Marais's name. We arrested a number of people at the warehouse and they are currently being held at the Central Police Station where they are helping us with our enquiries. Our intelligence reports suggest that a very senior politician in Kenya is involved. At the moment I cannot reveal his name to you. As soon as we can confirm his involvement we will be releasing a further statement."

With that he picked up the papers from the lectern and stepped down from the dais. Two policemen walked in front of him and pushed their way through the mêlée of journalists to create a pathway for Kalinga to leave the room.

§

One hour later James and Sean were on their way back to Mombasa. They had borrowed a Pajero from Edward Chidoli for the journey by road. Once in Mombasa, Sean would send Opiyo back to Dar with the Pajero. After returning it to Edward Chidoli, he could get the bus back. Sean was at the wheel. He took the highway from Dar through Kibaha and Mlandizi before turning north at the Chalinze junction for the 245-kilometre drive to Tanga, Tanzania's second largest seaport, for an overnight stop.

The tarmac road was in reasonable condition except for the occasional large pothole. Five hours later, having taken it in turns driving, they had driven through Manga, Mkata, Segara, Hale, Muheza and Ngomeni before eventually arriving shortly after nightfall at Tanga. They checked into the Mkonge Hotel on the seafront.

Throughout their journey, James and Sean had discussed the latest developments regarding Marais. His and the disappearance of T J, Martin and Chris were the main topics of conversation. They agreed there was a very good chance Marais had initially travelled to the relative safety of Kenya. In all probability he was taken in the Bora 20 up to Mombasa and then via a flight to Nairobi. Charles Bett would have certainly helped him to hide away there for a while. Bett though would be careful not to risk any more involvement with Marais now that the coup had been exposed. When his name was revealed by Kalinga as the prime suspect in Kenya he would have a lot of explaining to do to the President. With the number of disappearances of political enemies in Kenya, Bett would be in a very high-risk situation himself.

At seven o'clock the next morning they were on their way again up towards the border crossing at Horohoro. The condition of the tarmac road deteriorated from Tanga and it took them a good two and a half hours to reach the place. It had been an interesting drive and they had deliberately taken the route Marais's drug courier matatus generally took on their journey from Dar.

T J had told them previously that the couriers driving the matatus would telephone their police contacts at the border crossing, before leaving Tanga, to make sure they were on duty and to give them their expected time of arrival. This ensured a trouble-free passage across the border. If their matatus were ever searched it was only ever a half-hearted search to satisfy any suspicious onlookers. The couriers paid the border policemen on their payroll handsomely.

At Lunga Lunga, on the Kenyan side of the border, a similar system operated and the matatus would be waved through fairly quickly. This was in contrast to other ordinary people who were sometimes stuck for hours at the border dealing with all sorts of supposed formalities.

At both border control points, Sean and James handed over their Kenyan and British passports respectively, for inspection. Sean received a warm welcome from the Kenyan policeman on duty at the Lunga Lunga control point. They were soon on their way up towards Mombasa. As they reached a high point on the road south of Ramisi, Sean pulled over and stopped.

"James, let's have a five-minute stop here and you can admire the view."

They climbed out of the car and looked back at the panoramic view of Tanzania in the distance. The vastness of the land before them was an awesome sight to behold. Sean saw this as his chance to talk to James of the plan he had been concocting on the journey to cut off part of Marais's drug supply routes into Kenya. There was little he could do about the matatu route but he had an idea for the route through Benki Island.

"James, I wonder whether you would help me with an idea I have been thinking about ever since our conversations with T J about Marais's drug-trafficking activities through Benki Island."

James looked at Sean curiously.

"Go on."

"As you know Benki is one of Marais's major drop-off points via boat into Kenya for his trafficking empire."

"Hmm," James was considering this.

"Well, what are the chances of you helping me get to Benki Island and blow up or set fire to his store there? We can destroy all the drugs he has. If we do that and word gets out that has happened, surely Marais or his associates wouldn't risk continuing to use it in the foreseeable future. At least not until he has sorted out all his current problems," Sean said.

James raised his eyebrows. He had a habit of doing that when he wanted to bide his time to collect his thoughts.

"That's one hell of a project. How do you propose doing that? Why don't you simply let the Kenyan Police know about the drugs store and get them to raid the island?"

"James, you know as well as I do that thanks to Bett, Marais has many of the Mombasa-based police on his payroll. If there was any hint of a raid, Marais would be tipped off first and any drugs would be moved immediately!"

"Let me have a think about your idea. Come on, let's get

back to your place. I'm sure you're looking forward to seeing Achieng and all the other women in your life!"

He knew full well Sean was in a dilemma about Nikki and Njeri. Sean scowled.

"I don't need any reminding about that!"

There was very little traffic on the main highway and two hours later they were on the ferry from Likoni to Mombasa island. Once Sean had driven up the ramp from the ferry he headed straight back to his house in Nyali. It was almost two o'clock, so it was too late to collect Achieng from school. Akoth and Opiyo would already have done so.

Shortly before they reached home, Sean drove past the house of another of Kenya's well-known drug barons. Incredibly he was one of his neighbours. He pointed the house out to James as they passed by. The palatial residence was the epitome of overstated opulence.

On arrival at his gate he tooted his horn and waited outside. The askari on duty came out through the small side gate to check who it was. At first he didn't recognise the vehicle but when he realised it was Sean, a big smile appeared on his face. He quickly returned inside the compound and opened up the big iron gates for him to drive through.

Sean parked up and climbed from the Pajero. There were whoops of delight as Akoth spotted him from the kitchen window.

"Achieng, Achieng," she shouted at the top of her voice, "Baba is home, Baba is home!"

Moments later the kitchen door burst open and Achieng appeared, closely followed by Akoth and Opiyo. As Sean saw Achieng running towards him a big lump appeared in his throat. He was overcome with emotion. He bent down as she jumped up into his arms and flung her arms around his neck.

"Baba, Baba, I've missed you so much," she cried.

He felt the wetness of her tears on his neck as she broke

into sobs of joy. Akoth stood in the background wiping her floury hands on her apron.

"Mr Sean, it's good to have you back." She smiled and clapped her hands together excitedly. Opiyo stood next to her and saluted.

"Baba, Baba, promise me you won't go away again and leave me," wailed Achieng. She released her grip around Sean's neck and planted a huge kiss on his cheek. Sean looked at James. He knew full well he had other plans and he knew he couldn't lie to her as he had done so many times in the past to Louise.

"I have one more project to finish and then I promise I won't leave you again," he said quietly.

He put Achieng back down on the ground. He had only been away a short time but it looked like she had grown noticeably bigger.

"So when are you going away again, Baba?"

Sean gave James a sideways glance.

"In the next couple of days and then my project will be finished for good."

With that he took Achieng's hand.

31

THE FOLLOWING DAY the major Kenyan newspapers were full of stories about the Tanzanian authorities' warrant for the arrest of Victor Marais bankrolling a coup in Kenya. Incredibly Charles Bett was named as the Kenyan politician involved with him. Several investigative journalists from international newspapers had already uncovered stories about some of the businesses they were both major shareholders in. Bett's office had issued denials of his being involved in any criminal activities. So far he himself had made no comment on the allegations.

Such was the furore surrounding the reports in *The Nation* and *The East African Standard* that reports began to appear in the international media. The midday news on BBC Television in London and on the World Service contained brief details about the latest scandal to hit Kenyan politics. Other stories followed in newspapers and on radio and television news bulletins around the world. Kenya, which had the largest economy in East Africa, was consistently ranked among the most corrupt nations in the world by international organisations.

By early evening Charles Bett was left with no alternative but to appear in front of the media gathered at Nyayo House on Uhuru Highway in Nairobi to deny his involvement in the coup. He read from a brief statement prepared earlier by his lawyers:

"I, Charles Arap Bett, categorically deny any involvement in the alleged coup plot to overthrow our beloved President. I am outraged by these allegations against me and have instructed my lawyers to issue civil proceedings against any person or organisation who continues to make these claims. Have no doubt that I will be pursuing the individuals and organisations vigorously through the courts and I will be seeking substantial damages. I love my country and have been a loyal, trusted and devoted servant to my country and to my President. I have nothing further to say on the matter."

Sean switched off the television at the end of the news.

"Did you see his body language, James? If ever a man was guilty, he is!" said Sean, as he slumped back in his chair.

"I agree with you. I have never seen a man with such piercing, evil eyes. It was almost impossible to avoid his stare. His eyes seemed completely glazed over during the whole of his statement. He was doing his level best to contain his anger. He looks a very dangerous and ruthless man."

"Now will you help me to destroy the drugs store on Benki Island?"

"Sean, you are already in a very dangerous situation. Marais suspects you had something to do with the prison breakout. He will have done his research and will know exactly where you live. You are putting your life and your family at risk. Not only Achieng's but Louise's also. Men like Marais and Bett will stop at nothing to protect their business interests. Their network of criminal activities and contacts extends far beyond the borders of Kenya and Tanzania. My advice to you is to leave it well alone. You will spend the rest of your life looking over your shoulder if you cause any more trouble."

Sean looked grim as he listened to what James was saying. He was about to speak when James continued.

"Sean, we have all been well paid for our work in Tanzania. I say again I think you should leave things well alone. I have to leave for my next project in two days' time anyway."

"Come on, James. We're now quits. I feel I have repaid you for the help you gave me to find Akinyi's killers in Germany. Now it is my turn to ask a favour again."

James couldn't quite believe what he was hearing. Sean was trying emotional blackmail. He was surprised at his friend.

"Sean, what is it to you that we destroy the drugs on Benki?"

"The problem in Kenya is that more and more young people are being introduced to drugs at a younger and younger age. As they become more and more dependent it is causing a complete breakdown of the family structure. Corruption and collusion by policemen has undermined the war against them, Marais and Bett control most of the dealer networks in Kenya. It is becoming a huge industry and they are making obscene amounts of money from it. I see it as a way to cut off some of the supply before it even reaches Nairobi."

James stared long and hard at Sean. He took another sip from the beer he had in his hand. He scratched his chin and pulled at his left ear.

"Okay, Sean, but tomorrow is the only day I can help you. You'd better have a very good plan."

"I knew I could rely on you, James. Mark my words it won't take long for us to implement my plan once we are on Benki."

"What *is* your plan? How do you propose blowing up or setting fire to a drugs haul if you find it on Benki?"

"I was hoping you would help me with that. At least you will know how to use explosives."

James laughed.

"So where am I going to get explosives from in Mombasa at such short notice?"

Sean looked embarrassed.

"Well how about using petrol? We could soak the drugs in petrol and simply ignite the lot in one hit."

"It's as simple as that, is it?"

Sean looked annoyed with James's sarcasm.

"Pouring petrol over a pile of drugs shouldn't be too difficult. I don't have to be a fully paid up member of the SAS to do that!"

James smiled as Sean retaliated.

"Okay, okay. I will help but how do you propose getting there?"

Sean explained his plan. It was too obvious to cross to Benki from Bodo village, the normal crossing point from the mainland to the island. They would be seen by too many people.

"Opiyo has a friend Juma, who works for some of the tour companies. He regularly takes clients to Benki and he owns a small wooden boat powered by a fifteen-horsepower outboard engine. It's a wahoo, made from a mixture of fibreglass and marine plywood. We can travel across in that."

Juma would meet them at Ramisi Bridge where it crossed the Ramisi River on the main Mombasa-to-Lunga Lunga highway. The Ramisi Bridge was the highest point of navigation on the Ramisi, which rose in the Shimba Hills. From there it was approximately ten kilometres to the estuary where the river flowed into the Indian Ocean opposite Benki Island. Between the estuary and Benki there were numerous sandbars hidden below the surface of the sea. Juma was an experienced sailor who could navigate the waters easily. Once they landed on the island, Juma would lead them to the store where the drugs were supposedly held.

"Can Juma be trusted?"

"Most definitely, not only is he a lifelong friend of Opiyo's but they spent two years in the Kenyan Army together. In addition he and the other Benki islanders detest Marais with a passion."

"Tomorrow it is then."

"Thanks, James, I owe you one again," said Sean with renewed enthusiasm. "We will need some guns, James. I have some we can take with us."

He kept a shotgun and a Browning pistol in a locked gun cabinet at his house. James raised his eyebrows.

"How long have you kept guns at your place?"

"I've had them ever since I moved here. So far I have not needed to use them but they are a good insurance policy. More and more burglaries are committed every day now."

§

Sean rose shortly after the sun was up. It would be about an hour before Achieng awoke so it gave him a chance to prepare for their trip to Benki. When Achieng finally woke, he helped Akoth make her breakfast then drove her to school. He was a little apprehensive about meeting Nikki again but relaxed when he saw her reaction to his arrival. She smiled sweetly when she saw him and looked remarkably cool. She was dressed in her usual school attire of green Polo shirt and black skirt. It was a far cry from the way she dressed for their trip to the Tamarind.

"Good morning, Miss Greene," he said rather formally, "or can I still call you Nikki?" He lowered his voice slightly so Achieng wouldn't hear too much of their conversation.

"It's no problem to call me Nikki," she said as she put Sean more at ease. "How was your trip to Tanzania?"

"Oh, it was good and eventful."

"You and James wouldn't happen to have anything to do with the latest revelations of the Golden City and all that's being reported in all the newspapers at the moment?" she asked. She had her suspicions.

Her question caught him off guard.

"Don't be so ridiculous!" he responded rather more curtly than he intended. Realising how it must have sounded he apologised quickly. "I'm sorry but I didn't mean to sound so abrupt. I'm a little tired, that's all."

"It just seems a strange coincidence that you've returned shortly after all these revelations."

Before he had a chance to reply Nikki said, "That offer of dinner at my apartment still stands."

"I thought you would never ask again, after letting you down the last time. I would be delighted."

"Can you come this Saturday evening? Unless of course you have another engagement that crops up!" she teased him.

"Saturday would be good. I look forward to it. But now I must make a move." He looked at his watch. "Achieng, Opiyo is collecting you today. I will see you later." He waved at Achieng who was by then playing with a group of other schoolchildren. "See you Saturday, Nikki."

On his way home he filled his car up with fuel and also filled up two, five-litre jerry cans to take with them to Benki. He also picked up the daily newspapers at the Kenol station. The papers were full of stories about Bett and his network of companies. The front pages had photographs of him staring out from them. Back at home he was greeted by a very serious-looking James.

"Edward Chidoli has telephoned. There has been a break-in at the Golden City bank vault."

"Wow!" said Sean. "Tell me more," he said.

Apparently, some time after four in the morning, three armed men entered the offices to the bank vault and overpowered the guards. It must have been someone with knowledge of the codes to the safe because they were in and out in less than thirty minutes.

"They got away with an estimated $5,000,000. Part of it was the weekend takings and part of the money was a surplus that Marais stored there."

"Five million dollars! Has Chidoli any idea who was involved?"

"No, but he suspects Williams might have had something to do with it. He was the only one other than Marais and Chidoli who knew the combinations. Chidoli hadn't changed them since he sacked Williams earlier that day."

"That sounds a little too coincidental for it to be Williams. Surely he wouldn't have had enough time to organise a break-in so quickly? Maybe it is Chidoli himself who organised it. Maybe he has seized an unexpected opportunity."

Sean didn't realise the implications of what he had said. James was surprised at Sean's lateral thinking as it was something he hadn't considered.

"Yes, but Williams might have planned it well ahead of his arrest knowing that his days with Marais were numbered anyway. I think your suggestion of Chidoli being responsible is a little far-fetched."

James seemed to dismiss Sean's theory out of hand.

"Possibly, but aren't T J, Chris and Martin a more obvious choice?"

"Hmm," pondered James, "I must admit the thought had crossed my mind but I think we are letting our imaginations run away with us."

"Come on, James, we can discuss this on the way to Ramisi. Juma will be waiting for us."

Two and a half hours later Sean pulled over in a lay-by near the Ramisi Bridge. He had brought an askari with him to guard his car while they were gone. As they pulled up Juma appeared from under a coconut palm. He was chewing miraa, a local herbal drug that helped keep people awake. He greeted them with a big smile and took one of the five-litre jerry cans from the back of the car. The askari assisted by carrying the second. Juma was dressed in shorts with canvas shoes on his feet. He wore an oil-stained tee shirt that had several small tears in the chest. He looked an unlikely boat captain.

§

Five minutes later they climbed into the boat and were on their way down the river. The water was a murky, muddy brown and the channel very narrow and meandering between the riverbanks on both sides. A mixture of scrub and vegetation full of thickly spread mangroves overhung the river creating a secret world of shadows and shafts of sunlight. The phut-phut sound of the engine filled the air and mingled with the sound of birdsong. Several colourful kingfishers flitted to and fro.

The journey was long and arduous. There was an eeriness that surrounded them. As they continued downstream the river became slightly wider. A flurry of movement to the water ahead of them caused by a huge crocodile as it slid from the riverbank in search of prey made Sean and James more aware of the dangers that surrounded them. Juma continued to take things in his stride. It was an everyday occurrence for him to see crocodiles.

Occasionally they were confronted by huge tree stumps in the middle of the channel. Juma changed course to avoid them. As they rounded one bend in the river they were confronted immediately by one huge stump that reared out of the water and twisted towards them like a serpent's head. They all ducked to avoid the branches that spiralled down towards the water.

Two hours into their journey the river became clearer as they neared the mouth which flowed into the sea. The channel widened and the water began to flow much more quickly. Above them there was hardly a cloud in sight.

As they travelled into Benki Bay a light aircraft took off from the island and flew out across the headland near Ras Kidomoni as it headed directly out to sea. The drone of the engine became quieter as it disappeared into the distance before turning south towards Tanzania. A short time later it changed course and swung back round across the estuary almost directly above them towards Benki Island. The pilot dropped the aircraft low and skimmed across the water only two metres above the surface. He turned south again across the headland at Ras Wasini, on the mainland overlooking Wasini Island. He performed the same manoeuvre several times before eventually disappearing north in the direction of Diani Beach and Mombasa.

Sean had a dry burning sensation in his mouth. Juma slowed the boat down and cut the engine. He let the boat drift close to the shore opposite Benki. They had a clear view across to Benki from there. A couple of large dhows that were normally used to transport tourists across to the island were anchored in the bay. It was now high tide and there was no sign of any of the sandbars that appeared during low tide. Out in the middle of the bay the sea was becoming choppier.

It was now nearly half past five. Another hour or so and they could travel across to Benki under cover of darkness. As night fell, Juma started the engine again and turned the boat towards their destination. He guided it through several similar small boats as they neared the shoreline, eventually coming to a halt about a boat's length from the beach. He had pulled up alongside a sleek-looking speedboat, which seemed out of place among the wooden dhows.

In the background the rhythmic sounds of drumming from the village filled the night air. Juma dropped a small anchor into the water. He slipped over the side and beckoned to James to pass him the first jerry can. He lifted it above his head and waded towards the shore. He was only about five-feet-five and the water was up around his mid-thighs. James followed and Sean passed him the second jerry can. Sean jumped into the water, careful to keep the shotgun and the Browning pistol, that he had earlier wrapped in plastic bags, above his head.

Once they were all on the beach Juma gave a soft whistle that sounded like a bird calling. Moments later two men appeared. He indicated for them to pick up the jerry cans. He looked at James and Sean and he could see they were gravely concerned at the arrival of the two men.

"There's nothing to worry about, Mr Sean. They are here to help us."

Sean and James nodded their approval.

Juma led the way and they all trooped after him in single file across the beach and along a narrow pathway. First James, then Sean and then the two newcomers brought up the rear. The light from the moon was enough for everyone to see reasonably clearly. Sean carried the pistol and handed the shotgun to James, which he cradled in his left arm, holding the stock with his right hand. Several geckos scuttled across the pathway in front of them. The drums could still be heard in the background.

They walked at a steady pace for all of five minutes. Suddenly Juma held his arm out and indicated for them to stop. He turned and raised his index finger to his lips and beckoned for James to come to him.

"Mr James," he whispered. "Look over there and you will see the storeroom."

James peered over the top of a bush and he could clearly see a wooden building about the size of a small garage. It was enough to fit maybe two cars in it but that would be a tight squeeze. The roof was covered in makuti. The building was dimly lit. He was surprised that there didn't appear to be anyone guarding it.

"How many guards are there normally on duty?" whispered James to Juma. He began to remove the shotgun slowly from the plastic bag. He checked the safety catch and slipped it to the on position. Sean removed the pistol from his bag.

"Normally they only have two guards on duty. Sometimes we see a black guard but most of the time it is muzungus. My two friends here have been watching the store all day and there are definitely only two guards on the island at the moment. Two others left about an hour ago in a small plane."

James called Sean over and whispered a few instructions to Juma. They all knew what they had to do. Sean and Juma remained where they were behind the bush. James disappeared and skirted around behind the store. Minutes later he gave a shrill whistle to signal he was in position. Juma responded with a whistle too. With that he headed directly towards the front door of the store.

When he reached the door he gave a loud knock. There was no response from inside. He gave another loud knock. This time a white man appeared. He was very tall and well built. He wore a sweat-stained white singlet, revealing tattooed arms. His dark hair was closely cropped. He peered out into the dim light.

"What do you want, Kaffir," he barked at Juma in a thick South African accent.

Juma bowed his head slightly.

"Bwana, there is a problem with your speedboat at the beach. Come quickly."

The white man frowned.

"I hope you're telling me the truth. If you're wasting my time and I get down there and there is no problem I will give you a beating." He slurred his words as if he was slightly drunk. He called inside to his fellow-guard. "I'll be back in ten minutes, Jannie. There's a problem with the boat."

Juma led the way. Five minutes later the guard was staring down the barrel of Sean's pistol.

"You lying little Kaffir," he screamed at Juma.

"That's enough of that language," said Sean calmly.

Juma pulled the man's decorated arms behind his back and proceeded to tie him up. Once his hands were bound, Juma kicked him behind his knees and he tumbled face forward onto the sandy pathway. He let out a gurgled yell as he collected a mouthful of sand as he hit the deck. Juma smiled gleefully as he exacted his sweet revenge on the abusive guard. He began to tie his ankles together, pulling them behind the guard to tie his ankle ropes to his hands behind him. Then he rolled him over on his side and between him and his two assistants they dragged the big white man to the base of a palm tree and roped him securely to that. Finally he taped the now groggy man's mouth to stop him shouting. He gave the guard a gentle slap on his face with the palm of his hand, as if to confirm he was the one now in a position of power. Once he completed his work they all headed back to the store.

Juma gave out a low whistle to signal to James he was back. James was still lurking in the shadows. Once again Juma knocked on the storeroom door. This time another white man appeared.

"Is that you, Peter."

"No, bwana, it's me, Juma. Peter said to come and help him with the boat."

He stepped forward towards Juma and was about to grab him by the throat. In a flash James appeared out of the shadows and clubbed the guard over the back of his head with the butt of his shotgun, and knocked him out cold. He hit the deck with a loud thud. Moments later he was tied up in the same fashion as his compatriot. When Juma's two assistants appeared with the jerry cans they dragged the still unconscious guard away from the store and deposited him in the bushes about fifty metres away. By the time they reached them he was beginning to regain consciousness.

Meanwhile James, Sean and Juma entered the store. After a quick search it was apparent no one else was there. Within minutes they had uncovered a stash of heroin packed in brown sacks. What followed was the discovery of a huge haul of cocaine. James twisted a knife into a couple of the bags and white powder seeped out. He stuck his finger in and tasted it. He spat it out and wiped his lips with the back of his hand.

"Pure cocaine!"

He was experienced enough to know what it was from the time he had spent in the Colombian jungles training police to search and destroy many of the drug-manufacturing plants. He stepped back from the haul, picked up one of the jerry cans and began pouring the petrol all over it.

"Sean, get the other can and spray some of the petrol around the outside of the building."

Within minutes the whole place reeked of fuel. The store

was now a time bomb waiting to explode. Outside Juma had prepared a couple of bottles filled with petrol and stuffed with rags. James and Sean reappeared outside. James nodded at Juma who pulled a lighter from his pocket. Everyone stepped back. Juma lit the rags at the top of the first bottle and threw it into the store. The sound of breaking glass could be heard as it shattered on the stone floor. There was a loud explosion as the petrol from the bottle ignited and rapidly spread around the room. He slammed the door shut.

They all ran about twenty metres away from the building and Juma lit the rags at the top of the second bottle and tossed it onto the makuti roofing. It quickly ignited the thatch. A crackling sound could be heard as the tinder-dry roof burst into flames.

"Let's go," shouted James.

They all turned and ran back towards the boat. As they passed the tree where Peter was bound, James stopped momentarily and pulled the tape from his mouth so that he could breathe more easily.

"I'm sure your friends will be here to rescue you soon enough when they see their store burning."

Five minutes later they were scrambling back aboard the boat for the journey across the bay and back up the Ramisi. It wasn't something Sean relished as he thought of the crocodiles and the other hazards they might encounter on their way back in the dark. They looked back in triumph as they watched the flames from the burning store lighting up the night sky in the distance.

"Thanks, James, and you, Juma. I think we carried out a successful night's work."

"Yes, it was remarkably easy," remarked James. "I wish all my operations were as easy as that was."

Juma laughed loudly.

"I hope we've got rid of Marais and his drugs from our island at last. I hope he never comes back."

"Juma, let's hope for your sake he doesn't. Those two South Africans back there know who you are. Once they are released by Marais's men when they return to the island they will be after you with a vengeance," said James.

"Don't worry, bwana," Juma laughed again. "I've arranged for some of the villagers to release them in an hour. I think they'll be too scared to hang around for too long. They'll disappear for their own safety rather than allow themselves to be brought back to face Marais for not doing their job properly and letting the store be burnt to the ground."

"I guess you may be right about that," nodded James with a wry smile.

With that James pulled on the throttle and the boat increased speed back up the Ramisi.

32

A FEW DAYS before Christmas, Sean was waiting at Moi International Airport to meet James, Yolanda and their two children, Mark and Maria. They had flown from London with Sean's elder daughter Louise, to spend the Christmas holidays with him and Achieng. As they appeared through the arrivals gate, Sean and Achieng ran to Louise and embraced her. She was now a teenager and was growing into a beautiful young woman. Sean felt a pride he hadn't experienced before about her. Achieng was excited to see her sister and took her hand. She was talking non-stop as she pulled her towards Sean's car in the car park.

Yolanda, Mark and Maria looked very well. Sean hugged Yolanda and gave her a kiss on each cheek. He shook hands with Mark and Maria. James meanwhile had waited in the background. He stepped forward and shook hands with Sean. His handshake was as firm as ever but for the first time in his life Sean thought he looked haggard and mentally troubled. His left arm was in a sling.

"You are all looking so well, except for you, James. You look exhausted. What happened to your arm?" Sean asked with a concerned note in his voice.

James glanced furtively at Yolanda, who looked less than pleased.

"Oh, it's nothing. I'll tell you about it later."

James winced. Sean wasn't sure whether it was pain or because of Yolanda's apparent displeasure about his injury.

"We have a lot to catch up on. I have some news for you,

James, and I am sure you can fill in a few gaps since your departure."

Sean winked at James. It didn't go unnoticed by Yolanda.

"You two are incorrigible!" She scowled at them.

"Come on, guys, let's go," said Sean cheerfully. "You are here to enjoy yourselves. The party starts now!"

He took Louise's luggage trolley and headed towards the cars. Louise and Achieng had already climbed into the estate car that Opiyo had brought with him.

Sean had arranged a barbecue as a welcome party for everyone and after they had all settled into their rooms, he lit the charcoals. It was a beautiful clear day at the coast with hardly a cloud in sight. Sean and Opiyo had recently completed building a small swimming pool and the children had already jumped in and were having great fun splashing around.

Yolanda was the first to appear by the barbecue. She looked more beautiful every time Sean saw her. She was tall, slender and her light brown skin contrasted with the white tee shirt and shorts she was wearing. Her hair was cut shorter than she usually wore it.

"Is there a woman in your life at the moment, Sean?"

"Well, it so happens there is someone and she'll be here any minute now." He smiled proudly, as he glanced at his watch.

By this time James had also arrived and he caught the tail end of their conversation. James and Yolanda had both relaxed and their earlier digs at each other seemed long forgotten. Moments later Nikki Greene appeared. Sean left the barbecue he was prodding with a pair of tongs and walked across the grass to greet her. He kissed her affectionately on the lips then turned to his friends.

"James, you two have met before, but Yolanda, may I introduce a friend of mine. Nikki, this is James's wife, Yolanda."

The two women shook hands. Nikki looked stunning. Her blonde hair was tied back from her face. Her skin was a golden brown colour. She looked at ease in Sean's company.

"I would like to think I am a little more than a friend of yours, Mr Cameron." She gave Sean a dig in the ribs and laughed. Sean looked embarrassed and hopped from foot to foot.

"Of course you are more than a friend, my darling." He squeezed Nikki's hand to give her reassurance. He was not normally so tactile and Yolanda was surprised to see such a change in him.

"Nikki, perhaps you would like to take Yolanda for a walk along the beach. It will give you two a chance to get to know each other. Food will be ready in about half an hour."

"What you mean is you men want to talk without us around."

Nikki certainly seemed to have the measure of Sean. But she took Yolanda's arm and they walked through the small wooden gate that led to the beach. James pulled a bottle of Tusker from the cold box and twisted the metal cap off with a bottle opener, using his one good hand.

"James, what happened to your arm?"

James grimaced.

"It's possible, Sean, I have lost the use of my left arm completely. I injured it on my project in Iraq after I left here last time. It hasn't been the same since. All the tendons and ligaments have been damaged."

"Jesus James, I'm sorry to hear that."

Sean laid out some sausages on a platter. They stood adjacent to the barbecue and watched the glow from the coals.

"Working for Chidoli as Head of Security might be a good option now."

"Don't be so negative, James. That is unlike you. I am sure it will heal up eventually. Talking of Chidoli, you can tell me about him and the latest news at the Golden City in a minute."

In the pool, the children were enjoying themselves. Even though she was the youngest, Achieng was certainly the noisiest, as she did her best to try and organise a game of water polo. Sean watched his youngest daughter with mild amusement.

"It looks like Nikki is the woman of the moment then!" James teased.

"Come on, James. We get on okay. She's great company. It's early days yet. I don't know what will happen in the future," Sean replied as he gave almost every conceivable reason why he didn't have a future with her.

"I think there is more to your relationship than you are letting on, my good friend. What happened with Njeri?"

Sean went on to explain that he had contemplated long and hard about renewing a relationship with Njeri. After a good deal of soul-searching he had come to the conclusion that it was not a good idea to get romantically linked with her again, certainly not for the foreseeable future. He was genuinely fond of her but he was still deeply troubled by her behaviour in England and her working for an escort agency. She had chosen the easy option to make money by prostituting her body when she didn't have to. There were many other women who had an equally rough start in life but they didn't resort to that. Sean was still good friends with her and he saw her regularly. She knew about Sean's relationship with Nikki. At first she was extremely jealous but lately she seemed to have come to terms with it. She had also started a new relationship with a German who owned a water-sports school near her boutique. She had taken control of her life and her business was now very successful. James nodded his approval.

"I think you have made the right decision in that department."

The barbecue was now ready for cooking. Sean lobbed on the sausages from the platter and pricked the skins with a fork. They quickly began to brown on the heat. The fat sizzled as it dropped onto the charcoals. Occasional flames burst up around the sausages and the aromatic smell of barbecued meat cooking filled the air. Sean looked over at the children in the pool.

"Hey guys, time to get out of the water. Achieng, when you get changed, tell Akoth and Opiyo to join us for lunch."

He turned up the music on the CD player and took another sip from his beer. He was feeling good.

In the few weeks after he returned to England, James had been able to follow some stories in the British newspapers about the failed coup in Kenya. However there weren't any startlingly new developments and the papers had soon lost interest.

Two weeks ago, one of Charles Bett's major political rivals, Robert Owuor, had been mysteriously killed at his country home in Siaya, in Western Kenya. There had been a break-in but robbery didn't seem to be the motive for the killing. There didn't appear to be anything missing from his house. Owuor had been at home alone, except for his maid, who was also murdered. There were all sorts of suggestions that Charles Bett had something to do with the killing but nothing could be proved. The police were still carrying out investigations. Shortly after the killings, several senior politicians linked to Bett began to make accusations that Owuor was the man behind the coup plot. Those who knew Owuor personally and even some of his other political opponents knew the accusations were false and where they stemmed from.

The fact that Bett had survived, not only politically but also physically, since he was named originally as the politician involved with the coup attempt, spoke volumes for the corruption in Kenya and the power that he wielded. He had managed to persuade the President that he had nothing to do with the coup. The two of them were in fact inextricably involved in a web of businesses and that was probably the only reason why Bett was still alive.

"James, the tragedy of Kenya is that there is no commitment by anyone in the current government to fight corruption."

"Sean, I speak as a black man of Ghanaian origin. The tragedy of Africa and not only of Kenya is that we have had great politicians and great brains with the chances to change the course of our continent. We still have some very clever politicians and we always will. If some of those Africans were allowed to produce their own blueprints, without corrupt influences from outside or within, to prevent so many of our people languishing in poverty, then we could take our people out of their misery almost immediately. For the life of me I do not understand why ordinary Africans stand by and watch countries like Zimbabwe being destroyed by tyrants such as they are. The issues in Zimbabwe go far beyond the mass destruction of white-owned farms. The government there is destroying opportunities for almost every black Zimbabwean who is suffering daily."

"I agree with you entirely, James. I have many black Kenyan friends who are more than capable of running a corrupt-free country. There will be political change here but I think it will take at least another fifteen years."

"Have you heard anything about Marais? The last I heard was that he was back in Mauritius, where he was running his hotel complex.

"As you probably know there was a trial in Tanzania in his absence. Williams appeared for the prosecution and testified against him. Marais was found guilty of arms dealing. He received a sentence of six years, and with it a quarter-of-a-million-dollar fine. The Tanzanian government seized the few assets he had left in Tanzania and have since been fighting a legal battle to have him extradited from Mauritius to be brought back to serve his sentence. Edward Chidoli is now head of a consortium that is running the Golden City. As for the casino staff in New Bagamoyo Prison, they are still there and expected to have to complete their sentences unless they are paroled as a result of diplomatic relations with Britain."

Sean put some steaks and burgers on the barbecue. At that moment Yolanda and Nikki returned from their walk. The children arrived at the same time, dripping wet from the pool. Akoth and Opiyo brought out the salads that she had prepared earlier. Sean opened some bottles of champagne and poured everyone a glass. It was cause for celebration to have his daughters and his best friend and his family with him for Christmas.

"We will finish this conversation after lunch," said James.

Sean nodded and went about the task of serving everyone their food. The party went on long into the evening. One by one Akoth took the children to bed. Eventually Sean, James, Yolanda and Nikki retired to the veranda where they sat and watched the moonlit beach and the wonderful night sky above them filled with twinkling yellow stars.

"I spent months persuading James to contact Edward Chidoli and ask him if that job offer as Head of Security at the Golden City still stands," said Yolanda. "Eventually he relented and contacted Chidoli who offered him a six-month contract on a consultancy basis."

She sounded tired from her efforts.

"Hey, James, you should accept. Maybe we can operate a casino scam together and get away with millions. We could be set up for life!" Sean joked. "With you on the inside it would be dead easy!"

They all laughed. James clutched his left arm unconsciously.

"I kept telling Yolanda to give me a little more time but eventually I realised it would be a good opportunity to recover from my arm injury. My next operation is in the new year. As soon as I have it I will start at the Golden City."

"Did you ever hear from Martin again?" asked Sean.

Incredibly Martin had appeared back in England shortly after James had flown back to go on the Iraq project.

"He came with me to Iraq. I felt like sacking him because I didn't believe he was telling me the truth about his disappearance from Zanzibar. It was too late for me to organise a replacement for him, so I had no alternative but to use him."

"Did he ever explain his disappearance from Zanzibar with Chris?"

"No. I quizzed him on that but he claimed he and Chris simply took the speedboat to get back to England via Kenya."

"I still don't understand why Chris and Martin disappeared from Zanzibar in the way that they did. They weren't being held prisoner. So why tie up the guard and the cook?"

"We can't be certain it was them or T J who tied the guard up. It's a mystery to me too." James shook his head.

James knew nothing of Chris's whereabouts. Martin had said very little about what had happened to him. Martin had since bought a beautiful townhouse in Fulham. James had no idea where he had raised the money to buy it.

"He came from a moneyed family but I suspect he and Chris had something to do with the break-in at the Golden City!"

"If they did, then Chris at least deserved to use some of the money that was stolen from Marais. He could start his life afresh after spending all that time in prison in Mafeking as an innocent man."

"So you two did have something to do with the goings-on at the Golden City in June," said Nikki.

Neither Sean nor James responded.

At that point Yolanda stood up and wished everyone goodnight. She was tired from her journey. Nikki followed shortly afterwards. Once again Sean and James were alone.

"Did you ask Martin whether he had seen T J again or

whether he was the person who had helped them leave Zanzibar?"

"I asked him about that too but he swore that he never saw T J after we first left them at the villa on Zanzibar."

For a long time T J's whereabouts were unknown. He didn't return to the US Embassy in Dar, which claimed he had been transferred back to the States. However three months later he turned up in Kenya.

"My contacts at the British High Commission told me Charles Bett had employed him through the Kenyan government as a private consultant to a drugs enforcement agency they had set up to combat the rising drugs and crime wave in Kenya. They were under pressure from foreign governments and aid agencies to be trying to be seen to be doing something about it," continued James.

Sean stood up.

"I will be back in shortly. I have something to show you."

Minutes later he was back clutching a folder. He dropped it on the table in front of them and proceeded to show James a number of newspaper cuttings with photographs."

James picked them up and there sure enough T J was in one of the photos with a broad smile on his face, standing next to Charles Bett and the Attorney General.

"Wow!" exclaimed James weakly, trying to sound as though he had not known about the press reports. "Why didn't you let me know about these before?"

"When they were published I tried contacting you several times but on each occasion Yolanda told me you were away and she wasn't sure when you would be returning."

James shrugged.

The photos showed Bett and the Attorney General setting fire to a huge pile of cannabis plants. They had been seized in a drugs raid from a farm situated seventeen miles north of Mombasa. It was estimated they had a street value of millions of dollars.

"James, at least the government seems to be doing something about the drugs problem here in Kenya."

"On the face of it yes, but according to intelligence reports at the High Commission, although there was a big display of burning the ganja only a small amount of the real stuff had been placed strategically around the bonfire. The centre of the pile was merely full of sacks of ordinary grass cuttings. There was enough of the real stuff burning to give off the genuine smell of weed!"

Sean looked incredulous.

"You mean to tell me a large amount of the haul had been siphoned off."

"Spot on. At first rumours suggested that Bett had seized most of it for his own use to sell it to his underworld contacts on the streets of Amsterdam through a network of coffee bars there."

"That doesn't make sense. I thought it was legal in Holland to sell cannabis."

"Well it's not actually legal. An anomaly in Dutch law means that the coffee bars or licensed shops can sell the cannabis but it is a criminal act to acquire the stock to sell. Any cannabis not actually grown locally in Holland has to be smuggled in. Normally it comes from India, Jamaica, Morocco and other parts of Africa. A more credible reason is that Bett transported it to Nairobi where it is being sold on the streets there."

"I would agree with that. There is enough of an increasing market here without having to go to the trouble and taking the risk of shipping it to Europe."

"What is even more interesting and could be hugely embarrassing to the British government is that a Labour shadow Cabinet Minister apparently owns the farm to the north of Mombasa where the cannabis was seized!"

"Are you referring to Robert Browne? He is the only British MP I know that owns a farm north of Mombasa," asked Sean excitedly.

"I can't confirm that at the moment but don't be surprised if you read about an MP's resignation in the papers in the new year!"

"What will happen to him?"

"I suspect nothing much really apart from losing his job. It's unlikely any charges will be pressed against him. As you know his farm manager was arrested and is still on remand at prison in Shanzu and will probably take the rap for the cannabis growing on the farm. The MP of course will deny everything."

"Was he involved?"

"Again intelligence reports from the High Commission suggest he was involved and has several business interests linked to Bett and Marais!"

"If they were involved together why did Bett arrange to seize the cannabis from Browne's farm?"

James sighed. "Ever heard of a double-cross, Sean?"

"You mean Browne was expendable."

"Spot on again. What's more it will be hugely embarrassing to Britain."

Sean nodded his agreement.

"After all the criticism by Britain of how Kenya conducts its affairs, Britain will be looked upon in a very poor light, especially as a British MP was allegedly involved in a drugs racket! What's even more interesting is that it turns out that Browne's daughter, Lindsay, worked at the Palace Casino for Marais back in the 'eighties!"

"Is she the same Lindsay who was married to Tony Stanley?"

"Yes! Browne has had business interests with Marais and Bett for years and it was he who, unbeknown to Tony Stanley, pulled the strings to get him a job at the Palace in the first place!"

"Marais must have been well pissed off that Stanley ripped him off and then blackmailed him into handing over even more money when he unearthed the two sets of accounts. Browne too must have been very embarrassed his former son-in-law was involved in the original Bahamas cups scam."

"Right again, but back now to the present day. The Kenyan government is desperate to show that crime and corruption doesn't only happen in Kenya and the so-called good guys from the West are as culpable," replied James.

"I don't suppose it's the last we will hear of T J either," remarked Sean.

"For sure, guys like T J keep appearing when they see a golden opportunity to make a fast buck. He will have to be very careful though. When he's served his usefulness to the likes of Bett he will be in grave danger of being disposed of...literally! I would like to get that bastard for killing the security guard in Tanzania but the problem as you well know is that he could implicate us in the killing too!"

Sean paled but remained silent.

"I have some unfinished business with T J, that's for sure," said James menacingly.

It was now nearly midnight. James was tired from the flight and the alcohol had made him drowsy. He said goodnight and left Sean on the veranda.

He sat in silence for a while. Sean took it as an opportunity to contemplate his future. Although his relationship was developing with Nikki, he felt a sudden feeling of loneliness. He missed Louise when she was in England and he found it hard sometimes with Achieng because he could never be a replacement mother for her. His and her future in Kenya also depended on the political landscape in Kenya. At times he wasn't sure whether he had the desire to remain in Kenya and stand by helplessly while corrupt politicians lined their own pockets with little regard for their own people. His effort to destroy the drugs haul on Benki now seemed pathetic. Marais and Bett were still free men to pursue their criminal activities unhindered.

At times he realised how much better off he was than others. He knew then he had to remain and help create a future for Achieng in her mother country. His thoughts returned to Nikki. Maybe she held the key to his and Achieng's future.

33

THREE MONTHS LATER, Martin Donaldson left his house in Fulham, Southwest London, early one morning on his way to work. As he was about to climb into his black Golf GTI, parked in his resident's bay opposite his home, two masked men strode up the street towards him. One of the men called out to him.

"Martin Donaldson!"

Martin spun round slowly. He was halfway through opening the driver's door and turned towards the two masked men. Two automatic pistols were raised and fired simultaneously. Six bullets slammed into his head and chest. He fell forwards into the gap between the inside of the door and the driver's seat as a pool of blood filled the pavement around him. Eyewitnesses reported that two men ran off in the direction from which they had come.

Less than one hour later Chris Powell, alias David Smith, opened the front door of his house in South London. He was confronted by two men wearing motorcycle helmets. They calmly and clinically raised their automatic pistols and pumped six bullets into his head at point-blank range. Moments later they sped away from the scene on a motorbike. Chris lay dying in his hallway.

It didn't take long for detectives investigating both crimes to link them together. Forensic experts soon discovered all the bullets were fired from the same guns. Both killings bore the hallmarks of a professional hit.

Almost thirty-six hours later T J Delport died in a hail of bullets in what initially appeared to be another carjacking on the streets of Nairobi. After stopping off for a drink at a trendy bar in the suburb of Westlands he returned to his car for the short drive home to the house he was renting in the select area of Riverside Drive. As he pulled up at a junction two men dressed in what looked like police uniforms, waved him down with a flashlight as they stood behind a metal stinger that lay in the road in front of them. T J made the fatal mistake of stopping. As he wound down his window the two men raised their AK 47s and blasted him full in the face with four bullets. He died instantly.

Early the next morning Sean heard the news of the shooting on KBC. Within seconds he was on the telephone to James in Dar.

"James, have you heard the latest about T J?"

"Yes, Chidoli told me this morning. His contacts in Kenya have been keeping him informed about T J's movements in Kenya for the last nine months."

"Do you think Marais had something to do with it?"

"My guess is that he did. Not only that, Chris Powell and Martin Donaldson were gunned down in London less than three days ago!"

"What! I don't believe it! Tell me what happened!"

James told Sean all he knew about the shootings.

"So what can be done about it if Marais was behind the killings?"

"Not much at the moment." James paused. "But there have been some interesting developments in other areas."

"Tell me!" Sean demanded.

James went on to explain that the insurance company that had indemnified the losses in the original Bahamas cups scam in South Africa had suspected for years that Marais had over-inflated the amounts of money that had been ripped off by the croupiers.

"You mean the insurance company is still pursuing Marais after all these years?"

"Yes. They managed to persuade some of the croupiers involved in the original scam to sign affidavits to the effect that only about a tenth of what Marais had claimed to be ripped off was in fact stolen from the Palace Casino. The insurance company issued a writ in the High Court in Johannesburg last month. It was upheld and Marais was ordered in his absence to repay the equivalent of £3,000,000!"

"Isn't that a pointless exercise? Isn't Marais still holed up in Mauritius? They will never get the money out of him."

"Yes, he was still in Mauritius but the insurance company was determined to get their money and see him imprisoned. Two nights ago a group of South African policemen posing as a rugby team kidnapped Marais from his hotel complex and managed to fly him back to South Africa. He is currently being held in the maximum security wing of Mafeking Prison."

"Wow! Unbelievable!" yelled Sean down the phone. "So at last Marais will be brought to justice."

"Let's hope so," said James quietly.

"How can he get out of it now?" He's staring at a long sentence, particularly if he's linked to the killings of Chris and Martin."

"If enough evidence can be put together to link Marais to their deaths then he'll serve a long time. The Tanzanian authorities already have an extradition order in place for the crimes he committed in Tanzania. Only time will tell."

"I suppose it's down to whether he gets a clever lawyer to get him off on technicalities," suggested Sean.

"Marais has enough money to pay for the best but I think the net has closed on him for good. I'll keep you informed of developments."

James hung up the receiver.

When Sean put the phone down he sat and contemplated his conversation with James. If Marais was behind the killings he was greatly concerned that Bett had something to do with it too. The killing of T J in Nairobi was too close to home for his liking. His fears increased for his own safety and that of Achieng. He still wasn't sure how much Marais and Bett were involved together and whether T J had been working directly for one or both of them since his arrival in Kenya. Even though Marais was now in prison, men like him had plenty of money to arrange a killing at any time. Furthermore Bett was still one of the most powerful men in Kenya. The time had come for Sean to decide whether or not he would remain in Mombasa with Achieng. The problem was he still had unfinished business to fulfil his commitment to bring Achieng up in the land of her mother. He reflected on James's earlier warning that he would spend the rest of his life looking over his shoulder. He shivered at the thought. He felt a mixture of foolishness and anger for putting his and his family's lives in danger. He knew he would have to watch his back from now on. He briefly wondered whether he should return to England but he knew he would be equally at risk there. He had no alternative but to stay and take his chances in Kenya.

Also by Ian Manners

Where Do I Belong?

Where Do I Belong? is a shocking story of innocent lives and loves destroyed by racial hatred, international crime and an unequal world. It follows one man's search for justice – or is it revenge?

Sean Cameron seems to have it made. Tall, good-looking and a famous rugby international, Sean falls in love with a beautiful Kenyan girl in Germany. Just when his life seems complete, his girlfriend is brutally attacked by neo-Nazis and left to die – along with his unborn child.

When his efforts to bring the killers to justice are frustrated, Sean enlists the help of James Annan – an old rugby pal and the first black soldier to enter the SAS.

Your emotions are taken on a rollercoaster ride as the plot bucks and twists from the bars of Mombasa to the red-light district of Hamburg, and gathers pace as it hurtles towards its unexpected finale.

Reviews for

Where Do I Belong?

"Racial hatred, crime across international borders and inequality all rear their heads in this powerful debut... The action swings from Kenya to Germany and back again. Catch your breath while you can."
Bookworm, the best books to snuggle down with.
Pride Magazine, August 2004.

"As you read *Where Do I Belong?* your emotions are taken on a rollercoaster ride as the plot unfolds. With simple, clear language and a direct plot, the book is highly readable."
Coast Express (Mombasa, Kenya) April 2004.

"As a comment on race relationships and the way that blacks and whites view each other in today's world, this book (*Where Do I Belong?*) is very apt."
The Daily Nation (Kenya), April 2003.

"*Where Do I Belong?* is a riveting and captivating read with scintillating openness and vivid accuracy. The yarn is a gripping romantic adventure and comes with our strong recommendations..."
The People Daily (Kenya), March 2003.

"Reading *Where Do I Belong?* it would be so easy to forget that this is Ian Manners' first novel. For me it was a book that once started I could not put down until I reached the last page..."

"I am not going to give away any secrets. But I do recommend people to buy the book because it's a very good read..."

"Although this book is fiction, Ian has used it to put over a very serious message... Ian Manners has drawn on his own experiences to write a powerful novel."
The Swindon Evening Advertiser, November 2002.

"*Where Do I Belong?* is a gripping adventure story following one man's pursuit of the truth after personal tragedy. Sean Cameron is an action hero that will appeal to men and women alike."
Nicole Russell, presenter, *The Afternoon Show*, BBC Radio Berkshire.

"*Where Do I Belong?* is an exciting novel which keeps the reader's attention throughout...the book is a fast-paced and exciting story. It shows a detailed knowledge of African society and Kenyan cultural traditions. The issues of race and racism are sensitively addressed and for these reasons alone, we would recommend it to *Harmony* readers of all ages from teenage upward."
People in Harmony magazine (a multiracial organisation).